HOT ICE

JACK DUNCAN

Hot Ice

This book was first published in Great Britain in paperback during September 2019.

The moral right of Jack Duncan is to be identified as the author of this work and has been asserted by him in accordance with the Copyright, Designs and Patents Act of 1988.

All rights are reserved and no part of this book may be produced or utilized in any format, or by any means, electronic or mechanical, including photocopying, recording or by any information storage or retrieval system, without prior permission in writing from the publishers - Coast & Country/Ads2life.

Email: ads2life@btinternet.com

All rights reserved.

ISBN: 978-1689348898

Copyright © September 2019 Jack Duncan

For Maggie

FOREWORD

Anglola - Historical Note.

The Angolan Civil War lasted for 27 years from the time of Independence from Portugal in 1975 until the Official cessation of hostilities in 2002 although the country remains in economic and social turmoil with a massive refugee crisis and unrecorded minefields strewn throughout the faming areas

Angola has a land mass twice the size of France and under Portuguese Colonial rule was considered to be the 'breadbasket of Africa' Currently it imports approximately 90% of its food and domestic goods. Apart from diamond mining controlled by Endiama, the Angolan Government production company and CSO De Beers and oil production controlled by the multi nationals like Chevron, Fina, Texaco, Petrobas etc. it has no other source of income.

The tussle for Angola was initiated by the Communist and anti-Communist forces in Angola at the time of the Cold War which was further exacerbated by the involvement of the United States, the USSR, Cuba and South Africa.

A military 'coup d'etat' on 25th April 1974 overthrew the Portuguese regime. This was carried out by the combined forces of MPLA - (Popular Movement for the Liberation of Angola), the FNLA - (National Front for the Liberation of Angola) and UNITA - (The National Union for Total Independence of Angola).

Within one year the transitional Government of allies disintegrated and with economic aid, arms and troops on the ground from the USSR and Cuba. The Marxist MPLA under the leadership of Jose dos Santos took control.

UNITA under Jonas Savimbi, in opposition was financed and assisted with arms and 'military advisors' by the USA, Brazil and South Africa.

The Civil War was bitter with many atrocities committed on both sides. It displaced thousands of Angolans from the land who flocked towards Angola and established a refugee 'cardboard city of around one million between the Airport and Luanda City.

During this period both sides laid unrecorded minefields throughout the country causing a massive number of civilian deaths and amputees.

The heavy fighting continued until 1991 when a temporary ceasefire was brokered called the 'Bicesse Accords' This called for the immediate removal of Cuban, South African and all other Foreign Forces, the formation of a new National Government and Angola's first multi party Elections.

The Election was won by Dos Santos' MPLA gaining 49% of the vote. Savimbi's UNITA gained 40%. The result was hotly disputed by Savimbi who declared it a fraud and UNITA resumed hostilities on a guerilla war basis.

In 1993 the United nations placed embargos on Angola (Resolution 864) on petroleum and munitions shipments to UNITA however there were many other sources of both products and the guerilla warfare continued until Savimbi was killed in an ambush in February 2002.

There were many Foreign Mercenaries fighting with UNITA and two large Military Security Companies - Defence Systems Limited and Executive Outcomes supplying ex Military personnel in the role of Security advisors to the United nations, the surviving Embassies, Oil Companies, Diamond Companies including Endiama and the few remaining trading Agents in Luanda.

DSL employed many ex Ghurkha soldiers on these tasks. These 'private armies' protected the ex pat communities and kept them secure. Luanda in the 90's was a very dangerous city and due to the poverty of the massed population ex pats were targeted for their vehicles, wallets, wristwatches rings etc. if they were foolish enough to flout them in the face of locals, few such survived. It was not unknown, if an ex pat was stupid enough to have his car window open wearing a flashy watch, for a local to rush up and chop the limb off with a machete just to steal the watch.

UNITA was demobilised in August 2002 but remains a formidable political party in opposition in Angolan politics.

The country remains devastated by this long war of attrition. Rich in natural resources it is economically and politically in ruins with runaway inflation. Thousands of amputees and millions of landmines together with the displacement of millions of refugees is a national crisis.

Jose dos Santos is the longest serving President in any African country.

. . . .

The Author is a former Scots Guards Officer who also holds a Military and Commercial Helicopter licence and a Private Pilot's Licence for light aircraft.

After resigning his Commission, he held senior positions as Chairman, CEO, Deputy CEO, Managing Director and Director of many PLC

Companies in diverse disciplines and also CEO of two NGO Charities.

He has also started up and successfully run four of his own wholly owned Companies.

In the early 90's he was Managing Director for Defence Systems Limited in Angola and this novel is fiction but based on fact from his experiences towards the start of the first ceasefire between UNITA and MPLA.

Any resemblance to actual persons in this work is purely coincidental.

Prologue

The Jungle held its breath! No sound from the nocturnal creatures, no whining from the usual myriad of stinging insects, no rustle of wind in the dark impenetrable canopy of trees.

It seemed always thus in the seconds before an ambush was sprung.

The UNITA patrol of Savimbi's rebel army were almost in the kill zone. The smell of their unwashed bodies, strong tobacco and their unnaturally loud murmurings carried forward to the waiting Angolan Government forces, the 'Elite' called the 'Buffalos', together with their Gurkha Officer 'consultants', who had lain silently for the past five hours.

Jack Douglas, the Commanding Officer, formerly of the Scots Guards realised he too was holding his breath although he had been in similar ambush contacts many times.

Jack was on contract to the Angolan Government at the express request from Dos Santos, the President, who had come to know and respect him when he was heading up the Angolan unit of IDS (International Defence Solutions) in Luanda some years before. He carried the rank of full Colonel.

The lead in the UNITA patrol hit the black trip wire stretched invisibly across the path one foot from the ground, firing the magnesium and phosphorous flares, which outlined the enemy in stark silhouette against the blackness of the jungle.

All Hell let loose. A cacophony of harsh sound with a scything hail of death.

The patrol did not stand a chance. Automatic fire from the AK47's and one GPMG (general purpose machine gun) hosed the area. The illuminated figures had frozen in horror and disbelief just like red deer who when alerted, always stand stock still for ten seconds before taking flight.

Desultory return fire started up but soon silenced. The leading few men took flight down the track leaving the bodies of their comrades dead and dying looking like twisted dolls or bundles of discarded rags.

From the right came the bark of a second GPMG firing short bursts of 3 to 5 rounds. Good man Douglas thought, obviously curbing his enthusiasm to let rip with the whole belt which was an inherent problem with the Buffalos. This was coupled with the deeper bark of the .50 calibre platoon machine gun.

This was the 'Stop' group placed 400 metres round the bend in the track to deal with any escapees.

Cease fire. The pervasive smell of cordite hung still in the foliage. An eerie silence returned.

Douglas gave the order to sweep forward, clear the area through the killing zone and into the jungle on the other side. He gave a nod to Captain Mani Gurung, formerly 6th Gurkhas, to deal with the wounded. He moved forward cautiously with his 9mm Browning cupped in his hand in case there were any feigning injury. The count was fourteen dead and three seriously injured who were despatched with a 'coup de grace'.

This was total warfare as raw as one could experience. There was no possibility of medical assistance, nor of taking prisoners.

This was the way of it with both sides in this protracted conflict.

A textbook ambush - a job well done! The hard months of training were at last beginning to take effect.

The bodies were searched for Intel. but left where they lay for the animals and the jungle to take to her bosom. The weapons were gathered, anything useful kept, the remainder buried 500 metres off the track in the dense undergrowth - lost forever.

The jungle breathed again!

CHAPTER 1

The TAP 747 landed at Luanda airport in the early hours and taxied to the stand. The doors swung open and the sweet rotten scent of Angola pervaded the atmosphere.

Jack Douglas rose from his seat 1D in First class, the luxury upon which he insisted when tasked to West Africa. He was 58 years old, an impressive figure at 6ft. 3 ins. tall with a barrel chest and still a 34 inch waist. Deeply suntanned, what remained of his dark hair was offset by laughing hazel eyes. The chief flight attendant gave him a weary smile of farewell - she must be about my age, he thought, too old to be flying this route. She had looked after him well and ensured he had an adequate supply of Champagne during his flight - not his usual Bollinger but an adequate Laurent Perrier Rose.

He flashed her a quick smile as he shook her hand and thanked her for her kind attention.

He almost spoke his thoughts aloud as he gathered his flight bag. What the Hell am I doing back here? I left in 1991 never to return with a price on my head from UNITA.

The situation had changed in 2003. Savimbi the leader of UNITA was dead and Jose dos Santos was still President. Indeed he had a personal letter from him guaranteeing his safe passage in and out of the country. Jack knew exactly how much this was worth if the perpetual fluidity of the situation were to change.

"Bloody Hell" he said under his breath

Douglas had been out of the game for twelve years and living a quiet comfortable life in the South of Spain for the past seven of those years running his small Marine Consultancy. He also still maintained a house in London with Maggie Grosvenor, his partner for many years.

He had been co-opted into this task by General Bruce Kendall, the head of a 'black ops' section in the British Government and a close friend. The secondary reason was money, as he was running 'a little dry', with perhaps also the adrenalin buzz of being back in a risk situation.

He had been Managing Director West Africa of ISL (International Defence Solutions Limited) a formidable Security Company whose Board and Senior members were mostly retired Scots Guards Officers or 'G' Squadron SAS. Many joked that it was simply the commercial arm of the Scots Guards and that nobody had really left the Brigade. In some way this was true as the Company worked very closely with UK Government and the MOD. Douglas himself was a former Scots Guards Officer and his closest friend, also ex Regiment was Chief Executive.

In the early 90's when he had last been in Luanda, he had turned the station around from being a depressing loss making operation to one of million dollars profit in the first year. He had been pretty ruthless in cutting out dead wood and not suffered fools no matter what their Regimental background or long standing with the Company He had dismissed all found lacking. This had not endeared him to some Board members who had been Non Commissioned members of the SAS and who had an inherent dislike for 'Ruperts' the derisible name given to

Officers.

The operation then had covered a multitude of security and military advisory skills. Contracts were held with the British Embassy, United Nations, Endiama (the Angolan Government diamond mining corporation), CSO (De Beers), Chevron Oil, Fina, Texaco etc. providing physical and advisory security in all aspects of their daily operations. All Advisors carried arms, holding Angolan Government licences to carry concealed weapons, and ex Ghurkha soldiers were employed along with trained and armed Angolans - basically a private army with Government sanction.

All in the past, he mused. he descended from the aircraft and was immediately hit by the high temperature and humidity which jolted his memory and had soaked his shirt by the time he reached the tarmac.

There was a white Angolan Police Land Rover on the apron and a somewhat portly though recognizable Police Officer was walking towards him.

"Alfonso, you old rogue" said Jack "I didn't realise you were still alive let alone be meeting me. Good to see you" as he shook the proffered hand.

"Hello Jack, yes, I am still alive although you remember we were is some tight spots together in the early years. As you can see, I am now Chief Inspector"

"Well congratulations, how much did that cost you" he said jokingly.

Alfonso Carisco took off his Ray Bans and his eyes narrowed for an instant. "Nothing, in Angola now, bribery is not used for career advancement"

"OK, I hear you but your belly appears to have had a 'helping' hand"

The Chief Inspector gurgled, it was the only way to describe his laugh, he had always gurgled and Douglas suddenly felt he had never left this damned country as memories flooded his mind.

"Come, I have arranged Diplomatic clearance for you so we will go through the VIP lounge with minimum controls, you remember, to the left of the main Terminal."

"Yes, I remember, and I am grateful" Walking to the Land Rover he reminded Alfonso that his two aluminium cases in the aircraft hold would require special handling and that he had the necessary documentation.

"Not necessary, my friend" said Alfonso, "all is arranged, they will be delivered directly to your residence."

"What residence? I had thought the Hotel had been pre-booked"

"A re-organisation given the sensitivity of your visit and the task ahead. You know the house" he continued, "it was once the residence of the Managing Director of Texaco - you remember, the one who had the obsession of always washing his hands. What was his name?"

"Chuck Connel" Douglas answered "But I thought Texaco still maintained a strong presence in Luanda. Why have they given up such a fine villa?"

The house was probably one of the most secure private residences in the city, barring an incident in 1991 where Douglas had lost three of his men during an unconnected, failed MPLA operation to take out Savimbi, the UNITA leader whose house was in the near vicinity.

"Texaco has now moved their management to their base at Cabinda although they still retain their town offices and two apartments in the tower."

Douglas remembered the many meetings and briefings he had given to Connel in the top floor offices. This had been one of his most profitable contracts which he had negotiated to the delight of head Office.

In the early 90's the electric power was constantly interrupted so Texaco had installed two massive diesel generators in the building in order to maintain their satellite communications centre, lifts and air conditioning. Jack had used their facilities many times when the city power was down.

He said nothing more. He had only been briefed in outline before leaving London and was to be further briefed by the Military Attache at the British Embassy.

After a cursory check at the VIP Lounge to stamp his passport they drove out of the airport. Douglas noted that the sickly sweet smell of rotting refuse, sewage and filth, was as he remembered. There seemed to be some attempt to contain the mountains of refuse in open skips, but they were overflowing with the detritus of two million homeless souls who lived in the cardboard shanty town on the outskirts of Luanda. In these forsaken places there was no sanitation and only one water standpipe serving every few hundred people - no wonder it stank.

Luanda, once a beautiful city built by the Colonial Portuguese, was one huge slum. A few buildings in Government and main road areas struggled to maintain a reasonable dignity. The roads were even worse than he remembered. As they turned along the maritime road fronting the lagoon, he was amused to see the back of a truck sticking out of a large hole in the cobbled surface.

"How long has that been there"

"A few weeks only" said Alfonso "it was overloaded and fell through the old brick sewers under the road. But there are plans to move it soon"

Not surprising thought Douglas as nothing had been properly maintained for 50 years.

On his right the pink stone of the Government Bank, the Banco National de Angola, shone in the sun. This was a lovely old building and it was obvious a great effort had been made to maintain it, as with most of the other grand Colonial buildings along the banks of the lagoon which served as Luanda's natural harbour. 'The 'haves' and the 'have nots', he thought.

He noted there were only three oil platforms in the bay either in for maintenance or re- positioning. He could clearly make out 'Petrobas 111' on the side of the nearest which looked in poor state and was severely rust streaked. This was the rig on the Angolan shelf he had had to clear for booby traps and explosive devices after it had been occupied by the rebel UNITA forces. The crew had abandoned it during the height of the Civil War.

A sardonic smile played over his face as he remembered his number two on that operation was Abraham Dawson a main Board Director who had come out to Angola for a 'swan' and insisted he would help with the clearance. He lasted about forty minutes in the heat and confined space of the leg and Douglas and another member of his team had cleared the rig which took a further five hours.

This fellow had then returned to London claiming success for negotiating the new contract with Texaco which he had 'finalised', not Jack Douglas who had been working on it for the previous three months. The truth being that Dawson was one of the ex SAS men who had constantly tried to undermine and sabotage all of Jack's' work in 1991 after he had dismissed two of his old cronies from the Angolan station. He had sat in on one meeting with Texaco, the final contract approval, and not contributed a word, however being a main Board Director, he had signed the contract on behalf of IDS and thus claimed the success was his. Fortunately, James (aka Jimmie) the CEO, knew the truth.

"What are you smiling at Jack. Glad to be back in your old station. Now you can see how much Luanda has improved since you left"

"Just remembering Abraham Dawson's face after he had been down one of the legs of that rig in the bay and the state he was in. He had been halfway down inside one of the 120 feet legs in 95 degrees of heat and gave up emerging totally wasted, with his white hair plastered over his face, and covered in oil and rust particles. All too much for him as Billy and I cleared the other legs and the four storey platform - that gave me simple satisfaction"

"Agh I remember the white hair - he was an arrogant man" said Alfonso.

Douglas espied the British Embassy, another lovely old building on its rocky outcrop above the Lagoon and realised the driver was pulling into the pot holed road leading to the main gates. On arrival he almost wished he could see his old Ghurkha soldiers on guard in their distinctive light and dark blue DSL uniforms, slouch hat and gleaming service Kukris on the backs of their belts, waiting to check the vehicle. Alas No. There were two Marine guards in camouflage dress, with SA rifles slung over their shoulders one of whom approached the Land Rover in a leisurely fashion. He recognised Alfonso, didn't check Douglas' identity and waved them through.

Slack, he thought.

"What are we doing here Alfonso, I thought we were going straight to the house?"

"I thought you might wish to meet the Military Attache, Colonel Anstruther as soon as possible and thus took the liberty of arranging a meeting"

"Are you still Police Liaison Officer to the Embassy?"

"Yes" he confirmed "although it should be a more junior Officer, the Colonel personally asked for me to stay on"

Douglas realised it must be the same Anstruther who was Attache in 1991, he was a prat when John Flynn was Ambassador and probably even more of a prat now, couldn't possibly be so coincidental as to have two Officers with the same name in the same post.

With that he swung his legs out of the Land Rover and headed for the side office, the Military section of the Embassy.

The time was now 10.37 hrs. and the appointment and been made for 10.35. The English Secretary was the wife of one of the junior Embassy Officials who, with some embarrassment, stated that the Colonel who was very exact on timings had waited five minutes then gone through to speak to the Ambassador.

Would he kindly wait?

No I bloody well will not, thought Douglas, I am just off an eight hour flight then he swallowed hard and said.

"Yes, I shall but not for long" and sat down with Alfonso on the uncomfortable chairs in the vestibule.

This re-acquaintance with Anstruther was not going to be friendly.

10.45 hrs. No Anstruther!

"Come on Alfonso, let's get out of here"

"No, hold on Jack. Curb your justifiable annoyance, he'll be here in a few minutes" The Secretary kept her head down.

At that moment the secure steel door to the main Embassy buzzed open and there stood Edward Anstruther with a dark, slightly comical frown on his face. Anstruther was a small man, 5 ft 9 ins. but when last seen he had been reasonably fit. His Regiment had been the Green Howards. In the last ten years he had put on at least twenty pounds and his round face and plump body seemed to be struggling to release itself from his elderly service dress shirt and trousers. His 'stable belt' could hardly be seen under his belly. His rotundity made him appear even smaller against Jacks 6ft 3ins as he stood up to say Hello. No wonder they sent him back to Angola before retirement, he thought, as he would not have had a hope of passing his annual Fitness Test even in the Green Howards where he would have had to reduce his Rank to substantive

Major.

"Hello Douglas - you're here, Egh!"

"So it would appear Ed (he hated his name abbreviated) have you been here since I left?"

"Don't be ridiculous Douglas, as his frown darkened further. "Good morning Alfonso" he threw at the Chief Inspector. Come through here, I haven't much time now that the schedule has been revised. Judy could we have some iced water, or do you wish coffee Douglas"

"No thanks Ed" another glower.

Once in his office the ridiculous little figure sat down behind a large desk with almost nothing on it save two telephones. By the window was another desk piled high with files and trays in a state of disarray and it was obvious Anstruther had cleared his desk quickly to make him appear industrious, precise and very important.

Judy arrived with a pitcher of water and glasses.

"I don't wish to be disturbed for the next twenty eight minutes unless it is His Excellency" pointedly looking at his watch.

Jack stifled a laugh, Alfonso gurgled.

"Anything the matter Douglas" he said as the air conditioner belted out semi cold air at full chat which together with the oscillating fan made him appear more comical as the forced air lifted a sliver of hair from his damp forehead letting it flop over his eyes then lifted it again. This together with a small black moustache made him look like a fat Adolf Hitler.

"Yes there is. That's the fourth time you have referred to me as 'Douglas'. I have no time to indulge in your ridiculous games to bolster your inadequacies, your obvious lack of self respect and your lack of manners. You may call me Jack or Mr Douglas the latter being preferable.

Just who the hell do you think you are keeping us waiting after I have flown overnight from Lisbon because we were a few minutes late. You are not important. You are here to brief me if that is within your capability which I somehow doubt. I am here as a civilian with the full knowledge of the Angolan Government and under the auspices of the British Government on a specific matter of importance on which I am advised you have been given an abbreviated heads up.

Ergo! You work for me and don't you forget it. Now let's start again"

The Colonel's face had gone a mottled burgundy colour during the last few seconds.

"How dare you … I warned HE that you were a trouble maker when I was informed of your imminent arrival . . . ."

"Stop right there! You will brief me now on the current state of the displaced Guerrilla ops. around Luanda, where the balance of power lies in these groups and the geographical high ground held by the various factions. I also wish to know where they derive their political, financial and armament backing and who is considered the strongest opposition leader now Savimbi is dead.

Further I require the disposition of Angolan Navy operational craft, classification, readiness, armament, ammunition quantities and state of manning together with the exact number of Government hard skinned vehicles within a fifteen mile radius of Luanda.

You have, I know, been pre-tasked with my requirements thus if your brief is not ready you haven't done your bloody job which will be reported accordingly.

Now stop blustering and get on with it"

Alfonso sat with a whimsical look of slight embarrassment on his face. The air conditioner continued to try to jump off the wall in the sudden silence

"There is no need to be so aggressive" said Anstruther. "I am only trying to do my job"

"Well do it" said Douglas "and stop wasting my time"

Anstruther then proceeded to deliver a reasonably comprehensive brief of the current state of play which took almost two hours at the end of which Jack made requests for various files, photocopies and aerial photographs to be delivered to his house by 16.00 that afternoon.

When finished, Jack stood up proffered his hand to Anstruther and said,

"Now look 'Edward' you may not like it, I do not like it because I don't think you are up to it, but for the weeks we have to work together I have to have full access to your files and comms. Just remember in my current position I out rank you. In my former military career, I out rank you. You have been instructed to give me full support and assistance. If necessary, I will simply order you to carry out what I would prefer came from you voluntarily"

Anstruther faltered then took Jack's hand. "OK Jack, sorry I got a bit steamed up. I am sure you will be happy with the co-operation from this department now we have straightened out these few differences and I trust it will be suitably recorded in your final report."

"Right, come on Alfonso I need a shower and luncheon"

CHAPTER 2

Edward Anstruther sat fuming behind his desk. Although he had backed down in front of Jack's onslaught, he also knew that this was his last posting before retirement at, he hoped, the rank of full Colonel which would increase his pension considerably. He did not have a private income and had to exist for the rest of his life on this pension and on various 'acquisitions' he had made during his years in Angola. These acquisitions were contained in seven chamois pouches of illegally purchased uncut blood diamonds of value, around £150, 000, which were squirreled away in a deposit box within the control of a small safety deposit Company in South Kensington.

He had taken a risk in smuggling them out of Angola in the Diplomatic bag concealed in a Monte Cristo cigar box, purportedly a gift for his father, but the risk had been worth it as he had collected the box from his Father's house on his next UK leave.

Diamond smuggling from Angola has always been a serious problem, controlled as best as possible by the Government and De Beers, Central Selling Organisation who have the majority of licences to exploit the diamond fields. However, for every legal diamond exported there is one illegal smuggled out, bartered or used as payment for arms smuggled into the country.

Anstruther had courted the senior Security Officer at CSO and had managed to glean sufficient knowledge to make purchases knowing full well that if discovered, he would be cashiered from the Army and possibly lose his pension. For him it had been a great risk but greed overcame his normally cautious nature.

He had only two years of service before retirement and was considering another sally to the sordid streets behind the vast open market on the ridge above Luanda city to augment his collection. This would now have to wait.

He had never liked Jack Douglas and thought him a typically arrogant Brigade of Guards Officer born with the proverbial silver spoon in his mouth, educated at Fettes and Edinburgh University prior to being commissioned into the Scots Guards. Douglas had won the Sword of Honour at Sandhurst, been Senior Under Officer, played low handicap polo, and raced classic Maseratis. His family had substantial property in Scotland including a Georgian town house in Doune Terrace, Edinburgh and the 'family estate', 53, 000 acres of Ross-shire county near Alness with two Lochs and two salmon beats on the river Connon. A 'small estate' as he had once overheard Douglas describe the place but he knew that it was one of the most beautiful and sought after sporting estates in Scotland worth in excess of twelve million pounds.

He, on the other hand, had barely managed the minimum educational requirements to be admitted to Mons Officer Cadet School where he achieved a Short Service Commission, he had extended after the first three years and transferred to a Regular Commission when in the mid 70's many mid ranking Officers and Non Commissioned Officers left the Army due to the appallingly poor pay and conditions the disparity being 45% below civilian counterparts.

This exodus left a large gap and some officers who would not normally have been considered were granted a Regular Commission.

Anstruther was one of those and he had then made an indifferent career awaiting promotion through 'dead men's shoes' and not through achievement. He knew he was not a 'fast track' Officer and indeed was surprised when he was posted once again to Angola as Military Attache with the rank of Lt. Colonel. Although his rank was acting not substantive, a fact which he continually tried to conceal.

Eleven years earlier he had fallen foul of Douglas when Government Forces broke the cease fire and attacked Savimbi's palatial and heavily fortified villa on 'Millionaires Row'. The ensuing firefight was frenetic and uncontrolled, confused even further by the black darkness of the Luanda night.

The then Ambassador was that evening dining with Chuck Connell the Texaco CEO and big Jim Maclean the MD of Fina at the Texaco villa some 200 metres to the West. He was accompanied by Captain Manni Gurung in the armoured Daimler with a back up of three ex Ghurkhas, and two Angolan Guards employed and trained by DSL, in a V8 Range Rover.

Jack Douglas had prior intelligence of the possibility of an operation against Savimbi and passed this on to Anstruther with the express instruction that the Ambassador cancel his evening engagement and that he would warn Jim Connell at Texaco. Anstruther dismissed the whole notion of a break in the ceasefire, relying on his own sources that everything was peaceful and that the Government had reduced its Alert State.

Thus Anstruther did not advise HE. Douglas expecting this might be the case had tried to see the Ambassador personally but was advised he was out on the island water skiing with his family and would not return till late afternoon. As he was due in Cabinda he left a message asking the Ambassador to speak to Manni Gurung who he had thoroughly briefed ordering them to 'tool up' if there was any exit from the

Embassy that evening. Apart from their standard sidearm, the Jericho 9mm automatic on their belts, they were all to carry AK 47 assault rifles and a GPMG. The General Purpose Machine Gun is a standard Infantry support weapon in the British Army and is extremely effective and hard wearing. Belt fed 7.62mm, that night the belts would be made up with a tracer round every third instead of the normal, every fifth.

The fan was hit at 22.30 hrs. when a Karl Gustav anti tank round blew open the gates of Savimbi's compound followed by an assault by two Companies of the 'Ninjas', Angola's special forces, supported by an ageing Russian T52 tank and four BRDM armoured personnel carriers.

The small UNITA bodyguard was taken by complete surprise and retreated to the main house where Savimbi and two of his Senior Officers were ensconced. Once inside the heavy doors were barred and fire was returned from the steel shuttered upstairs windows. The forward area was now bathed with spotlights and although the Angolan forces vastly outnumbered the defenders, heavy casualties were inflicted. UNITA then opened up from the roof with a heavy .50 calibre machine gun - discretion proving the better part of valour the attackers rapidly retreated through the gate in disarray.

Sporadic fire was kept up from the gateway for the next fifteen minutes.

Douglas had just landed by helicopter at the airport and was on his way back to the city when the sky was lit up by the firefight. He raised Manni on the radio and received a situation report confirming the assault and that the Ambassador was with Jim Connell contrary to his advice, As yet there was no advance towards the Texaco villa. He was told that 'the Colonel' was en route with the three SAS troopers stationed at the Embassy.

Anstruther arrived shortly afterwards and after a hurried discussion with the Ambassador and the SAS team leader, as there was a lull in the firing, he decided to pull back to the Embassy. Manni told him that he had orders from Douglas to stay put as there was no direct threat to their position and no fire had been directed towards them. He was over ruled and ordered to assist with the evacuation. The convoy was made up behind the steel gates of the villa. In front was Anstruther and two of the SAS troopers, second was the armoured Daimler with HE, Jim Connell and Manni., taking up the rear was the DSL Range Rover with Jim MacLean, Corporal Stevens and two Ghurkhas. The tailgate was down and a GPMG set up on the floor to give covering fire.

There were no street lights and the villa lights had been killed as had most of the lights in neighbouring buildings thus it was very difficult to see any troop movements outside the walls.

The gates were quietly opened, no fire! So far so good. The plan was a high speed left turn away from Savimbi's villa and race down the single track road away from the earlier firefight. Only the leading vehicle would have its lights on to protect the Daimler until they were well clear. Just as Anstruther gave the order to go the bellow of a straining diesel engine was heard but instead of checking again or aborting he pulled out accelerating away and the convoy had to follow, straight in to the path of another T52 tank crawling up the steep slope to the road.

There was simply nowhere to go as the road dropped away in a 2oo foot fall on the offside and walls of the other buildings hemmed them in on the nearside.

Brakes were jammed on all three vehicles skidding to a halt with the Daimler crunching into the rear of the lead Rover, only the roar of the tank engine punctuated the night as it approached the top of the slope. Fortunately the tank could not engage with its main armament due to the angle of the incline but had opened up with the turret machine guns which were slowly but inexorably creeping lower.

Chaos ensued. Anstruther had stalled his Rover and was desperately trying to restart. Nobody had control until Manni got out of the Daimler ordered the Range Rover to reverse back past the gates to cover the Daimler, then with a shout to Anstruther to follow, ordered the driver to hard reverse back in to the villa compound. As this was going on the tank machine guns found the lead Rover and shredded the rear. Miraculously nobody was hurt and all legged it back towards the villa.

In the interim the Government forces at Savimbi's villa, thinking it was either UNITA reinforcements or an escape break and seeing their own tank firing, opened up on the Range Rover which had now commenced covering fire with the GPMG for those on foot. Tracer rounds were bouncing everywhere. The Range Rover was hit and the gunner killed, one of the Ghurkhas running back to the gates was hit in both legs and went down hard. There were still five on foot running for cover when to their incredulity they saw the gates swinging closed in front of them. They yelled and hammered on the gates whilst trying to take cover on the open ground and return fire but they remained closed until a sustained burst of fire from the tank lifted two of them off their feet. Suddenly one half opened and the survivors fell through dragging the wounded.

It transpired that whilst Manni was shepherding the Ambassador and civilians back inside the villa, his first priority. Anstruther had shut the gates knowing his own forces were still on the outside but fearing being overpowered.

Corporal Stevens launched himself from the Daimler shouting "What the fuck are you doing, our boys are still out there"

Anstruther screamed. "I am in command, it is my decision"

At that Stevens short chopped him across the neck and kicking him out of the way opened the gate - too late!

A measure of calm ensued. The Angolan forces had stopped firing having no further targets. The tank was slewed across the road highlighted by the burning Range Rover.

Manni and Corporal Stevens took stock, tended to the wounded as best they could and put two of their remaining force on the walls to observe and report.

Manni raised Jack on the radio telling him the grim news of the ballsed up escape and the death of three men. At the time Jack had teamed up with the UN Security Chief, Joe Walsh a tough, ex New York cop and was in his white UN Toyota Landcruiser sporting two large UN Flags on the whip aerials spotlit from the vehicle roof. No one could mistake the vehicle for anything than what it was, and it had been allowed through to the bottom of the hill below Millionaire's Row. It was now 23.4o hrs and it had been reported that there was no movement or fire from Savimbi's villa for the last thirty minutes.

Douglas had remonstrated with the local Commander to allow him access to the Texaco villa with a squad of Angolan troops to protect the Ambassador however these repeated requests were curtly refused as ' we had fired on his troops'

In the next few minutes a tentative probe forward was carried out by the Ninjas. As soon as they were near the villa they opened up with a crescendo of automatic fire. There was no returning fire. The T52 was brought up to bulldoze the gates after which the villa was found to be empty Savimbi having usind the diversion caused by the Texaco villa debacle to escape through his cellars which connected to an old sewer leading out to a manhole 200 metres to the rear. Only one dead UNITA soldier remained.

On this discovery permission was given for the Ambassador and civilians to return to the Embassy under the protection of the Angolan Army.

Everybody was furious: The Angolans were furious with the failure of their own troops, with the British, with the Americans and with DSL

The Americans were furious with the British and the Angolans.

The Ambassador was furious with Anstruther

The SAS were furious with Anstruther

Douglas wasn't furious just deeply saddened that a British Officer's incompetence and cowardice under fire had caused the un-necessary deaths of three men. If they had stood their ground as he had ordered Manni rather than attempting a thrown together escape plan all would be alive and unharmed. However Manni had been over ruled. . . .

His eyes steeled. Retribution is a dish served cold!

The mopping up operation got in to full swing at first light. The mauled vehicles were recovered and arrangements made for the bodies of the two Ghurkhas flown back to Nepal that evening and the SAS trooper to the UK the following day. The Ghurkhas would be given a full pension by DSL and assistance with an honourable funeral. Nothing however could replace a loved husband and father.

Anstruther had received a severe reprimand, reduction to his substantive rank of Major and R.T.U'd (returned to unit) a week later. Once back at his Regiment he struggled in various indifferent postings till he eventually became Company Commander of Headquarter Company.

The blot on his Confidential report infuriated him and although the truth had dulled over the years, in his own mind he blamed DSL and Douglas for the failure of his escape plan and the ignominy which followed.

. . . .

Colonel Anstruther stopped day dreaming at his desk and brought himself back to present day.

"Judy, I'm off to lunch. What's HE doing?"

"He is down at the pool with Mr Belguerro, the managing Director of Endiama. I think they are talking about diamond smuggling"

Endiama was the Angolan Government diamond operation controlling mining, retrieval and marketing and was headed by the charismatic Belguerro who had been MD for fourteen years and was a close friend of the President. The long Civil War and the lack of production in the Northern mines had almost bankrupted the Company and ergo, the Government, however Belguerro still maintained his private Lear Jet, private Jet Ranger helicopter. His two Mercedes 500's, his huge family villa near the Presidential palace and a lovely house on the spur of the lagoon, the home of his mistress and children. A powerful man.

"Well, I'll just pop down and see if HE wishes my input on any matter"

"Colonel. . . . . ." Judy said then stopped.

"Yes, What?"

"Oh nothing" Judy well knew that Anstruther had been informed of the meeting and that there were to be no interruptions but it wasn't for her to remind him.

On the other hand Anstruther had a hidden agenda. He had met Belguerro at several official functions and knew him for the rogue he was. He wanted to try to ingratiate himself with the man as there may be some service he could provide in the future.. For example, couriering a small parcel to London courtesy of a Diplomatic Passport. He had heard that Belguerro was getting ready to retire and although he had significant stature and assets in Luanda he had been advised he was trying to build up his assets offshore.

Interesting, he thought as he passed through the French doors to the Embassy gardens

Chapter 3

Alfonso drove Jack to the 'Texaco' villa as it was still called. Not much was said as they passed Savimbi's house, still a desolate and pock marked shell with locked gates and razor wire spread along the walls. As they approached the gates of his house the bullet and cannon holes were still evident although they had been painted over quite recently.

The gates were closed so Alfonso blew the horn, a few seconds later they were hauled open without any check, by a bleary eyed Police sentry who from his appearance had either been asleep or was high on the local Ganja. Alfonso let fly a string of rapid Portuguese, the sentry visibly quailed and rushed off to find his partner who was 'off watch'

What a joke, thought Douglas, the place is wide open. If there is any attempt at an incursion these two sorry souls will run a mile.

"Alfonso, I appreciate the provision of your men but is this the best you can do?"

Alfonso grimaced, "sadly at the moment, yes, we are stretched very thin. I appreciate they don't look much but at least they will cover the gate and they are uniformed, armed Police, the visible deterrent. . . . That is if they keep awake"

Douglas looked at him, "slight confusion here, how does the visible deterrent work when they are locked behind the gates? The only person therefore to see them is me"

"Ah, yes. Hadn't thought of that. Do you want one positioned outside?"

"No that will simply bring attention to the villa being occupied. I will talk to them later"

At that moment the front door opened and a small, powerfully built man immaculately dressed in white shirt and trousers with burnished black shoes, even in the perennial dust bowl that was Luanda, came towards the Land Rover.

Alfonso introduced him as Sergio and Douglas shook hands with the wiry little man who made a slight bow. He had an unusually strong grip. He further explained that Sergio ran the household and was employed by the Chief of Police, He is an excellent man, speaks English and French and was also a Commando in the Portuguese Army where he became equivalent to your Company Sergeant Major.

Douglas glanced at him once again this time noticing that for a man in his late 40's he did not carry any surplus weight or flab under his shirt, his bare forearms were well muscled.

You also have a housemaid and cook called Anna who is Sergio's sister thus her honesty can be vouched for. They both have their own quarters in the villa.

"Thank you, Alfonso. The house seems to be in a better state of control than your gate guards" Alfonso started to bluster. "No Alfonso, I am only joking. I am grateful for your arrangements, really! "

Sergio suddenly rattled off a torrent of fast Portuguese at Alfonso about the 'lazy dogs'. Douglas had never mastered Portuguese and could only remember a few words.

In Angola it was even more difficult as the language was interspersed with many words from the seven tribal dialects in the country dependent on geographical area. He however understood the gist of the delivery and it was obvious that Alfonso was not pleased as he rattled back at the end of which Sergio simply turned back to the house with a polite 'excuse me' to Douglas.

It looks as if Sergio is not overawed by Alfonso's exalted position of Chief Inspector, mused jack. I wonder exactly what his true role and position is. I shall have to have words with him.

Alfonso apologised for speaking Portuguese.

"Not necessary old friend, it is I who should apologise for not speaking Portuguese"

During this heated exchange a feeling of darkness had encroached on his mind. He obviously remembered the three who had fallen here eleven years ago and indeed could still define their faces distinctly as they had been some of the longer serving. He had, many times, been a guest of Manni Gurung and his boys for a curry supper in their quarters at the rear of the Embassy where they formed the permanent guard. He always attended the Ghurkha religious and regimental festivals and he remembered with a wry smile, the speech he made as Commanding Officer, in Ghurkhali during the festival of 'Dipthwala' although he could not speak a word of the language.

He had written the speech in English, Manni had translated it and then coached him phonetically. Seemingly it had been a great success as most seemed to understand his attempt and the ferocity of the dancing and celebrations which followed went on till dawn. The Ambassador was an honoured guest who had no compunction in sitting down to supper with private soldiers. Good man, thought Douglas, retired now with a well earned Knighthood.

The feeling of unease did not leave him as he entered the villa.

"Jack, your cases should be upstairs. I have to leave you now "

"Thanks Alfonso, have you arranged my 'carrying certificate', the Licenca de Uso e Porte de Arma de Defensa"

Alfonso confirmed he had already arranged to renew his old Licence number 873 as all his information was still on file and he would collect the new documents from the Ministerio de Interio that afternoon. "Do you have two current passport photos?" he asked

"Yup, in my wallet, here. The old Licence had my three handguns on it the Makorov, Tokarev and the Jericho. You had better add on an AK47 serial number to follow"

"OK. I will have the new Licence for you this evening. Remember Jack, automatic shotguns like your infamous Mossberg are still illegal in Angola - stupid, I know when everyone carries an AK47 but that is the law"

"Would I bring an illegal weapon in to Angola" said Jack with palms upraised.

"Yes you would but I do not wish to know. You have been given the 'official' warning"

"Drop by this evening for a drink around 20.00 hrs"

Alfonso nodded, put on his cap, touched his Malacca cane to the peak and departed.

"Sergio" Jack shouted. Sergio emerged immediately from the dining room. "Sorry shouting didn't know how to summon you" Sergio indicated the various bells situated in the walls and said "It is your house Sir, If you can't find me simply walk in to the kitchen"

"Fine, do you have any Champagne? "

"Of course, Senor. I was given explicit instructions, and everything is available in Luanda at the right price"

"Krug?"

"I have a bottle of the non vintage already chilling in an ice bucket. Would you like it upstairs or in the drawing room?" Jack chuckled to himself at the use of the slightly old fashioned but correct 'drawing room' as he always used it and could not a call a room a lounge or sitting room. Maggie was always making fun of him for his, at times, pompous and certainly old fashioned use of English but that was him, that was the way he had been brought up and he would not change.

Indeed the villa boasted a most impressive drawing room.

"Upstairs please Sergio. I will unpack and take a shower"

Douglas went upstairs to find his two re-enforced cases with triple locks, placed on a large rosewood kist at the end of the bed. The room was exquisitely furnished with pale blue silk carpets and drapes, reproduction Sheraton desk and chairs with a large chaise longue covered in dark blue damask in front of the double French windows which led to a covered terrace. The floors were white marble with rose coloured flecks. The air conditioning fluted quietly. Definitely a woman's hand in the decoration trying to remember Jim Connell's slightly built Texan wife. No, this was all new and even smells new. . . .

He hefted both cases on to the bed. Should contact Kendall, he thought.

Opening his larger case he started to unpack his clothes. A discreet knock at the door and Sergio entered without waiting for a response carrying a heavily misted silver ice bucket on a silver tray spotless white napkin folded over his arm and walked to the desk. Douglas noted he had immersed the long crystal flute in the crushed ice so that the glass would be equally chilled.

Sergio wiped the moisture from the glass, checked it was perfectly clean and with a practiced hand, unscrewed the bottle from the cork with a soft plop. He poured an inch of the amber liquid into the glass, sniffed the cork and satisfied presented the glass to Jack to taste.

The effervescence of this fine wine was softly bubbling filling the flute with its scent. Jack held the glass under his nose and inhaled the aroma he knew so well.

"Excellent" handing the glass back to Sergio without tasting.

Sergio filled the glass to the shoulder and handed it back to Jack who immediately took a large swallow, then a second emptying the glass.

"The only way to drink the first glass Sergio" as he handed the glass back for a refill. "Assault the taste buds and the palate then savour the second glass." He smiled. He didn't smile often these days but Krug and Bollinger always made him smile and certainly lifted his mood. He and Maggie normally drank Bollinger as a pre prandial libation - another of my pompous phrases he thought as he lifted the second glass in a silent toast to Maggie in his minds eye.

"Will you be dining in tonight Senor" said Sergio

"Yes, a light supper then an early night. I have a busy day tomorrow. Chief Inspector Carisco is stopping by for a drink around 20.00 so let's say supper around 21.00 hrs.. Could you ensure our gate guards remain awake"

"I have already spoken to them Senor. Be assured they will stay awake. . . . a slight hardness had crept in to his voice."

His shower having refreshed him, Jack closed and locked his bedroom door then unlocked the smaller case. Inside protected by black foam rubber was the latest Satellite communication system with a scrambler and keyboard. It even had an inbuilt GPS, The actual equipment was surprisingly compact and light unlike the huge satellite comms. he had in 92 which almost required its own vehicle to carry it around.

Communications could be made by voice, fax or email all totally secure as, when ready, the signal or voice transmission was encoded and sent in 'burst' at incredibly high speed to be automatically interrogated and decoded by the recipient. The aerial was embedded in the lid of the case.

Jack wished to speak directly to the General, and as it was now 19.30 knew that he would probably be at home at his house in Eaton Mews in Belgravia. Time lines to London were the same as Luanda was approximately due South of Greenwich.

He lifted the receiver, hit the scrambler and dialled the number.

"Kendall" came the gruff answer.

"Hello Bruce, just checking in"

"Thought you might give me a buzz this evening, how are things?"

"Fine" said Jack "you neglected to tell me that prat Anstruther was the Military Attache once again"

"I thought you would like that little surprise, are you two getting on or burying hatchets in each other's heads. You don't have to like the chap to work with him. Seriously Jack. I know what you think of him and about all his past cock ups. If I had told you he was your liaison would you have accepted the task so quickly"

"Possibly not, anyway enough Bruce. You may not know Alfonso has installed me in the old Texaco villa and . . . "

Kendall interrupted. "I know, it was my suggestion, much more secure than the Hotel and away from prying eyes even although it has bad memories. Is Alfonso Behaving himself and earning his retainer"

"Yes, so far, but then he should as the income he gets from you is twice his Angolan salary and paid offshore - very nice. Back to Anstruther, how much is he in the loop?"

"Hardly at all Jack. He has been instructed to give you all possible assistance in your 'tasks' and the sensitivity has been impressed upon him and the Ambassador"

"Good. I don't want him involved in any part of the Operation. How much does HE know?"

"As much as he should know within the Diplomatic envelope. When you meet keep to the basics he does not wish to know the detail although is aware of the nature of the operation and the consultation with the Angolan Government. Presume you are seeing him tomorrow?"

"Yuh, hopefully around 10.00 but not as yet confirmed"

"Right, keep your head down. Bye" and Kendall cut the connection.

Douglas closed and locked the case as he heard vehicle tyres crunching on the gravel. 19.55, Alfonso's on time for once . . .

Sergio knocked again on the door. "Senor, Colonel Anstruther is in the ante room and wishes to speak with you. Shall I show him into the drawing room?"

"Yes you had better otherwise he may be affronted by being kept waiting in the hall. I shall be down in a sec. By the way Sergio this room is to be kept locked at all times as are the windows and shutters. Are there duplicate keys?"

No Senor, all the bedrooms have only one key although I have a master. Sergio now dressed in a white Mandarin Jacket and black trousers retired and was heard speaking to Anstruther.

A few minutes later Jack Douglas carrying his last glass of Krug entered the drawing room.

Anstruther was standing by the windows underneath one of the air conditioning vents running his hand through his sparse black hair. Running was not the operative word, it was more like swimming through his hair as he was perspiring greatly and there were dark patches of sweat under his arms and in the small of his back.

"Good evening Edward, you wish to speak to me? "

"God this country is a hell hole" he said, no greeting! "nothing ever bloody works although you seem to be all right. My bloody air con. Packed up this afternoon and will not be fixed for at least two days. Bloody typical. I hate this place "

"Why did you accept the posting" said Douglas.

"Err, I was instructed"

"I see, now to what do I this unexpected pleasure" Jack asked with a twinkle in his eye.

"Now, see here Douglas. . . . ."

"I have already warned you about the use of my name. This is the last warning, don't do it again"

"Sorry, Err, Jack" he offered tentatively, "but it's been a bloody day"

Sergio was hovering. "Ah Sergio, would you open a bottle of Bollinger and give a glass to the 'good Colonel'. You probably drink gin Edward, but it is far too heavy in this sort of climate don't you think"

Without waiting for an answer Jack sat down. "For God's sake man sit down and relax. Why are you here?"

"I was tasked to supply you with an Embassy vehicle on Diplomatic plates and specifically a Range Rover. We have only one Range Rover and that is mine so I have to give that to you and make do with a bloody long wheel base Land Rover without air con.. Why do you need a Range Rover and why can't you simply hire a four wheel drive from Hull Blyth?"

"You swear a lot Edward, pressure of work?" he left hanging in the air.

Sergio arrived with the Bollinger who opened it, sniffed the cork and proffered a glass to the Colonel. He had gulped half the glass before Jack raising his glass in a toast said "your health"

"Err, Health" muttered Anstruther. Sergio withdrew.

"Right Edward. Why I have to have a diplomatic, reliable vehicle is no concern of yours. You were ordered so to provide not asked so to do. Furthermore my task here is also not your concern. You have been ordered to assist me in any way I see fit and that is exactly what you will do. I have confirmed all this tonight with General Kendall"

Damn, Douglas thought, slipped up there, now he knows I have direct communications.

"When I wish to use your comms I shall do so. I am also on the Embassy VHF net and we have working telephones which will suffice for the time being"

"Ok, If that's the way it is . . Thanks for the drink. I have my driver outside with the Land Rover, here are your keys. Try not to bend it, spares are hard to get. I don't suppose you will sign for the vehicle"

"You suppose correctly. By the by could you confirm with the Ambassador's secretary re my appointment at 10.00 tomorrow. If I don't hear back from you, I will assume it is confirmed.

"Goodnight Edward" at that Sergio showed him to the door as Alfonso Carisco entered tossing a cheerful Hello to Anstruther.

"One last thing Edward" he paused with one leg outside the Land Rover. "Be a good chap and phone or radio through if you wish to come here, it may not be 'convenient' Do not presume to turn up unannounced"

Jack turned and walked back to the drawing room where Alfonso was already quite at home with a large glass of whisky and soda clutched in his hand.

"What are you smiling at?"

"Oh nothing. You know you really shouldn't wind up the Colonel so much he is a bit like a terrier - dangerous when cornered"

"It's difficult not to" said Jack. He is a pompous incompetent but I suppose you are right" as he poured himself a glass of Bollinger, lifting it to the mirror in front of him in silent toast

"Have you got the firearm certificates"

Alfonso withdrew the certificates from his pocket signed by the Chief Commandante, countersigned by himself and with two lines initialled but left empty for the acquisition of any other weapon. His Jericho 9mm and Makarov automatics had been already added. He only retained these sidearms at the direct intervention of General Kendall as after the knee jerk reaction from the Dunblane shooting he had had to surrender all his legally held handguns for destruction. Even his late Father's Webley Service revolver by Dicksons of Edinburgh, encased in an engraved oak case all because of one deranged person and the wimpish Labour politicians. Quite wrong!

Handguns were even more readily available than before on the black market and he knew of two pubs in Glasgow where £200 would purchase an unmarked revolver automatic with 20 rounds of ammunition.

"Do you need anything else"

"Yes an AK47 preferably Czech, folding stock and two banana magazine s. 200 rounds of 7.62 ammunition"

The Chief Inspector simply nodded - "tomorrow"

"Thanks Alfonso, help yourself to another whisky. I would like to meet the local Garrison Commander who supplies the protection detail for the diamond convoys. Captain Ramirez I think you said. What's he like?"

"He is a good Officer and a professional soldier with a thirst for promotion. His present appointment as head of the diamond security detail will give him his majority in another year and guarantees his promotion to Lt. Colonel at the end of his tour. He will then probably command the Special Forces training battalion and by God do they need 'training'. This is his main problem, his troops are better than most of the Angolan Army but do not have, what do you call it. . . 'the killer instinct'. They are not as dedicated as he is, partly because of poor pay and conditions and partly because of poor equipment. They are reasonably trained but they do not go through re-training as it is considered to be time consuming and expensive, also there is no one to replace them if they were to re-train thus they are rusty and since the cease fire have become quite slack in their duties.

Ramirez does his best but his two Lieutenants are hopeless, one is a Political appointment who won't work the other is fat and lazy who can't work."

Jack chuckled at his description. He had always liked Alfonso and his easy manner but knew that behind his slow speech was an intelligent mind and a professional Policeman. He also had the ear of the Chief of Police, a distant relative, and through him the ear of the President himself.

Jack knew that Ramirez had studied at Sandhurst and unlike so many foreign cadets who were simply awarded their Commissions at the end of training, he had worked hard and been made up to a Junior Under Officer.

"Could you set up Luncheon with him at the Barracuda tomorrow"

"I am sure that will be acceptable. If you wish I shall call him now"

Jack nodded. Alfonso strode over to the telephone in the hall helping himself to a third whisky en route. Hmm. he thought, he seems to know his way around this house pretty well. I wonder if it is wired. I better have it swept tomorrow.

A few minutes later Alfonso returned "Confirmed. He said he will be there precisely at 13.00"

"Good could you use your influence and book a secluded table on the terrace?"

"Oh, it is impossible to book a table at such short notice but if I were also invited . . . . ."

"You are invited you old rogue. I would never hear the end of it if you were excluded from luncheon at the best restaurant in Luanda"

Alfonso chuckled. "Thank you my friend, a poor policeman cannot normally dine at such expensive places. I shall bid you Good night"

After his friend had left Jack dined quietly on grilled swordfish and salad, finished his Bollinger and prepared to retire.

"Thank you Sergio. Breakfast at 07.30 and I would like to speak to you afterwards"

"Certainly senor. Good night."

CHAPTER 4

Dawn. 07.10 hrs. Douglas had slept well, now dressed, he opened the terrace doors to check the day, A mistake!. The temperature was already in the 80's and the humidity stifling. He rapidly closed the doors stood under the air conditioning for a minute then went down to breakfast.

The table was already set with a jug of freshly squeezed orange juice together with a pot of strong aromatic coffee.

Sergio appeared from the kitchen.

"Good morning Senor, what do you wish for breakfast? I have fresh fruit, ham, eggs mushrooms, cold meats, cheeses or cereal and yoghurt if you prefer"

"Morning. Great" said jack. "fresh mango and yoghurt if you have it, followed by two poached eggs, ham and grilled mushrooms. Brown bread toast and marmalade". The important decision being made he pondered the day ahead.

Finishing, he complimented Sergio on an excellent breakfast, asked him to leave everything for the moment and come into the drawing room.

"Sit down Sergio"

"No Senor, I prefer to stand"

"As you wish but this is just an informal chat to get to know you a little better"

Sergio inclined his head, said nothing but remained standing.

"Firstly, thank you for the way in which you have prepared the house it makes my job much easier knowing I can relax here with good food and wine in a secure environment. Alfonso told me you were in the Portuguese Army, indeed a Company Sergeant Major in the Commandos. It is somewhat odd that you now appear to be the Major Domo of a luxury villa looking after the likes of me but directly employed by the Chief of Police. Are you instructed to report back on my conversations and movements"

"No Senor. My task is to ensure you have a pleasant stay, are correctly looked after and assist you in 'every' way. This includes your personal security. Anna is a good cook and I enjoy the dual role"

"I see, do you carry a gun"

"Yes, a Makarov" lifting his trouser leg and exposing a neat ankle holster"

"Are there any other weapons here?"

"Yes, there are six AK 47.s with 2000 rounds of ammunition and an American .50 calibre machine gun with 1000 rounds which is in a cupola on the roof covering the area directly in front of the house. There are also four Browning 9mm automatics. The British Army issue. All apart from the machine gun, are locked in a steel gun cupboard bolted to the kitchen wall. I have the only keys"

"Quite an arsenal" said Douglas "and who has the discretion to release these arms"

"At my discretion Senor, and to whom I deem necessary and qualified."

"You have a very good command of English, almost unaccented. You didn't learn such in depth colloquial knowledge in the Army"

"My Mother was English. She was born in Winchester and a lieutenant in the WRACS when she met my Father who was a Captain in the Portuguese Cavalry on secondment in England. I say secondment but I believe he really only played polo for most of his eighteen months. Mostly at Smiths Lawn with your Household Brigade"

"I take it by your voice you didn't approve"

"No, My Father left the Army after he was married and returned to the family Estates in the North of Portugal, on the Costa Verde near Vianna de Castello. We were modest wine producers and thus comfortably well off however he was always away travelling the world playing polo - South America, Britain, Germany even Russia. He ran two strings of ponies and simply did not have the money to maintain his lifestyle so he started selling off parts of the vineyards ending up with only the main house and stables which he also mortgaged for his sport which had now become a fixation. I was eighteen when he came from England and announced to my hard worn mother that he was bankrupt but had been having an affair with an English Lady with whom he was in love and was leaving to live with her. She was very wealthy and would ensure he could continue his love of Polo which he was still playing at decent handicap even although his years were marching on.

My Mother was heartbroken. We moved to one of the Estate cottages and she died a year later. She just gave up."

A light of recognition to this somewhat scandalous story flickered in Jack's mind.

"Sergio, I did not mean to intrude in your private life. Please forgive me."

"That's all right Senor. I prefer that you know my background and therefore may give me trust"

"Believe me" Jack continued, "I have an important reason for asking. May I ask, is your family name De La Cruz and your Father, Luis?"

Sergio gasped, the mask slipping from his face for a moment.

"Now will you sit down" Sergio sat in one of the high wing brocaded armchairs opposite Douglas.

"Yes, that is my family name but how did you know?"

"I too played Polo Sergio, sadly no more, too old and couldn't afford it anyway but I played against your Father and indeed played on the same team a couple of times. He was a very good player. When did you last see him?"

I have not seen him since I was eighteen,"

"Good Lord. Well you may not know, the Lady your Father married was Lady Caroline Marden, She had Estates in Yorkshire, near Malton and in Wester Ross in Scotland. A steel heiress and very wealthy."

"Yes I believe that was the 'woman' "Sergio said with tight lips.

"I am really sorry to have to tell you, your Father died some five years ago. I was at the funeral"

A cloud passed over Sergio's face and his head went down for a few moments. Regaining his composure he straightened his shoulders, slipped the mask back on his face and asked "How did it happen?"

"They both died in an horrific car crash in Yorkshire returning in the small hours from a Hunt Ball. Luis was drunk so Caroline drove although she had also been drinking. She was driving an old Alvis convertible and simply came round a corner and ploughed in to the back of a lorry on the side of the road which had had a puncture. The roads there were very narrow. They were both killed instantly as was the farmer who was at the rear changing the wheel.

If it is of any consolation they would not have felt a thing as a second vehicle appeared on the scene minutes afterwards and the driver tried to give first aid but it was obvious that they were dead from the quite shocking injuries.

Silence for a minute. "Thank you Senor, Will that be all"

Jack nodded, adding. I am really sorry, I liked Caroline and Luis a lot"

Sergio walked to the door. He seemed to have grown smaller and aged in the last ten minutes. Poor chap, Jack thought, what a small world, well the last half hour would either have Sergio on my side or firmly against me.

Jack Douglas drove the Range Rover through the Embassy gates at 09.50 after a cursory check from the Marine sentry. Not good, he thought - sloppy, even although he recognised the vehicle. Too sloppy by half, but not my problem.

He walked to the massive front doors of the Embassy which was also the Ambassador's residence just as Judy Wiltshire walked out accompanied by a thin mousy man about the same age who seemed to be in a bit of a mood.

Her face brightened to a lovely smile when she saw Jack.

"Good morning Mr Douglas, I see you have the Colonel's Range Rover" she said with another impish grin"

"Yes, he was good enough to lend it to me for the duration of my stay"

"That's not what I heard" she said quietly. Oh, Sorry, Mr Douglas I would like you to meet my husband James. He is the Commercial Attache."

"Yes I know, How do you do" as both men shook hands.

"I have just re-confirmed your ten o'clock with Rosie, HE's secretary. Must run, we are going shopping and James insists I do not go alone"

"Quite right" said Jack.

Unless things had changed greatly, but he didn't think so as Alfonso had only told him yesterday of a Portuguese man who had his arm chopped off at the wrist whilst stopped at traffic lights, window open, arm on the side, just to steal his watch. The somewhat macabre side of it was although it looked like a Rolex it was only a cheap 30 dollar copy so he lost his lower arm for being a poseur.

Douglas was ushered in through the two security gates to the Ambassador's office which was one of the original grand public rooms, indeed as the ornate ceiling went through two floors it was really a saloon with a breathtaking view over the lagoon and out to the islands beyond the spur. Brings back memories of happier times, he thought as he looked down and saw the old Ghurkha quarters to the left of the formal gardens towards the rear gate.

"Good morning Sir" as The Ambassador stood to shake hands.

"Good morning Mr Douglas, do sit down. Has Rosie asked if you would like a drink?"

"Yes, and no thank you"

"Fine. Let's get straight on. I know you had a close relationship with this Office when you were here in the 90's and the Ambassador was a personal friend. I have read some of the summarised files.

I just wish you to know that I am unhappy about this quasi clandestine operation even although sanctioned by both Governments. Mr Belguerro is a friend of mine and I think it wrong that he is not fully briefed. This story that you are to simply check the diamond convoy security does not hold water"

I also think that it is quite wrong that your General Kendall and his unaccountable section can bulldoze the Foreign Office to go along with this deception even although he has the ear of the Prime Minister".

Here we go, thought Jack.

"Sir the story is quite feasible as I was in charge of Endiama's diamond security for two years and that there is now almost daily pilferage from the mines and the transport.

Informing Belguerro in detail would defeat the Exercise.

Secondly, General Kendall is certainly not 'my' General but is a very well respected Officer holding down a senior, vital and difficult position. I don't think he is even the PM's General - that is why his independent section is in existence. He answers only to the Security Services not the Home Office which is a sieve of leaks and misinformation.

There is a definite leak at senior level of movements and stock whereabouts of uncut diamonds. This may be Endiama, CSO or a number of other possibilities. Angola is awash with contacts, and informers. I know the Embassy employs several moles in various organisations. . . . .

"That does not concern you," interrupted the Ambassador, "What I am saying is the less I know about your activities the better"

"That suits me perfectly. The less you know about my operation decreases the potential of a leak from this building and that certainly goes for Anstruther"

"What! Are you implying sensitive information is passed on from this Embassy?"

"Let's just say 'careless talk cost lives'. "Good Day, Sir"

Jack got up and walked out of the 'saloon' leaving a flabbergasted and angry Ambassador staring at his back.

"Well, that went well" he thought with a sardonic smile.

"Thank you, Rosie," he said as he walked past her desk to the outside and his waiting vehicle where an Angolan was leathering off the bodywork.

"Thanks very much."

"Yus Suh. It just finish (click) up as he shambled to attention and threw up an untidy half salute. Yu is remembering me Suh. I is (click) Paul. I's worked for (click) you back (click) then.

Indeed Jack did remember him. Paul was Chocque, he couldn't remember the spelling, and he had the unusual clicking sound interspersed through their language and the patois of English and Portuguese.

"Yes Paul, I do remember you as he extended his hand. How are you? "A great grin broke over Paul's face showing his few remaining broken and yellow teeth as he shot his hand forward and languidly but energetically pumped hands up and down. "How is your brother?" Jack could not remember his name but knew he had lost a leg below the knee from a landmine which were spread indiscriminately throughout the country.

"He gone Suh. Some (click) three years gone"

"I am sorry to hear that"

"Suh. You here (click) back for long time? You here give (click) Paul a good job like before, not Embashy, not good Coolnel (click) not good coin. I good (click) driver"

He was actually an appalling driver but Jack just said, "Sorry Paul I am only here for a couple of weeks but you look after yourself" and he hid a 20 US dollar note in his hand, two weeks pay, as he shook hands, which was quickly transferred to his grimy pocket with another huge grin.

During this exchange Anstruther had been watching from his office window. He had already spoken to HE on the telephone and knew the irritation caused.

Walking across the courtyard he said. "Hear you ruffled the old man's feathers. Not a good idea, better to keep on his good side"

"You can do that for both us Edward" and drove out of the Embassy.

Descending the road he turned left on the causeway which linked Luanda to the spur.

The original Lagoon road curved all along the bay from the spur, the Ilha de Luanda, to the docks and had once been a lovely palm lined dual carriageway with impressive Portuguese colonial buildings all along the landward side. It was now rutted and full of axle breaking holes although in a slightly better condition than when Douglas was last here.

Four lanes of traffic tried to squeeze in to two lanes and driving was as he remembered - push out, gun the engine, use the horn and don't look back.

Just as he turned towards the causeway a large Black Toyota Landcruiser bulldozed past him air horns blaring causing him to squeeze over and fight for space with a canted, overloaded Bedford truck. Well, it had once been a Bedford but had 'benefited' from being cannibalised from other marques during its life. As the truck lurched to the left he squeezed through and looked again at the Toyota. Green Government plates, could be a Government Agency or one of the many Ex Pat Operations who had paid the extra fee to get green plates. All the Oil Companies had them as did most of the other large European business.

As it reached the roundabout after the causeway the person in the rear passenger seat opened his window and looked up as if something was being pointed out to him. He realised he knew the face from way back. As he pulled on to the spur he remembered, 'Gallagher'. Sean Gallagher had been highly placed in the IRA - an evil bastard. Jack had locked horns with him when he had commanded a helicopter flight of 662 Squadron, IV Guards Brigade in Armagh.

What the Hell is he doing here?

He dropped back as the road on the spur was a normal carriageway. They passed the Naval barracks and docks then just before the primary school the Toyota veered right throwing up dust and disappeared down the track. Douglas knew that it led to an old wharf and the Hotel ship 'Hispaniola' which had been moved in to position in 1991. It was now 12.15 hrs. and the Barracuda Restaurant was across the road on the seaward side so he allowed his curiosity to rest for the moment.

He pulled the Range Rover in front of the long low restaurant building. Immediately he stopped he was besieged by ten or twelve filthy jabbering urchins. These were the street kids, no parents just gangs to look after them. Fortunately he knew the form. His old IDS compound, the Campo Hydroportos was only two hundred yards from here and he often frequented the Barracuda in early years.

"Quiet" he roared, even if they didn't understand English they got the idea. He picked out two of the boys, one about twelve with a wall eye who seemed to be the leader and a younger crippled boy. Beckoning them towards the vehicle he said 'Guarda el Coche' in Spanish which they understood and immediately the older boy established proprietorial rights by taking up position sitting on the front bull bar with the other boy stationed at the rear. His vehicle was now safe from theft or pilfering, until a bigger boy came along he thought.

The Barracuda was an anomaly, definitely the best restaurant in Luanda, probably in Angola. It was Portuguese owned although it was rumoured that it had Government backing. It had survived twenty years of civil war and was beautifully situated at the end of the long peninsular finger which completed the Western side of the lagoon.

The decoration, ambiance, food and service were excellent and could rival many of the best restaurants in European Capitals. There was a lovely long verandah on the seaward side overlooking the beach which was private and kept spotless secured at each end by armed guards wielding large night sticks to keep the locals from intruding.

The Barracuda had been a haven of civilisation during his earlier tours and looked as if it still was. Douglas remembered many an evening sitting on the verandah with his number two, Dickie Baird after a particular 'bastard of a day' sipping very cold Vinho Verde (champagne was in short supply in these days) and watching the huge orange ball sink quickly below the horizon at 18.30 every evening.

Extraordinarily beautiful! Sunset was always the same time in Angola and the night really fell. There was no dusk, one minute it was light, next, pitch dark. It caught a lot of people out when they first arrived in country as there were few street lamps and only generators lit the few buildings on the Ilha.

The sad part about this restaurant was that prices were equally European and way over the top for Angola. The oil men would drop 200 dollars, the acceptable currency, for dinner for two. Very harsh on the Angolan waiters who were lucky to earn twenty dollars a week, and that was considered 'well paid', however they rarely showed any resentment at the ex pats paying the equivalent of two months wages for one meal. You couldn't possibly pay in the local currency, the Kwanza which was virtually worthless due to rampant inflation. The only way the currency was traded was in 'bricks' of 1000 Kwanza notes. You never counted them and never got change. Prices were, two bricks, four bricks etc. one brick in the early 90's equated to around 4 dollars US. Going shopping was a nightmare.

The Maitre approached Douglas as he walked through the doors. He had half expected to see the old Maitre who had always looked after him so well. Alas he had then been in his 60's and had either retired or passed on. "I believe. . . . ."

"Yes Mr Douglas, Good afternoon. The Chief Inspector telephoned your reservation and we have managed to give you a fine table. He described you on the telephone and said you would be here around 12. 30.

Would you care for a drink at the bar or go straight to your table?"

"I will have a bottle at the Bar which can be taken to the table"

"As you wish Sir" with a slight bow and in rapid Portuguese, the Sommelier was summoned whilst a waiter guided him to his chair at the bar..

"Bollinger if you have it, the non vintage, lots of ice and chilled glasses"

"Certainly Sir" as he tucked the unopened wine list back under his arm.

There were few people at the Bar as it was still early and Jack sat in the corner back to the stone wall with the sparkling sea on his right. Here he could see the entrance way and partly in to the Restaurant which at the moment appeared to be almost empty. Managed to reserve me a table indeed, I bet the place will only be half full he smiled.

His wine arrived, was opened and poured. He took the 'nose'. Nothing really like Bollinger, so distinctive. He raised his first glass in silent toast as he always did.

Alfonso arrived in the company of a very impressive young Army Officer in immaculate uniform.   So this is Captain Francisco Ramirez.

. . . . .

Chapter 5

The harsh Falls Road accent of Sean Gallagher cut across the suite on the Hotel ship 'Hispaniola'

"For fuck's sake Ger, pull your finger out. You are pissing money away in the Casino trying to impress that French bird. We are trying to keep a low profile on this job"

"That's a load of shite Sean and you know it." Gerry McGafferty replied "Nobody knows us in this God forsaken place. I don't take orders from you and I am not about to start now"

Gerry McGafferty was a very hard man and was once one of the IRA's top 'enforcers' i.e. he was a 'hit man' and Gerry liked his work. Aged 54 he was not an imposing figure and passing him by would not merit a second glance. One of his many nefarious skills was to be almost invisible. He was a master of disguise and could change his appearance and add or subtract twenty years of age simply by changing his body movements. He had fifteen confirmed kills to his name and a couple of dozen knee cappings. He had shot his first man when he was eighteen and was still dyed in the wool IRA. Since the cease fire he had moved to the shadowy world of International arms dealing whilst maintaining close contact with the many factions in Ireland still requiring arms and explosives for clandestine operations or the resurgence of active cells in the former IRA.

Sean Gallagher was 55. He had been the main Quartermaster for the IRA and had been entrusted as paymaster for all foreign arms acquisitions. He had been Number 4 on the most wanted list in the Headquarters of the now defunct Royal Ulster Constabulary and that of the British Army. In the earlier years his had been the mind behind several successful assassinations and bombings including the murder of Lord Louis Mountbatten. He was another ' quite hard man'.

Unlike the disgraceful hand out of pardons by the British Government to known IRA murderers like Michael McGuiness under the Good Friday Accord, McGafferty and Gallagher received no such pardon and were still classed as 'persons of significant interest to the British Security Services.

"Awh right" Gallagher growled "but you remember. I'm in charge of this Op and I am telling you, go canny and lay off the booze"

McGafferty looked at Sean through cold, hooded eyes. He half opened his mouth revealing tobacco stained teeth as if he were going to reply then thought better of it.

"I hear yuh. I'm off"

"Where you going? We have the final meeting with those UNITA boyos this afternoon"

"To get a drink OK!" not a request, a statement.

No it was not OK thought Sean but he let it go. It was only 10.30 in the morning. Trouble brewing there!

Gallagher and McGafferty had been partners in crime for over thirty years. They did not particularly like each other but held a grudging respect for the history and the cold heartened decisions and actions both had made over the years. The only sentiment they had was for the old IRA which held them in loose partnership, and of course, the money!

Sean Gallagher had negotiated to buy two container loads of arms, ammunition, landmines and Semtex explosive from one of the many breakaway ex UNITA factions still roaming and raiding as they pleased in the vast unpopulated areas of Angola since the end of the Civil War. It was simply too difficult for the Government Forces to round them up and frankly they couldn't really be bothered as long as these gangs kept the thuggery, looting and rape in the Northern areas and did not threaten the diamond recovery operations.

This particular Group needed hard cash and didn't have access to the source of uncut 'blood diamonds' they had milked during the war. They were now simply a bunch of thugs selling anything and everything from arms to slaves.

Yesterday his contact told him they had access to the latest American anti-personnel mine, similar to a Claymore and Sean had added a hundred of these lethal and very effective close quarter killers to his shopping list.

These mines were ideal for ambush of infantry or indeed soft skinned vehicles as the shaped charge devastated all within a 140 degree arc. They were designed to maim thus tie up forces and air support in recovery of the grievously wounded. At close range it would be as if both barrels of a shotgun had gone off simultaneously six feet away and would rip a body in half.

A nice little bonus though Sean.

Back home on the Emerald Isle the IRA had completely disarmed (as far as the Public was aware) and Jerry Adams and McGuiness were now ensconced in Stormont as the political arm of Sinn Fein. As in Angola, there were still hard line cells in existence consisting of the diehard old thugs who lay in wait for the 'Cause' to be resurrected and still carried out mischief behind the scenes. Some of this shipment was destined for

Ireland, some to Basque Separists, some to a new subversive group in France, the rest to his warehouse on the Cape Verde Islands, which lay adjacent to the coast of Angola.

It had been increasingly difficult to purchase arms from the old sources of Libya, Iran, the Balkans or the devolved Russian States. Too many watchful eyes since ISIS had caused so much more security to be in force throughout the world.

Few eyes kept a dedicated watch on cargoes coming out of Angola, Sierra Leone or Zaire.

The one group with whom he would have no dealings was ISIS who were, in any event, awash with arms. This was not from any political, religious or soft heartened reason, simply for his own safety.

Bloody mad 'towel heads' he thought.

Gallagher had a long association with the old UNITA rebel forces and had purchased arms from this source twice in the past, all for the IRA. This was his first personal acquisition but he was using the same agent he had used before, one Alfonso Ponce.

He was not overly concerned that he was dealing with a very hard line faction of the old UNITA as long as he got his delivery on time and in good condition.

They had been here for almost two weeks and it had been frustratingly slow organising the collection and delivery to two containers hidden thirty kilometres North of Luanda. Today was supposed to be the last collection day. The containers would then be driven to the docks where Hull Blyth would handle the Bills of Lading as 'used Marine diesel engines'. The arms would be stacked in the centre with each end loaded floor to ceiling with filthy old engines and parts purportedly going to Germany for rebuild.

Few Customs Officers would dirty themselves clambering over the top and if they did all they would see would be more engines up to the roof as a false mezzanine floor had been built to support some of the smaller engines above the arms cargo.

Sean had arranged with Christopher Armstrong, the Hull Blyth Agent, to prepare the necessary paperwork and be present on the dock to facilitate the final, casual Customs inspection prior to the containers being sealed and swung inboard. Armstrong did not know and did not wish to know what 'extra' cargo was in the containers.

The ship was the 'Maria Luisa'. She looked like one of the many tired old rusty African Traders plying the West coast shelf but she was in fact only twelve years old with powerful, well maintained engines. The seemingly rust streaked sides was in fact a clever camouflage paint. The perceived lack of maintenance and the deck clutter were simply a ruse to depict an old worn ship.

At 8, 000 tons she had a flank speed of 26 knots.

Registered in Liberia she ran her nefarious tasks from South Africa to Europe under a canopy of nominee Companies which completely hid her true ownership.

His containers would be the last loaded, the ship would be singled up, diesels fired ready for immediate departure.

The payment to UNITA would be made in three drops. One third this afternoon when the containers were fully loaded and inspected by him with Gerry carrying out a check firing on some of the weapons. He would then padlock the containers with his own stainless steel locks until they arrived at the port to ensure none of the arms or indeed all of the arms were not offloaded in transit. He also had eight special seals to secure the main end doors. These would be removed by him prior to Customs inspection.

The second payment was to be made in the docks after the containers had been Customs sealed.

The third made aboard ship once the containers were securely on board, just prior to departure.

Sean had paid Armstong the Hull Blyth handling fee with an extra 1,000 dollars to ensure 'smooth passage' through Customs control. He expected the bulk of this money would be retained by Armstrong as he was known to 'take a bung' on 'iffy' cargo. However as far as he was concerned it was two containers of used marine diesels, whether he pondered why an Irishman would buy engines to be shipped to Germany was best left alone.

Gallagher checked his watch. 11.40 hrs. Better find Ger, he thought and get down to the dock to meet the transport.

He carried a lightweight beige blouson jacket over his arm which would be necessary to wear once he had retrieved his pistol from Ship Security at the bottom of the gangplank. This was a well run operation. No firearms were allowed on board save the black uniformed ship's guards who patrolled the decks day and night armed with Heckler Koch light machine guns and who were definitely not locally trained. Most of them seemed to be South African ex Military as were the two gorillas he had employed in Windhoek in Namibia as his bodyguards and who occupied the suite next to his.. He knocked twice on that door and carried on up to the main deck.

Just behind him the two minders emerged ready to go.

"Morning Mr Gallagher" they chorused

"Morning boys, as per yesterday's brief. Inspection and first payment today as he lifted the briefcase in his left hand. Keep close, stay loose. I don't trust these buggers"

"Bloody Kaffirs" said Pieter, one of the guards. "can niver trust these bestards" he added in his clipped accent.

"That's enough. I don't give a damn what your personal feelings are. You're paid to do a job, just do it and shut up"

He turned to Jouhan the other guard and told him to get Mr McGafferty. "He's probably in the bar"

Gerry emerged from the bar smelling of whisky

"Jesus Gerr, could you not just stick to beer in the morning?"

"What's it to you. I can hold my drink" Sean just looked at him coldly. If truth be known he was a bit scared of Gerry who at times could go off at half cock for no reason but he was the senior man and McGafferty had to accept it. He would just have to watch his back.

"Come on then" and he walked down the gangplank preceded by the 6ft 4ins tall Pieter with the very slightly smaller Jouhan taking up the rear.

They entered the security Reception where two of the black uniformed guards unlocked a large steel barred door behind the desk entering a small room lined with steel numbered drawers similar to a safety deposit vault. One of the guards alternately inserted the plastic card from Gallagher and turned a key in the lock on each box then said.

"Gentlemen, if you would come in one at a time and retrieve your weapons. No one enters until the one inside has left. You will not load your weapons until you are clear of the ship. Is that clear" They all nodded.

Sean went in first as the second guard moved to the side with both hands on his machine gun covering him but with his 'oppo' out of the line of fire. He picked up his Browning 9mm, another magazine and a box of 50 rounds. He favoured a butt forward shoulder holster instead of the more upright holster as, once used to it, it was much quicker to draw and fire. He put the straps over his shoulders, inserted the weapon and put on his light jacket.

As he left Gerry entered, picked up his Colt Magnum, he favoured a revolver, much less likely to jam and it had two speed loading cylinders.

He wore this in a conventional rig under his arm "Fuck, I've forgotten my jacket"

"Well, you'll just have to wear it under your shirt and leave the buttons open. If you like I'll buy you a gold medallion at the market to complete the image" Sean said with a smile.

McGafferty actually smiled himself - "Yeh, yeh, big joke"

Pieter and Jouhan followed the procedure both hefting 9mm Desert Eagles and both also wearing ankle guns, one a .38 revolver the other a Beretta automatic.

"Right lads, all tooled up? I think we better have one up the spout just in case and all loaded and cocked their weapons chambering a round in to the breech.

At that time a black Toyota Land cruiser stormed on to the wharf spinning a cloud of dust from its oversize tyres. . . . .

CHAPTER 6

Luncheon at the Barracuda was progressing well. Having finished the Bollinger, Douglas had ordered a bottle of Castel Garcia, a Portuguese Vino Verde, to wash down the lobster all three had ordered.

Francisco Ramirez spoke good English and they were now on Christian name terms. The first course consisted of a well presented spinach and avocado salad with anchovies and goats cheese which had been placed in the centre of the table for each one to help himself.

To put the Captain at ease, Alfonso had been rabbiting on about his and Jack's past association and he had visibly relaxed after his first glass of wine although still formal in his speech and manner.

"Francisco, Alfonso has told me of the well trained troops you have in the Diamond Security Company and also of some of your slight problems with your junior Officers"

Francisco's eyes lost their warmth and he shot a look at Alfonso as if to say, 'why did you tell this man of our internal problems, ' but then turned to Jack and said,

"Yes, they are good men but because we work twelve hour shifts there is little time to re-train or even take them to the firing range for practice. Half of my men have not fired their weapons in over a year. This is not satisfactory, you understand, but although I have asked my Commandant many times for a period without 'deliveries', it has not been possible.

Again for security purposes we are not informed of actual timings for a delivery until the aircraft is en route so we are on duty every day.

I have three platoons, each of thirty men and one platoon is required for each convoy and for security at the airport when the diamonds arrive

Thus you see my problem. There are no replacements available with the level of skills of my men though these skills have not been practised for some months. All my men are put through a rigorous screening to ensure they are honest and of the correct calibre."

"I see" said Jack.

At that moment the lobster arrived and conversation stalled as both halves of large mouth watering lobster were placed in front of each man together with a new potato salad and a tomato, onion and basil salad. A small bowl of the Chef's own mayonnaise enhanced the presentation.

"This looks good" said Alfonso as he got stuck in. . .

"Bon appetit" said Jack. The lobster was indeed, excellent.

After a few minutes silence and contented eating Francisco Ramirez continued,

"I have been informed that you are to review our security procedures for my Government although I am mystified why you have been brought in, even with your past experience and knowledge, when I am sure a senior Angolan Army Officer would have been just as able to carry out the task.

I mean no disrespect Mr Douglas, err. . ., Jack, but it appears that if you recommend various changes or improvements you do not have the authority to implement them, whereas an Army Officer would ensure these changes were made. . . Unless, of course, there is another reason for your presence in Angola about which I have not been briefed."

Alfonso kept his head in his lobster.

"Your first point" said Douglas. "It was thought that an external unbiased source would be more effective in taking an overall view of the complete operations from sorting 'up country' to arrival at the Bank. A source which could not be contaminated by friendship, personal. Political or Military aspirations.

Your second point. Yes, there is a secondary reason why I am here which has been discussed and agreed at the highest Government levels of both our countries, unfortunately this is 'need to know' and I can not disclose any further information at the moment."

Francisco looked slightly miffed. "I see, well, it has not been confirmed yet but I am expecting a delivery this evening if you wish to accompany me. I am Duty Officer today"

"Thank you, that will be grand as I want to get matters moving as soon as possible. I shall simply come along as an observer."

Luncheon finished, Douglas paid the ridiculously high bill and all three men rose from the table. The Maitre made his way over asking Alfonso if all was well and if they had enjoyed their meal.

"Senor Douglas is host today he said not me"

"Excellent" said Douglas "apart from your prices which are extortionate" The Maitre raised his shoulders in a small shrug "it is the taxes and import costs Senor Douglas, all imports are expensive in Angola."

"Agreed, but not that expensive, you must be making at least 200%

profit but of course you know everybody will pay as the food is excellent and there is nowhere else"

The Maitre, shrugged again with a smile and had the good grace to say nothing more.

The three men shook hands at the door, Alfonso and Francisco thanking Jack for lunch with Francisco advising that he would telephone later to confirm timings and that he would pick him up at the villa if the delivery was scheduled for tonight. He turned towards a beaten up Army UMM with one of his soldiers leaning against it. On seeing his Officer he came, quite smartly, to attention and saluted. Not bad, Jack thought.

Walking towards his Range Rover the two street lads were still sitting on the bonnet which was now in the shade of a tree. He took three US dollars from his pocket, gave one each to the delighted boys and a second dollar to the elder asking Alfonso to tell him he wanted them to guard his car every time he came to the Barracuda as they had obviously done a good job and even cleaned all the dust off the windows.

Alfonso rattled something else to the two boys who looked a bit sheepish then scampered off.

"What was that all about?"

Alfonso chuckled, "Oh I have to scare them every now and then. One of Fina's cars was stolen form here last week whilst some of the boys were supposed to have been guarding it. Indeed they could not have prevented the theft but instead of telling the owner who was in the restaurant, they ran off and hid. By the time the theft was discovered the car was long gone and hasn't been seen since - probably up country somewhere. It will be run into the ground then cannibalised and abandoned. The thieves will then simply come to Luanda and steal another one. It happens often and we have only managed to recover three vehicles in the past year.

You must be careful of your Range Rover as these are highly sought after. Last year a V8 Land Rover was stolen from the British Embassy, quite blatantly, simply driven out by one of the Embassy employed local drivers - vehicle and driver never seen again. Not bad for two weeks work, Eh!"

Jack laughed, "yes I did here something about it. That would have put egg all over the face of the great Colonel Anstruther.

Right Alfonso, one more thing this afternoon. Do you remember a man named Papa Rock? He used to work for me and lived near the Naval base on the lagoon".

"Of course, I remember. I see him quite often. We can call at his house on the way back"

"Ok, I'll follow you as I can't remember which one of the alleys leads to his house. There has been quite a lot of new construction on the Ilha since I was last here".

Five minutes later the two vehicles pulled up in front of a small single storey house with a garden at the rear running down to the lagoon. There was a small dock and an 8 metre rigid raider with two large outboard engines, pulled up on the beach. An old Isuzu Trooper jeep languished in a lean to.

I remember this house now, thought Jack. One hundred yards to the left was the somewhat grandly named 'Luanda Yacht Club' where he had kept the Texaco high speed launch.

"I think we are in luck, both the boat and his jeep are here," and with that he opened the door, walked straight in calling Papa's name "Papa, I have brought an old friend to see you".

As Jack entered, a mountain of a black man emerged through the house from the beach wiping his hands on an oily cloth. He had a cap of white hair above his heavy shoulders and bull neck.

"Jack, Jack Douglas" he cried launching himself at Jack and encircling him in a bear hug.

"Steady on Papa, you'll break my back" Papa Rock released Jack then grabbed his hand in one of his large paws and pumped it up and down grinning all the while.

"L0 Alfonso" he said, "what are you doing back here Jack. You said you would never come back when you left in '92. God it's good to see you. How have you been? Are you back with the 'Company'? How long have you been in Luanda?"

"All in good time" Jack said giving the old man a playful punch on the arm, an arm which was still hard muscle.

"Wait till I get some beers from the ice box. Come out to the back"

All three walked through the house to a small verandah which thankfully was covered and threw reasonable shade. There was an old cracked leather armchair and a rope hammock. The other furniture consisted of an upturned hogs head barrel, a wooden crate for a table and a wooden chair whose back had long since disappeared thus becoming a four legged stool.

Papa handed round the beers then fell into the armchair which groaned in protest. Condensation had already formed thickly on the ice cold cans.

An outboard motor with its cover off was strapped in to a 50 gallon drum full of water. Tools lay scattered around. This was the object on which Papa had been working.

John 'Papa' Rockwell was British. He had come to Angola in the late 70's as a driver for the Elf Oil Company. He was now 62 years of age and huge. Apart from a thickening of his waist he looked in good shape. He was over six feet in height and had been heavyweight boxing champion in the Royal Navy. With a 48 inch barrel chest he must have easily weighed seventeen stone. His skin colour was purple black. A truly, black, black man.

After the reunion excitement had died down, Douglas explained why he was back and that he would like to hire Papa and his Rib, if it was running, for the duration of his stay. He also wanted Papa to drive for him.

"If it's running? What do you mean if it's running? Don't let looks fool you," indicating with his can, "these are two 150 horse power Yamahas on the transom, only two years old. It will best 50 knots and out run anything here."

He had purposely sanded off the insignia and dulled the covers so that the 'rag trade' as he called the local thieves would not think them worth stealing although both engines were anchored to the deck eyes by thick steel cables. The rubber works and hull had also been artificially aged.

"That's mine as well" he said, pointing at a gleaming 12 metre Chris Craft gently swinging on its mooring just offshore. Although a 'Tupperware' boat as he referred to glass fibre, it was a double skinned hull with inbuilt buoyancy tanks and twin 425 horsepower turbocharged diesels. "That does about 45 knots, very strong and virtually unsinkable."

"OK, OK," Jack said with a smile. "I didn't mean to offend your obvious Marine Engineering skills and competence" indicating the old outboard in the barrel.

"Oh that, that's not mine, just doing a favour for a fisherman friend to see if I can coax another few hours from it but it is really 'goosed'"

"Do you still have all your diving gear?"

"Sure" said Papa, "all recent and in good working order. I still have your tanks and equipment you left me although the wet suit is a bit perished in places"

"Great, we may have need of it "

"What are you up to Jack? Or is that a question the answer to which you don't wish me to know. Well, you always had a pretty good budget so you can afford my 'enormous' fees" he chuckled.

'Papa' had got his name when he first came to Luanda. He married a local girl who bore him two sons in three years, sadly, Mary his wife and the first born boy, John, were killed when the car he was driving at night, overturned on one of the back country tracks. Papa lay under the car badly injured with his dead family around him for over 30 hours. A passing truck driver eventually spotted the wreck, pulled him clear and took him to a local Doctor who patched him up. He carried a 'railway track' 18 inch scar across his left shoulder and chest.

Although mentally in anguish, Papa survived and doted on his other son Mark until he contracted tuberculosis and jaundice, dying, aged seven years.

After this second tragedy Papa went 'on the bottle' and was drunk for about three years. He lost his job and only existed by fishing from an old boat he had bought and refitted. One night whilst fishing and drinking, or drinking and fishing he came across a half submerged canoe some three miles out to sea. With his bleary eyes and a flashlight he examined his find but could only see a bundle of rags in the bow. He was just about to turn away thinking that it had been abandoned when the rags moved. Dam rats, he thought but then a small hand and a bony arm appeared.

He hooked the canoe alongside and discovered to his amazement a tiny little girl, completely naked and half dead from exposure. She looked about three years old but he later learnt she was actually six.

Papa took the girl in, nursed her back to health and having been unable to find any relatives, adopted her.

That day he stopped drinking hard liquor.

He never married again but over the course of the next twenty years he took in and gave life back to seven other orphaned children to whom he was 'Papa'. Most were now up and away with families of their own. Only one of the boys, Malcolm who he also adopted, stayed with him, and worked with the boats.

Naomi, the little girl found in the canoe is a successful Lawyer in South Africa.

The 'Rock' part was from his name and the fact that his sheer bulk resembled a large black rock whose muscles were almost as hard.

Hence,   'Papa Rock!'

They stayed for two hours yarning and catching up.

Eventually Alfonso was called away on Police business and Jack got up to leave grasping his hand. "It's good to see you. Consider yourself on the payroll from today, we can discuss terms later.

It would be easier for me and more sensible if you were to move in to the villa if that's OK. Can Malcolm run things here?"

"Sure, it will be nice to have some luxury for a change and see how the other half lives. ."

Chapter 7

Gallagher, McGafferty and the two minders were bouncing down a dirt track in the dust covered Landcruiser approximately twenty five kilometres North of Luanda. A camouflage painted long wheel base Land Rover had joined them two minutes ago but was hanging back about three hundred metres to keep out of the dust stream. There appeared to be four or five heavily armed men in the vehicle.

Gallagher was informed by the driver that that was Senor Ponce and 'friends'.

"Good" grunted Gallagher and made an unobtrusive sign to the other three to be ready.

Another five minutes and the Landcruiser swung off the road on to an almost invisible track leading to a large coppice of trees where it braked to a halt. Sitting under camouflage nets was the bulk of a forty ton articulated truck with a tri axle container trailer. The dust slowly settled in the oppressive heat and the outline of another unit became visible behind the first.

There were a dozen or so badly clothed but heavily armed men lounging around another Land Rover wearing a form of raggedy military uniform.

These were the breakaway UNITA rebels, thought Gallagher. They don't look much but he knew they had been brutalised by many years of war and were very dangerous indeed.

Nobody moved - the only noise being the fans of the air conditioning unit in the Landcruiser whose engine was still running.

The following Land Rover pulled up about twenty metres to the rear effectively blocking any escape route and the occupants debussed, spreading left and right, weapons ready.

This was the signal for the UNITA boys to come to action and they also fanned out across the front of the leading truck, weapons ready.

"What the Fuck" said McGafferty, "are we in the middle of a firefight? Let's get out of here"

"Shut up Ger" said Gallagher.

The air was very still. The Landcruiser engine had stopped and only the ticking of the hot engine broke the silence. Gallagher slowly climbed down from the vehicle signalling the others so to do but keep close and hands away from weapons.

Alfonso Nunez Ponce, the Broker of the deal and the main gun runner in Luanda strode past them without a word and approached one of the UNITA soldiers standing slightly apart. He was unarmed however his four boys had taken up positions to give him instant covering fire if necessary and be able to find cover.

He stopped a couple of paces from the leader and a heated exchange ensued in one of the local dialects with much arm waving.

Ponce stepped back and spat on the ground. There was a growl of disapproval from the UNITA rebels and his adversary's hand moved to the holstered weapon on his side but then relaxed slightly.

The static in the air was tangible making Gallagher's hair stand up on the back of his neck and forearms.

Ponce turned around and walked towards the group at the Landcruiser.

"Alfonso, Gallagher said softly, "this looks like the gunfight at the OK corral. What's the problem?"

"OK corral?" I don't understand, but that prick over there wants to renegotiate terms. Seemingly he thinks his superiors are not paying him enough for this type of operation and he and his boys are not used to being in one place for a long time. He wants a slice!

I'm sorry Sean but we have a problem."

"Did you confirm that all our weapons are here?"

"Yes, he says they are all here. Some of the AK's are still in the manufacturer's waxed paper and grease."

"Now here's the situation" said Gallagher, "we have a contract price out of which you are making a hefty commission. That's fine, that's your slice as Agent, but my contract price is firm and any extra that bastard wants comes off your end, understand? And Alfonso, smile and give me a kiss"

"What...?"

"You heard, I like a kiss when I'm being screwed! Now go back and tell your friend it won't wash, and I know he will be in deep shite if he doesn't come back to his Lords and Masters with the contents of my briefcase.

And... Alfonso, don't ever try this with me again"

Ponce walked away with a scowl on his face.

"Who the fuck does he think he's dealing with" said McGafferty.

"Steady Gerr, Alfonso made an error of judgement but I am sure it will not happen again"

Ponce approached the UNITA leader who after another heated exchange ordered his troops to take cover. They scrabbled in the dirt and came up in the firing position but held their fire.

Ponce had dived off to the left and was now scurrying back to his own men who also had weapons to their shoulders. The Irish contingent had taken cover behind and below the land cruiser. Not good thought Gallagher there's almost a full tank of fuel in this bloody vehicle. At least it's diesel!

The men on the ground were now arranged like three points on a triangle with the land cruiser at the apex and Gallagher's position most exposed.

Nobody moved. A tense silence.

"Ponce, get your arse over here" Gallagher called. Five minutes later Ponce and one of his own men crawled in from the left using the vehicle as some cover.

"Alfonso, this is fucking ridiculous and is going to get someone killed. We all want this deal to go through and we'll all make money so let's stop fucking about. Go and tell your friend that he is really pissing me off and if he doesn't stand down his men, we'll take them all out and just take the fucking weapons"

McGafferty and the two South Africans had found a couple of AK's in the back of the Landcruiser and were now spread out finding shallow cover. Even if the AK's ran out of ammo they were all so close that well aimed pistol shots would be just as effective as wild automatic bursts which the rebels were used to firing meaning the rounds went high and to the left. They never took the butts in to the shoulder.

Ponce shouted across the bare baked ground.

"Ask him to come over here. He can take two of his men with him."

"He fears a trap" said Ponce.

"All right. I will stand at the back of the vehicle in the open with no weapons, you beside me but signal your men to be ready."

The UNITA leader and two of his men stepped warily forward weapons at the 'high port'.

"Right Gerr, tell our boys to take out the two guards, you hit the leader but don't kill him. Alfonso as soon as we open up tell your lads to take on the remaining rebel soldiers."

"But you can't do this" said Ponce, "these are people I work with"

"You should have thought of that before you tried to double cross us you greedy bastard. Just thank God you are still alive."

It happened with extreme precision. The two guards were taken out and the leader collapsed to the ground having a taken a thigh shot from McGafferty which he placed so that it did not cut the artery. A masterful shot.

The leader was dragged behind the land cruiser at the moment Ponce's forces opened up

Taken by surprise by the speed of the happening, three of the rebel soldiers were killed immediately, three fled and the remaining four threw their weapons down, raised their hands and asked for mercy.

The maelstrom of fire stopped.

"Ponce, tell your men to make safe their weapons" and with a sign to his three compatriots Gallagher ran forward to the front Artic to find the three dead and another dying. The ones who had surrendered were cowering on their haunches by the trailer wheels.

"Scout back a bit and see if you can find the ones who broke out" he said to Pieter and Johuan, "but watch out for bloody landmines"

A shot startled the stillness as McGafferty gave the Coup de Grace to the wounded soldier.

Ponce and his men joined them. "This is bad" he said

"Yes it is and it's all of your making "as he turned and viciously struck Ponce across the face with his pistol. "If I didn't need you, you would be dead. Your life is mine - do you understand?"

Ponce glowered at him from his crouched position wiping the blood from his cheek but nodded as his men helped him back to his feet. He shrugged them off and looked at Gallagher with hate filled eyes and Gallagher knew he had made another enemy. Just what he did not need!

Meanwhile the UNITA rebel leader was being attended to by one of his men who had surrendered. He turned out to be one of the HGV drivers, the other he said was dead. They had not been UNITA but had been ordered by the leader to stand up with a weapon to swell the ranks.

"Gerr, take this guy and check out the weapons, Test fire as many as you wish and take a couple more AK's for us with a box of ammo." The minders had returned with a 'no contact' for the scampered rebels. "Take the boys with you I will all right with this toe rag" indicating the wounded leader.

"Now you, let's get started. What's your name" No response. "I know you speak some English as I heard you speaking to the driver".

No response. "OK, well your no use to me and I haven't time to tend your wound" as he cocked his Browning.

"No, No Senor. I have a little English"

"That's better, your name?"

"I am Luis, I am Lieutenant"

"Why did you try to get more money?"

"No Senor, I did not. Alfonso told me you were only going to pay half of the contract price and we had to be strong so that you paid the agreed price"

"And the extra" Gallagher said, "was to be split between you and Alfonso?"

"No Senor, I am a poor man and a freedom fighter. I have no home and no family what would I want with money?"

"Then why were you arguing with Ponce?"

Luis said nothing. . . . "Or were you to take us out, steal our money and sell the arms elsewhere. The Lieutenant's eyes gleamed for an instant. "Thought so, you are a bad liar and a worse thief. Pity you can't plan worth a cuss" and he shot him between the eyes.

The others came running back at the sound of the shot. "No probs" said Gallagher "get on with the checking".

"What have you done" said Ponce, "UNITA will now hunt us to death"

"No laddie, they'll hunt you. Your friend Luis told me the truth and I shall tell the UNITA Paymaster when I meet him at the docks. In the interim the first payment stays firmly with me.

You have buggered this up. . . You get out of it and if you're thinking of pulling that pistol you better turn around and think again".

Alfonso did and found himself staring down an awfully big hole which was the muzzle of Pieter's Desert Eagle

"On your feet. You are going to get us through the docks and on to the ship. If you do that I will let you live, if not . . . ."

Gerry McGafferty returned with Jouhan reporting that all the weapons seemed to be in good order, some new as they had been informed. The rest of the arsenal including the landmines, present and correct. Two of the men were replacing the mezzanine floor and sliding the small engines on top. "Poor bugger" he said as he looked at the Lieutenant.

Ignoring him, Gallagher said. "Right, let's get rolling."

"No can do" said McGafferty, one of the trailers has two tyres shot through, could have run on one but not two down. The driver is changing them now with Ponce's men but you should see the spares no tread and the canvas showing through. We'll be lucky to make the Port. The other tyres are not much better"

"OK, we'll just have to go easy. Who's driving the other rig?"

"I am, with one of Ponce's men who speaks English. Can we not get rid of that backstabbing bastard Ponce?"

"No we need him to get us through the Docks. Just watch your back".

"Aye. It's your back I'll be watching not mine. I don't think he likes you. . . ."

The tyres changed, the rigs roared through the quickening fall of darkness. McGafferty, Pieter with Ponce driving were in the lead Landcruiser followed by the lead Artic with Angolan driver and Jouhan then McGafferty driving the second rig with the last surviving Angolan. Ponce had ordered his men to clear up the mess, burn the bodies and take the Land Rovers back to his hidden warehouse where they would be repainted, renumbered and sold.

Matters were not going well for McGafferty. The inspection had been a total cock up, bodies all over the place and he had not paid the first instalment. Instead of the trucks going to the Port tomorrow night as planned they were now en route twenty four hours early, under their control but with only Ponce as their means of getting through the roadblocks and City checks especially now travelling at night as nobody travelled at night for fear of hijack.

He signalled the trucks and pulled off the road about four kilometres from Luanda, the City lights clearly visible.

All alighted and McGafferty waved the Angolans forward with his own men.

"We have a wee problem" Gallagher said.

"Aye that's true, arriving at the docks twenty four hours before our boyos are on duty. "

We have two options. Both options mean we all work together to finish this operation no matter what personal clashes exist. If you don't accept that then you leave the Company. . . . . Permanently!" continued Gallagher looking at McGafferty for acknowledgement.

"Ponce translate"

"No need, they both understand English"

"Good, that makes matters easier. As we have not paid the first instalment for the cargo every one here will be paid for this extra night's work, apart from you Ponce"

"First option is to barrel on through as if we were expected tonight and try to bluff our way in saying it was the Dock's mistake not ours"

Ponce interrupted, "can't do that all the transport permission papers are dated tomorrow. The first road block will impound the trucks or shoot out the tyres if we try to break through"

"OK. Alternative is to laager up here and run at first light, at least the papers will be in order even if our men will not be on duty in the Customs shed until the evening"

Ponce interrupted again. "No. If we stay here we run the risk of being discovered by a Government patrol and without the necessary permission we will be arrested and we can not arrive at the Docks outwith the expected time window, as none of the day Officers know of our pending arrival and will simply not let us in.

We must have special permission to park up at the side of the road overnight".

"Even in a breakdown?" queried Gallagher

"No that is OK, but none of our papers match allowing us to be here, broken down or not, at this time and day"

"How difficult is it to get this overnight permission?"

"Not that difficult" said Ponce, If you know the Officers you simply go to Police Headquarters with the truck manifest, registration and Insurance and a small 'gift' to achieve the necessary permission".

"How small a 'gift'?"

"Two hundred US dollars per truck should do although you better give me five hundred in case there are other expenses"

Gallagher looked at Ponce. "You better be on the level with this. Gerry will go with you and we will wait here. Jouhan you go too, you speak the language, make sure our friend here is not out of earshot when speaking to the Police".

"Sure Boss" Jouhan said as he eased his frame off the truck mudguard.

"Right, here's the money. Get back as fast as you can and bring some food and water. How long will it take?"

"Probably a couple of hours" said Ponce, enjoying the fact that he was almost back in charge.

When they had left Gallagher checked his locks on the two containers giving one set of keys to Pieter who he posted on the first two hour sentry stag. He settled down to snooze with the two Angolans who now seemed quite content with switching sides and their new role with the prospect of earning US dollars. They seemed untroubled that two hours earlier they had witnessed him murder a man in cold blood.

Ponce parked the Landcruiser outside Police Headquarters and all three alighted.

Jouhan issued another reminder to keep things on the level and he and McGafferty followed him into the Station.

Inside chaos reined. There were people everywhere, Different uniformed Police, Military and civilians flowing this way and that. A steel cage was packed full of prisoners awaiting due process. There were rag tag human beings lying on the floor and the few benches. A central dias held a desk reminiscent of an old court room bench behind which sat two harassed Angolan Police officers with a queue of about twenty people awaiting attention. The noise was the terrific, the stench, appalling.

One large, fly blown, ceiling fan languidly stirred the fetid air.

It was so bad that McGafferty retched in his throat.

"Jesus" he said, "I've been in better cow byres".

Ponce bulldozed his way to the front of the queue elbowing the front man aside who looked once and recognising the head of one of the gangster families, stepped aside without a word. There were a few murmured objections from the queue but another look from Ponce, with his recently damaged face, quietened these mutterings.

In rapid Portuguese he told the desk Sergeant he wanted to see the Duty Officer and that he and his associates would wait in the Administrative Office till he arrived. At that he turned and walked across to a frosted glass fronted door, opened it without knocking and the three entered the rather more wholesome atmosphere. The office was simply furnished but boasted an old, rattling air conditioner in the corner.

Ponce sat on the desk the other two taking the only chairs. Five minutes later a Police Lieutenant opened the door and walked in. It was obvious Ponce knew this man as he immediately smiled and various courtesies passed back and forth.

Ponce explained his predicament with Johuan translating for McGafferty. The Lieutenant smiled and indicated there was not a problem.

It was unfortunate that his foreign associates had been inconvenienced by the breakdown of one of their trucks but he would issue the appropriate documentation if he could have the manifests and registrations. Hopefully the problem would be repaired in the morning.

"Did they wish a Police presence overnight?"

"No, that will not be necessary. We have our own security".

Having handed over the documents the Lieutenant got up to leave. . . .

"Just a minute me old son" said McGafferty. "Tell this man to go and get his forms and come back here. Our documents remain where I can see them. He can issue the permissions in front of us.

Ponce duly translated. The Officer nodded his acquiescence but said regrettably that there would be a fine to pay as their current documentation was not in order together with a fee for the new permissions.

"How does he know that, he hasn't even looked at our documents."

This exchange had been in even more rapid Portuguese but Jouhan had understood all of it especially the amount of the fine where he had asked for fifty dollars a truck not two hundred. This he reported to McGafferty who told him to say nothing for the moment.

"How much does he want Ponce?"

"As expected, two hundred dollars per truck"

"I see" said McGafferty peeling four hundred dollars off and handing it over. "Don't suppose we will get a receipt?"

The Lieutenant returned with various documents, a wooden embossed stamp and ink pad. Ten minutes later with a flourish of a signature he completed the forms and stamped them twice, Handing two to Ponce he folded the third and put it in his pocket. Ponce turned his back to obscure the payment and handed over an amount of dollars to the Policeman which disappeared into his trouser pocket.

Just as the payment was being made the door crashed open making all four men jump and in walked Chief Inspector Alfonso Carisco with two of his heavily armed men.

"I was told there was some form of conference here involving Foreign Nationals" he said, addressing the Lieutenant who had immediately sprung to his feet.

Chapter 8

Douglas had arranged to meet Alfonso on the Hispaniola at 21.00 hrs. He wanted to check out the old ship and renew his friendship with Sylvette who he had confirmed was still 'in situ' and perhaps play a few hands of Blackjack. Essentially, he was on an intelligence gathering exercise combined with a little relaxation.

He told Sergio he would not be in for supper and gave him the evening off. At 20.30 he slipped a light cotton jacket over his shouldered Jericho 9mm climbed in to the Range Rover and drove across the causeway to the ship.

There were few vehicles on the quay car park at this early time so he picked his spot with care reversing alongside the gang plank Reception area where the Range Rover was bathed in bright spotlight.

Having been relieved of his weapons, patted down and given his plastic key for retrieval he walked up the gangway to the well lit ship festooned with white bulbs, bow to stern and to the highest points on the mast and rigging.

A blast of cool air met him as he opened the sliding doors to the main deck.

Better air con than I can remember, he thought and looking around he could see that the ship had recently been re-fitted to a very high standard. Some one has spent a shed load of money on this old girl, as he made his way to the stern bar area.

The Bar was quite spectacular. It was semi circular and opened out to the aft deck where there were rattan tables and chairs with a few sun loungers spread around. This led down to a half deck above the stern which held a decent sized swimming pool bathed in concealed, low intensity, aquamarine light.

The Bar area was panelled in burr elm which gave off a serene golden glow in the diffused lighting from the wall sconces.

The carpeting was deep pile beige with the blue ship motif repeated every three feet. The Club armchairs were in navy blue leather.

The effect was of conservative elegance, and was very relaxing to the senses. Light classical music played softly from hidden speakers.

There were only two other guests in the Bar although two barmen and three waiters were in attendance.

He picked his spot, at what used to be his usual table, with his back to the bulkhead facing half forward from where he could see the two entrance doors and the aft door to the stern deck. Old habits die hard, he thought.

He ordered a bottle of Bollinger non vintage from the waiter, wincing internally at the exorbitant price.

As Alfonso had still not arrived, he took his glass having made his usual toast, and as the evening was not too humid went out to the deck instructing the waiter to carry the ice bucket outside. Douglas had once left an opened bottle of wine on his table many years ago where certain illegal substances were added which nearly cost him his life. He would never do that again.

He sat in one of the rattan chairs sipping his wine enjoying the clarity of the evening and the twinkling lights of Luanda across the lagoon. The breeze was offshore so the air was not tainted by the sour smell of the City. He reached to pour a second glass when he sensed someone was watching him although there was no one else on deck. He scanned the shadows - Nobody! A bit paranoid old chap, he thought then his senses picked up a delicate perfume.

"Well Jack Douglas" said a soft female voice, "it's been a long time". The voice came from above on the starboard side.

Standing up he saw the source of the voice standing on a small deck above his. The female form was silhouetted by the bulkhead lights behind and the thin clinging material of her calf length dress left little to the imagination. Long dark hair cascaded down each side of her face making it difficult to identify the speaker.

"Hello Sylvette" he said with a slight intake of breath, "won't you join me?" He had always been very fond of Sylvette. She was an attractive, sophisticated woman in her early forties. They had become friends soon after the Hispaniola arrived in the Lagoon when she originally worked as a Croupier. She was soon promoted to Casino Manager due to her professionalism and charm.

He knew she carried an American passport and had been married once, for a short time. She was in fact of French/Swiss origin and also had a Swiss passport.

After an initial flirtation he had told her about his attachment to Maggie Grosvenor with whom he had been in love for thirty two years. The friendship had settled to an even keel although they still mildly flirted due to the obvious mutual attraction.

He enjoyed her company. She had been his hostess on many occasions in the early years and knew that matters would have been different if he had not been committed.

All these old thoughts crowded through his head as he waited for her to descend from the deck above. It was a pleasurable anticipation to listen to her heels clicking down the companionway ladder then, emerging from a concealed door which he had noticed earlier, discreetly marked with the words 'Private - Crew Only', she was there!

She was quite beautiful he thought as she walked towards him her auburn hair shimmering in the light. He could now see she was wearing a midnight green silk 'sheath' which would be the only way to describe it. This accentuated her figure, the swell of her hips and the rise of her smallish uplifted breasts the nipples of which were standing out slightly in the evening air.

Not that he was noticing, he thought, as he walked towards her, bent down, kissed her on both cheeks then gave her a hug.

"You are prettier than ever" he said. "The years have been kind".

"You don't look too bad your self for an old man" she said with a smile and a twinkle in her deep green eyes.

Douglas had always loved her eyes. At times they became iridescent. At other times deep pools of dark green in which one could become totally immersed. On their first meeting he had thought she was wearing coloured contact lenses but later learnt they were her natural colour.

She eased her dress on her hips and sat down in the proffered chair crossing her bare, lightly tanned legs.

"Still Bollinger Jack, and no doubt still the same toast. I presume you and Maggie are still together.

"Yes and Yes," said Jack. "Here's to both of you. It's good to see you."

"What about you Sylvette? Married, engaged, partnered?"

"No. There have been a couple of liaisons however I am single but almost married to this old ship. I am now the Managing Director and a shareholder so am very comfortable thank you. Partners, I have found, will always disappoint you in the end."

Jack looked at her face and saw slight lines of sadness. You have been badly hurt lassie, he thought but not for him to probe.

"Why have you come back here? I was told by that old rogue Alfonso that you were back in town and couldn't really believe it. You could have kept in touch, you know - not a word for eleven years and then you just walk onboard as if we saw each other yesterday. Not good, Jack. You don't treat friends that way"

"I deserve that. You know I am dreadful about keeping in touch and the last few years have been somewhat traumatic. I never expected to come back here and thought you would have been long gone back to Switzerland, but that's no excuse. . . . ."

"Quite right" she said "No excuse and it hurt to be cut off. You didn't even say Goodbye"

"You may recall I had to leave the country rather quickly. There wasn't much time to pursue the niceties of departure but I am truly sorry about not sending a letter or a card for your Birthday. It's not as if I could forget being the day before mine"

"I remember, Alfonso told me a bit about your final escapade here - you really were one of the last Buccaneers, however I suppose I can forgive you."

"Thank you, but not 'Buccaneer' - last of the 'Privateers', a small distinction but at least we had the sanction of HM Government in those days"

"And do you still have it?" asked Sylvette. "Is that why you are back here? Don't you think you are a bit old to still be playing Cowboys and Indians "

"Possibly, but needs must. I could use a couple of bagfuls of money right now as I am somewhat financially embarrassed with my Company in Spain."

"Still the same Jack Douglas, no doubt still dreaming of buying that island and shutting yourself off from the rest of humanity. You always did play your last £ or give it away to someone you thought in more need"

"Whoa," Jack said raising his hands in front of him "I am not exactly the 'White Knight'. How about you? You said you now own part of this ship. Do you stay here year round or manage to get back to Switzerland or America for some time?"

The conversation swayed back and forth as both caught up on each other's lives. A second bottle was ordered when Douglas realised that Alfonso was over an hour late. Just as he was about to find a house phone to call him, Alfonso strode purposefully across the deck towards them.

"Good evening Sylvette, as beautiful as ever. You should not be in the company of this rogue"

Sylvette stood to greet Alfonso kissing him lightly on both cheeks.

"Jack, sorry I am late, but I have been at Headquarters and have some very interesting information. Perhaps Sylvette would give us a few minutes? "

"Sure" she said with a slight pout. "I don't want to be involved in your 'war games". She got up and walked to the bar.

Alfonso then told Jack of his finding his namesake, Alfonso Ponce at Police Headquarters with Gerry McGafferty, trading US dollars for amended travel documentation for two trucks parked up on the outskirts of the City.

The manifests state 'used Marine Engines' but it was obvious that this was cover for other 'cargo'. He knew Jack had spotted Sean Gallagher which now placed two dangerous and senior ex IRA men in Luanda in the company of a known arms dealer. What was more, they were staying here on the Hispaniola with two or three minders. He also told Jack that he had spoken to Customs at the docks and to Hull Blyth, the shipping Agents, who had confirmed two containers from Ponce were due to be loaded on to a ship called the Maria Luisa expected to dock tomorrow afternoon and due to sail the same evening.

"What are you going to do?" asked Jack.

"Nothing for the moment. We know the location of the trucks and we know the time due at the Docks. As far as the Government is concerned it is a legitimate export cargo even if half of the containers are filled with weapons. It means simply there are less in Angola."

Angola was awash with weapons and armaments of all types and origins but the bulk was from the USSR who had used its influence when the Portuguese had left to establish Russian and Cuban training Officers within the Angolan forces. A mass of arms had then been sent from Russia and although the 'advisors' had long since left, arms had still continued to pour into the country. A Kalashnikov AK47 in good order with two full magazines could be purchased on the street for 10/12 US dollars.

"I will report this back to the UK" said Jack. See if you can get more intel. on the composition of the weapons load and thanks Alfonso"

Alfonso stood up as Sylvette returned to the table.

"Not staying?"

"No forgive me. Duty calls. Enjoy the evening." and he took his leave.

"I am not even going to ask" she said

"Good because I can't possibly tell you however, I would like to enlist your aid"

Jack then told her of the men who had aroused his interest and could Sylvette keep as close a watch on them as possible, informing him of their movements.

"I can do better than that. Most of the public areas are under CCTV with sound mikes concealed throughout the ship. Indeed most of the suites are also rigged for sound so we can eavesdrop on your friends"

"Great. I had noticed the extensive re-decoration. Now walk me through to the Casino and be my lucky charm like old times".

- - - - - - - - - - - -

Sean Gallagher was not in a good mood, truth be known, he rarely was. Although they had control of the cargo the trucks were still parked out in the middle of nowhere with inadequate defences and with the UNITA rebels probably looking for revenge for the cock up that had killed so many earlier in the day.

They were now in Gallagher's state room planning the next move although Ponce was not a happy man and had only, grudgingly agreed to continue to save his large commission.

Ponce had said that all Hell would break loose when UNITA did not receive its first payment, found that the trucks were no longer at the RV (rendezvous point) and discover the deaths of their men. He reckoned they had until first light before the alarm went out and they activated their agents in Luanda. It was now 23.00 hrs. so that gave them some eight hours.

"OK" said Gallagher turning to Ponce. "Use your sources to try to get a message to UNITA that we had no choice in our actions sadly dictated by the greed and duplicity of their own men. Explain that there was never any intention not to pay the first tranche nor to take lives which became a regrettable necessity. The deal is still on and they will get their full payment at the Docks tomorrow night with a bit extra as compensation for the dead men's families. We moved the trucks as a security measure only and they are now under our control with arrival at the Docks as planned.

Ensure they don't move against us before we have a chance to meet face to face, further explain if necessary, and pay them their money. Right?

Now bugger off and get that through."

Ponce glowered at him fingering his damaged face. "I will phone you later if I have made contact"

Gallagher slammed the door on his back and double locked it. I don't trust the little shite he thought but knew he had no alternative. He peeled off his soiled clothing leaving them on the floor and soothed his head and body in a long hot shower ending by turning it cold for the last few minutes. Much refreshed he kicked his dirty clothes in to a corner and re-dressed in a white open neck shirt and a beige cotton lightweight suit.

God I'm hungry he thought realising he had had no food since breakfast. He unlocked and re-locked his door with the good, old fashioned key and headed for the Casino for a steak sandwich, a bottle of wine and a few hands of Blackjack.

Douglas had been playing for half an hour and he had been steadily winning. He was now ahead some 1, 200 dollars from his original 200 dollars stake. Sylvette had stayed with him for ten minutes but was now doing the rounds of the other tables speaking to her guests. The Casino was filling up and there were probably forty people, mostly European, playing the various tables.

I wonder if Sylvette had told his Croupier to give him an edge, he thought. . . No, too much of a businesswoman but I'll just check it out.

He had 1oo dollars on the table, three cards in his hand totalling nineteen. He called for another card which was flicked across to him, the four of spades, bust! as his hundred dollars disappeared. So mush for that theory he mused.

Sylvette appeared beside him. "Not a clever draw Jack."

"No. Lost concentration for a moment" She smiled at him

Gallagher was sitting at one of the small tables on the periphery of the room eating his steak sandwich and drinking a very good Portuguese Douro wine - Duas Quintas Reserva 1994 - an excellent full red, and was on his third glass. His mood had lightened and he was feeling more at ease.

He looked around the room to pick his table, saw Sylvette at one of the Blackjack tables where three men were playing and two chairs were empty. He knew she was management having met her when he first arrived. She was standing beside one of the players with her hand resting lightly on his left shoulder.

He emptied his bottle of wine into his glass and approached the table.

"Hello Sylvette" he said as he sat down across from Jack on his right side.

"Good evening Mr Gallagher. Did you enjoy your meal?"

Gallagher grunted his answer and asked for five hundred dollars in chips nodding acknowledgement to the three other players.

Sylvette who knew them all, introduced them in her professional manner. Douglas did not shake hands.

They played for another fifteen minutes when the man on Jack's immediate right decided he had had enough and gathered his chips to cash in. This opened the space to Gallagher who had been sitting two along. There were only three now playing and it was half past midnight. The other player caved leaving only the two of them.

Gallagher asked for a new deck and whilst the dealer was gathering the old pack he gazed at Douglas inquisitively. "What line of business you in?"

"Surveyor" replied Jack "Mine Surveyor for Endiama."

Oh, Diamonds egh" said Gallagher.

"No. Diamond 'Mines'. What about you Mr Gallagher?"

"Import/Export" was the guarded reply as the dealer shuffled the new pack asking Jack to cut.

"I wouldn't have thought there was much to export from Angola" said Douglas.

Gallagher caught Jack's eye but said nothing. After two hands he said, "have we met before Mr Douglas? You seem to be vaguely familiar" He appeared to be searching his memory.

"No, I don't think so, you may have seen me around the ship" Jack lied.

Sylvette interjected. "Mr Douglas is an old Angolan hand and is well known here"

"Is that so" said Gallagher, but it was clear that he was still slightly troubled.

CHAPTER 9

Douglas returned to the villa in a troubled frame of mind. His task in Angola was quite clear - he had to try to trace the loss or theft of diamonds which were appearing in the hands of certain terrorist factions by reviewing the current security and transport arrangements. He felt sure he could establish where they were going and who was responsible although he also had a secondary, hidden agenda.

The emergence of senior ex IRA personnel in Luanda complicated matters.

The following morning Sylvette telephoned asking him to come to the ship as soon as possible. He told her he would be there by noon as he had an invitation from Captain Ramirez to see his troops training and inspect the vehicles used in the diamond convoy.

He weaved his way through the early traffic in the Embassy Range Rover heading for the military barracks on the outskirts of Luanda, on the airport road, arriving at 09.00 hrs.

He was expected, even so the gate guard took several minutes examining his papers and the vehicle before lifting the barrier and directing him to Ramirez's Company lines.

As he braked to halt Ramirez stepped out of an administration block dressed in desert lightweights which were already heavily stained with sweat.

"Good morning Jack, would you like coffee or a cold drink before we start?"

"Morning Francisco, no thanks, let's get on although it looks as if you have already been busy"

"We start at 07.00 hrs every day" Francisco said, First parade inspection of vehicles and equipment at 08.00 then the morning drill normally starts at 10.00. I have delayed the inspection this morning in order that you could accompany me.

As you know we use three soft skinned vehicles for the convoy although the diamond carrier is a lightly armoured hardtop with bullet proof glass and run flat tyres. The other two are standard military specification 110 Land Rovers with extra steel bumpers and steel wire covers for the windscreen and windows. The carrier is a 3.9 litre V8, the others turbo diesels."

At that he strode around the corner of the barracks block to an open sided, hanger like, building where ten vehicles were drawn up with their individual equipment laid out on canvas groundsheets in front.

Quite impressive, thought Jack as a Company Sergeant Major brought the crews to attention and with a smart salute to Ramirez reported the Company present and ready for inspection then fell in alongside.

Douglas dropped back a couple of steps as each Section Leader produced his vehicle service books and went through any problems with Ramirez. The vehicles were all quite new and in good condition, surprisingly well maintained.

He thought, these soldiers certainly know their jobs as far as presentation was concerned although their personal appearance was not up to the same standard. Their weapons however were clean and lightly oiled, again surprising for the Angolan Army.

The AK 47 is renowned for being almost 'soldier proof' and will normally still fire rusty, dirty or covered in mud.

The CSM at Ramirez's order had one of the mounted GPMG's, dismounted and stripped in front of the vehicle. The soldier was proficient and the weapon was spotless with no wear in the barrel or breech.

Only two of the vehicles were V8 and armoured, the diamond carriers, and Douglas inspected the rear of each one. Two strongboxes were fitted in the racks on the armoured floor and were chained through the handles by stainless steel chains and padlocks to rings welded to the floor..

"Who carries the keys?"

"No one" replied Ramirez, "once they are chained in place at the airport they can only be unlocked by a Bank Official when they arrive at the Banco National. He holds duplicates, the originals return to Huambo with the aircraft Courier.

Good policy, thought Douglas noticing that the Carriers had armoured rear doors with no windows.

He also noticed there were two hinged roof vents in the rear - no air conditioning.

He didn't comment but logged in the obvious vulnerability. Big V8 engines could easily carry air conditioning units and that would secure the diamond carrying compartment.

"Who carries the key to the rear door?"

"I do" stated Ramirez, "but the internal Guard can also open from the inside if a problem 0ccurs."

The inspection completed, the men were given fifteen minutes to re-equip the vehicles, return them to the hanger, and have a quick 'brew'.

"I have arranged for one of the other Companies to carry out a dummy ambush on the convoy to show you how my men would react if brought under fire. We shall use the driver training area at the rear of the barracks which although unrealistic due to lack of buildings, keeps our training away from prying eyes".

Good comment, thought Douglas, Ramirez seems to know his stuff.

A dry river bed had been chosen for the 'ambush'. As the diamond convoy drove through the steep sides the attacking Company effectively sealed it in by charging one of their vehicles broadside across the front as the track rose level, with two more occupying the high ground on either side in a pincer trap, a further attack vehicle stopped fifty yards to the rear. All the attackers mounted machine guns pored fire into the convoy. Their men had de-bussed, spreading along the heights and automatic fire from their AK's was also hosing the area.

The defenders escort Rovers returned fire the occupants having taken cover and impressively, using disciplined short bursts would have taken out many of the attackers.

The first vehicle suffered a simulated explosion, the defenders blew smoke and with their own men clinging to the welded hand rails along the roof, roared in reverse charging the lone attacker vehicle blocking their escape. The rear escort stopped alongside the attack vehicle, again simulating having pushed it aside with serious damage, the crew then baled out climbing on to the sides of the diamond carrier, holding on for dear life, which turned and roared away to safety with two of the crew being thrown off as it hit a massive bump in the track, leaving them rolling in the dust but mercifully uninjured.

Lack of realism was made up by enthusiasm both by grinning attackers and defenders who very rarely had the chance to use blank ammunition and thunder flashes, thought to be an un-necessary cost!

The cacophony of sound ceased, the smoke drifted away and everybody congratulated each other on 'killing' so many of the enemy. Ramirez thanked the young Lieutenant commanding the attackers who dispersed and turning to Douglas said that he thought over two thousand blank rounds had been expended in fifteen minutes.

"They do get carried away but this is the only simulated exercise they have had in nine months. I am pleased however most of my men held to a disciplined rate of fire".

"Yes, they did, I thought the exercise was carried out well" not saying that if it had been real the three vehicles in the diamond convoy would have been disabled within the first two minutes, the rear in the convoy, blocking the escape of the Carrier as it had been travelling far too close. He was however, impressed.

"Thank you Francisco, please pass on my congratulations to your men and perhaps a couple of cases of beer when they come off duty?"

"Un-necessary, but thank you for the offer. Those not on roster will have the rest of the day off once they have cleaned up their vehicles and weapons"

"OK, your call", as he shook hands by his Range Rover, "now please excuse me I have another appointment".

Driving out to the Hispaniola he mulled over what he had just witnessed. Ramirez seemed to have an able and well equipped unit and if morale had been down, today's little exercise seemed to have cheered up the troops. A good Officer!

Arriving at the ship he realised he was covered in dust from the 'ambush'. Surrendering his ankle gun to Reception, all he was carrying today, he beat himself down and made straight for the first bathroom to wash but could do nothing about the sweat stains on his shirt or the oil stain on his right trouser leg he had picked up off one of the vehicles.

He went up to the stern Bar ordering a bottle of Bollinger and asking the barman to inform Miss Dubois that he was here. The barman returned with the wine informing that Miss Dubois was temporarily engaged but would be down in ten minutes.

Precisely ten minutes later Sylvette entered through the crew door.

Jack rose to greet her, kissing her lightly on both cheeks. Sitting back down he proffered a glass of wine.

"Thank you, never too early for Champagne".

She lent forward exposing the tops of her exquisite breasts. Jack's eyes were drawn downwards before he got a grip.

"Your IRA friends are up to no good. They have had two meetings with Alfonso Ponce a notorious gun runner and gangster. They have two containers of arms near Luanda which are due to be loaded on to a ship called the Maria Luisa tonight. It appears they bought them from one of outlawed former UNITA factions but there was trouble at the pick up and several men were killed.

Ponce has managed to smooth the ruffled feathers and has offered an additional payment of 20, 000 US dollars as compensation without first clearing it with Gallagher, who is furious, otherwise UNITA are prepared to take the guns back by force.

I am afraid the recording is only piece meal as they kept walking between suites and only Gallagher's state room is wired for sound.

Come up to the Security Office on the next deck, you can hear the tape and see the CCTV of Alfonso Ponce"

Jack picked up the ice bucket, the two glasses and followed Sylvette to the crew door which opened on to a practical steel companionway up to the next deck.

"It's a good job you are not wearing a skirt today" he said with a smile looking straight up at Sylvette's well proportioned rump.

"Don't be so rude" she said laughing, "keep your mind on the job"

"Oh, but I am".

They passed Sylvette's sumptuous private quarters, through a bulkhead door locked with a sophisticated swipe card system and into a cabin where two operatives monitored an array of screens showing various areas of the ship, Reception, the wharf and what looked like some of the private guest suites. The equipment was very modern and expensive. Introductions made, the voice recording was replayed but there was nothing more Jack could glean. He was then shown the CCTV footage of Ponce arriving on board and in the restaurant this morning.

Evil looking bastard" he said, noticing the livid weal down his cheek.

"He is evil and very callous"

"Can I have these tapes?" Jack asked. "Quite frankly they are more dangerous to you leaving them here".

"Yes, I agree" and she instructed the nearest operative to give them to Douglas.

With his thanks to the two Security guards, Jack followed Sylvette through another locked bulkhead door which led discreetly to the main staircase of the ship. Still carrying his ice bucket, the glasses now inside, he suggested they return to the aft deck and finish the bottle. Once seated he told her that she had to watch her back. The two Irishmen were serious trouble and would think nothing of harming her if they suspected she had information on their operation.

"You worry too much Jack. I can look after myself. I have been dealing with 'hard men' from all over the world for the last fourteen years"

"Be careful" He said, "these men are killers! Murderers!" and taking her hand he thanked her for the information and left.

Retrieving his Makorov he drove back to the villa to report to Bruce

Kendall.

Alfonso Ponce was quite pleased with his morning's work. He had met with a very angry group of rebels, taking along twelve of his own heavily armed men as a precaution.

After much shouting and gesticulating the two senior 'Officers' sat down with Ponce in the rear of one of the vehicles and hammered out a new deal with the opposing forces warily circling each other, weapons ready, like stray dogs round a bitch.

The rebels would not interfere with the delivery to the Docks provided each of the 'Officers' received 5.000 dollars and the complete payment on arrival alongside the ship, Customs cleared, but before the containers were swung inboard.

Ponce had agreed to their demands without reference to Gallagher and this had caused the explosion from the Irishman at breakfast on the Hispaniola.

"An extra 20, 000 dollars, where the fuck do you think I am going to lay my hands on that kind of money, "he blustered knowing full well he had an extra 100, 000 dollars as his contingency fund.

"You better be on the level Ponce and not trying to pull another stroke".

"I assure you Sean, it took me over an hour to persuade them to accept this amount. They wanted 50, 000 to start with".

As Gallagher calmed down, Ponce then delivered his master stroke.

"They want the money delivered to them today by 13.00 hrs. as s sign of good faith, after all you have the weapons and they insist it is delivered by me alone as they no longer trust you.. Further they want the whole shipment payment dockside not the last payment on board as previously agreed. They suspect a double cross".

Gallagher knew he was over a barrel.

"All right, I'll get your $20, 000 but you better be straight with me otherwise I shall see you in Hell. Tell your friends they will get half the arms payment on the dockside and the final half on board ship once the containers are on board and that is final."

Ponce agreed to collect Gallagher that afternoon and take him out to the trucks which he assured him had not been bothered by anyone although a Police patrol had driven by in the small hours without stopping.

In his Landcruiser he unbolted the steel door under the rear carpet, extracted $10,000 from the briefcase he had been given by Gallagher and drove to the RV with the other $10, 00o

That's part payment for this he said to himself, fingering the livid scar on his cheek

---

Douglas had been speaking to the General on the secure phone for ten minutes explaining the IRA situation. Kendall confirmed that he had heard something was in the wind.

Some ex IRA hard liners were trying to re-arm. He advised Jack that strong Diplomatic pressure was being applied to the Angolan Government to increase gun security and try to remove weapons from the various outlawed militia groups on the streets. These were nothing more than armed thugs.

It was also vital to remove arms out of the hands of children some as young as nine years old.

These were the main conditions on a substantial British and EEC aid package already agreed but not implemented.

Kendall would immediately advise the Foreign Office to pass to the Angolan authorities who would deal.

Jack remonstrated with him for a few minutes. He advised Bruce that there was not enough time for the usual channels and he also knew that somewhere there would be high ranking Officials in the loop on this type of operation. They would be bound to pass on a warning.

Kendall thought about it for a few seconds.

"Right, you seem to be impressed with Ramirez and he has the ear of some honest Senior Officers. Tell him he will be the best front man to stop this shipment but under no circumstance do you become directly involved and do not involve our Embassy"

Douglas signed off, contacted Ramirez who was still at his Company lines and asked him to meet him soonest at the villa on a matter of some importance.

Edward Anstruther had just arrived for his meeting with Christopher Armstrong the senior Hull Blyth Cargo Agent. Armstrong didn't much like the Colonel but played the occasional game of squash with him.

Sadly, at 46 he had become a heavy drinker and Anstruther always ensured there was a plentiful supply of alcohol to loosen his tongue, perhaps making him indiscreet about a certain cargo.

Christopher knew he became loose tongued when he drank but could not help himself. He had been with Hull Blyth in Luanda for thirteen years, was the senior Cargo handling Agent but knew he would go no further as he had been passed over for management jobs due to his excessive alcohol consumption. This had led to depression compounded by the illness of his wife Grace who had recently been medivac'd to England for cancer treatment. They had no children and he now found solace in the bottle.

They were lunching at the Blue Moon Chinese restaurant just off the causeway, the opposite end of the spit from the Barracuda and a favourite haunt of Anstruther's for clandestine meetings.

Armstrong had been at his desk bottle already and was 'well on' when he arrived.

"Christopher, my dear chap. How are you and how is Grace?" said Anstruther getting to his feet from his preferred corner table.

"'Lo Edward" said with a lopsided grin, I'm OK. Grace is just the same, thank you"

"Well, come and sit down, have a drink and forget about the world for a while".

Armstrong became increasingly inebriated and when Anstruther called for coffee and large Brandies he could hardly stand up to go to the Gents. The conversation had turned to Port activity and Anstruther had learned of the arrival of a well known smuggling ship, the Maria Luisa, that evening. He had also been told there appeared to more armed men around the dockside container yard than usual.

Christopher had further dropped into the 'pool' the fact that he was handling two containers to be loaded on that ship for some 'very shady characters' - all transactions in cash with special instructions for bills of lading.

With this useful information secured, Anstruther poured the hapless Armstrong into his Discovery and with "you'll be all right to drive old boy?" beat it back to his office.

Armstrong could hardly see the steering wheel let alone the ignition. Fortunately, he dropped the keys on the floor and fell asleep being found in the same position by his Secretary some four hours later.

Anstruther tied to contact Alfonso Carisco to inform the Angolan authorities about the possible 'iffy' cargo in the two containers marked for Germany but could not reach him. He was put through to the Duty Officer who was the same Lieutenant who gave Ponce the false papers for the trucks. He blurted out his information for which the Lieutenant thanked him and assured him it would be given to the Chief Inspector as soon as possible, instead of which he immediately contacted Ponce's organisation to advise that the cargo had been compromised and that the authorities would be watching the Port.

The Ambassador was still at luncheon when Anstruther requested an audience. This had been granted although HE was slightly nettled by the interruption as he only took forty five minutes for his repast. His own quiet time during which he gathered his thoughts.

Anstruther unfolded how, with his efficient intelligence gathering and network of spies, he had managed to unearth a possible illegal cargo departing tonight on the Maria Luisa and that he had informed the proper Police authorities. Pausing, expecting a pat on the back he was somewhat dumbfounded to be told that it was not his job to become involved in internal Police matters. He was the 'Military' attache not a London Bobbie and should act accordingly. Such interference just clouds issues. Report it to London on the normal channels.

Back in his office, somewhat abashed. He reported through to London.

Half an hour later an URGENT/IMMEDIATE signal flimsy was placed on his desk from the MOD.

'Re your last tx (transmission). Already aware and assets in place. Under no circumstance, repeat no circumstance, become involved or advise local Police authorities'.

Oh! Oh!.

CHAPTER 10

On returning to the villa Douglas was handed an 'immediate' signal flimsy by Papa Rock which had come through half an hour previously. It was from the General and authorised him to assist Captain Ramirez and his special forces who had been tasked to ambush the arms shipment and arrest the key players when they arrived in the Docks, that evening.

He again contacted Ramirez who was already rehearsing his men for the task and asked him to come to the villa PDQ . (pretty damn quickly).

Captain Ramirez barrelled into the courtyard in a cloud of dust some twenty minutes later.

"Francisco, I hope you don't mind my input, but our Governments have decided we should work together on this one and I for one wish to nail these particularly nasty thugs. "

"Not at all! I welcome your assistance - you know these men and their capabilities better than me although I have been fully briefed."

"Right, we haven't much time. Come inside and we will firm up the plan"

The two men entered the dining room and sat at the table where Papa joined them with sketching paper and pencils.

Ramirez opened the discussion.

"The ship is scheduled to leave harbour at 21.00 hrs. tonight and we believe that the last two containers with the arms will be swung on board about 20.00. One of my men is posing as a stevedore and watching all movements around the containers. There are three armed guards in civilian clothes, probably ex UNITA rebels, patrolling the area. These guards are only carrying hand guns although assault rifles may be close at hand.

It is also apparent from the conversations overheard that the final money exchange between the IRA people and UNITA is to take place on board the ship once the containers are inboard, thereafter the mooring lines will be slipped.

My plan is simple - I shall go on board with the Port Authority personnel, and a replacement Pilot who will be my Company Sergeant Major.

There are two gangways, one amidships and one at the stern. I will have a small hand picked unit, only a dozen men, in two civilian vans near the ship. Once the containers are inboard they will debus, four will remain on the quay to dispose of any ground resistance, the remaining eight will board the ship by the stern gangway, fan out towards the bridge and secure the ship.

In the interim we will have found and arrested Gallagher, McGafferty, Ponce and his UNITA associates.."

"Fine" said Douglas, may I suggest you position two men with a light machine gun in the dockside crane in case we need covering fire. May I also suggest that I act as the Marine Pilot to leave the CSM free to command the rear boarding party. It will be dark and I shall enlist Papa's skills to ensure my skin colour is suitably adjusted.

Papa I want you to be in the rigid raider in the harbour near the ship in case we have any problems. Take Sergio with you.

Francisco, I presume you have asked the Navy for assistance?"

"Yes, they are on standby."

The three men covered detail for another ten minutes then Ramirez left to brief his troops, to return with his squad and a Pilot's uniform for Jack at 18.00 hrs.

Ramirez returned with his troops in the two vans at five minutes to six, He handed Jack a navy blue sweater, blue serge trousers, a black web belt with a holstered 9mm Browning automatic and a Navy cap.

"This is the normal rig for our Port Pilots and before you ask, they always carry sidearms. I have also 'borrowed' a set of papers for you" handing over an Angolan passport, Master's Licence and Port Authority ID.

It was now 18.20 and it would be fully dark in a few minutes. Ramirez gave the order for his men to load their weapons and he and Douglas climbed into the front of the lead van beside the driver.

All Ramirez' men had discarded their normal uniforms and were now dressed in black overalls, boots and black berets. Each man carried an AK47 with a holstered Browning on his webbing belt which also carried three spare magazine pouches, water bottle and field dressing. Although all were dark skinned Angolans they wore camouflage cream on their faces to stop perspiration shine.

A tough looking group, thought Douglas, as the small convoy headed to the Port.

Douglas and Ramirez would be dropped at the Harbour Master's office to await the time to board the ship. The two vans would take up position on the quay towards the stern. Ramirez would signal his men to go on his handheld VHF radio.; If no contact 'H' hour would be

20.45 .

Extra armed Police had been provided by the Chief Inspector who were stationed strategically throughout the Dock area in case the UNITA rebels, had clandestinely, infiltrated more men.

At 20.30 they left the office with one of the Port Officials who had been briefed to stay behind on the quay and walked towards the 'Maria Luisa' whose diesels were already fired up for an immediate departure. Ramirez's undercover man had witnessed the containers being swung aboard and lashed down as deck cargo, not secured in the hold. He had also reported that Alfonso Ponce, the gun runner, had gone aboard with an unknown Angolan.

Douglas estimated that there would be five or six men on the bridge including the two South African minders and that most would be armed. the element of surprise would be vital. Ramirez called his squad to confirm a 'go' at 20.45 hrs. All was set!

As they approached the amidships gangplank two men emerged from the shadows. It was indeed the two South African heavies who were apparently awaiting their arrival. They briefly shone a torch in their faces, checked Douglas' credentials, radioed the Bridge and allowed them to proceed.

"That's a bit of luck, I thought they would have been onboard. Your boys will take them out if necessary"

Ramirez grunted and acknowledgement.

They boarded the ship and then climbed the external companion ladder to the Portside Bridge wing, the opposite one from the quay and the one through which anyone on the Bridge would not expect them to arrive, which also gave the covering machine gunner a clear field of fire.

Douglas looked towards the stern and thought he glimpsed shadowy figures making their way forward. So far so good. He glance in through the Bridge window and saw the Captain, a Helmsman at the wheel, Ponce, Gallagher and the unknown Angolan incongruously wearing black lens Raybans. He held up five fingers to Ramirez as they drew their weapons and stepped through the door.

"Good evening Gentlemen" Douglas said, "all hands where I can see them, no sudden movements and step towards the centre of the wheelhouse away from the console. Ramirez had gone to the rear of the Bridge, Douglas closed and dogged the steel bulkhead door.

"What is this?" exploded the Captain, "are you mad?" obviously thinking Douglas was still the awaited Pilot

"Quite sane Captain, we are here to arrest these men and impound your vessel for smuggling. This is Captain Ramirez from the Angolan Army and we already have troops onboard your ship, resistance is futile so let's try this without unnecessary blood shed or loss of life."

An explosion from the aft deck shattered the silence followed by a cacophony of automatic small arms fire. It was obvious that Ramirez' troops were being heavily engaged by the crew or the UNITA rebels and they could expect no immediate assistance from that quarter.

The curtain covering the entrance to the radio room at the rear of the bridge was suddenly pulled aside. McGaferty stepped over the coaming, weapon in hand and with one swift move headlocked Ramirez from behind ramming the muzzle of his pistol to his right temple.

"Now then, nobody move! Get his weapon Sean" he said to Gallagher.

Another exploding grenade caused a momentary loss of concentration. Ramirez raked his booted heel down McGafferty's shin and stamped hard on his toes. The grip around his neck was relaxed and as he twisted out Douglas shot out the overhead Bridge lights. He then threw open the door and both he and Ramirez dived out onto the flying Bridge with shots pinging off the metalwork behind them. He slammed and dogged the door from the outside.

Fierce fighting continued on the stern although the level of fire had diminished. Douglas' peripheral vision caught three figures making a break for the aft gangway dragging a fallen figure with them. He realised that it was the surviving members of Ramirez' assault party and as he watched a long burst of machine gun fire came from the dock crane to cover their retreat.

"That didn't go quite as we planned, Let's get out of here"

Wait" said Ramirez, as he pulled Jack back into the shadows of a steel deck vent. "I will radio the crane gunner to advise him we are coming off at the stern otherwise he will continue shooting at anything that moves."

Ramirez contacted the gunner and carefully explained where they were and that two more 'friendlies' would be coming off at the aft gangplank. This was acknowledge by the gunner who shifted his aim, peppering the bridge and foredeck with short controlled bursts.

As this was transpiring, the deck vibrations increased as the diesels rumbled up in revs. The bow started to swing out as the head line was cut or let go dropping the midships gangplank to the dock with a resounding crash.

"Now or never" said Douglas as both men jigged around deck obstacles racing for the aft gangplank. Their movement caused a volley of shots to follow them and Ramirez went down with a sharp cry, a round through his upper arm.

"I'm all right, go on" as he crouched up ready to continue his run.

The coaster continued to swing outwards and the aft gangway also crashed to the dock. The ship was free and unfettered by mooring lines.

"Right, over the Port rail" shouted Douglas, "jump out as far as you can from the side and swim away from the ship, We must avoid the undertow from the propellers. Understand? I will help you."

Ramirez nodded his comprehension.

"Radio the gunner to switch target to the fore part of the aft deck to give us cover." This Ramirez did and as the gunner opened up both men sprinted for the rail and dived or indeed half fell into the water.

The ship was now gaining forward momentum and both could hear the thunk, thunk, thunk of the big props coming towards them as the barnacled, rusty hull slipped by above.

"Swim" shouted Douglas, as even with him assisting they were both being remorselessly sucked back towards the ship and the stern.

Just as he thought they must be finished, there was a deafening roar of high power engines and Papa barrelled out of the darkness in the rib placing himself and the boat between the swimmers and the increasing speed of the hull.

"No time to lift you" he yelled. "grab the handlines on the pontoons and hang on. I shall tow you out" As soon as the two swimmers were secure to the port side of the rib with Sergio helping Ramirez, he racked up the throttles and surged away from the ship thrashing past.

Once in the darkness of the lagoon Papa throttled back, put the engines to idle and both exhausted men were pulled from the water and rolled into the rib floor. Ramirez was now bleeding profusely as Sergio slapped a field dressing on his arm tying it tightly.

The ship was now well clear of the berth and as they looked at her stern they clearly saw McGafferty standing there giving the two fingered salute to their last position.

"What a cock up" said Douglas.

"It's not over yet my friend, and by the way thanks for saving my life"

"Think nothing of it" responded Douglas with a smile as he punched Papa Rock on the arm. "and thanks to you, you old rogue for pulling us out of the excrement" as Papa handed them both blankets and a welcome hip flask.

As Douglas took a long pull from the flask feeling the fiery local Brandy course down his throat, the bellow of a ship's horn split the night. Two powerful searchlights immediately picked up the coaster's Bridge bathing it in naked light.

A Tannoy crackled loudly. 'Maria Luisa', This is the Angolan Navy. Heave to and wait to be boarded. You have no permission to leave Port and have used illegal weapons'

The coaster did not slacken speed and the men in the rigid raider looked on as if they were extras on a film set.

Again the Tannoy crackled, 'Heave to immediately or I will open fire. There will be no warning shot'.

A spotlight stabbed back from the coaster lighting the Angolan Navy minesweeper which appeared to have more rust than grey paint but which was steaming about 20 knots, six hundred metres on the port side on a converging course to intercept 'Maria Luisa' before she cleared the Lagoon. Although somewhat bedraggled she still looked very business like indeed as her forward gun turret turned to bear on the coaster.

The gun belched and a star shell lit up the scene in stark detail.

The gun fired again, this time with HE (high explosive) and scored a direct hit on the Bridge superstructure which almost disintegrated.

Douglas then saw the minesweeper go hard astern as she was approaching the shallows.

The fleeing coaster, still at full ahead but out of command and control veered to starboard and ploughed hard on to the sandbank with its engines still racing, the props throwing up a huge mud and sand wash from the stern as they bit in to the bottom. Her engines screamed then started breaking up as the ship died.

The sea was lit by the minesweeper's searchlights as they watched the death throes of the ship. With fire blazing from amidships, she settled on the bank. A sudden quiet as her broken engines at last fell silent and the props became still, the blades sticking some two metres out of the water.

Dreadful to watch the death of a ship no matter what the circumstance, thought Douglas.

"There must still be some of the crew alive. Francisco, will the minesweeper effect a rescue?"

"Papa is speaking to them on the radio now, mine was lost in our nocturnal swim, they have already launched two cutters and she is standing by. I don't think they will board until first light as if the fire reaches the Semtex she will blow in half. They will simply encourage any remaining crew to take to the water and pick up any trying to swim away.

She went aground in a very shallow part of the harbour and survivors could probably walk to shore after a short swim so we have contacted the Chief Inspector to provide shore patrols."

"OK Papa, let's go home. I am freezing and Francisco needs a hospital, We shall review the situation in the morning."

Papa gunned his motors and headed towards his dock on the other side of the Lagoon with a half wave, half salute to the minesweeper. Ramirez was talking in rapid Portuguese to the Captain to whom he also gave a wave with his good arm as they sped past.

Turning to Douglas he announced that he had arranged for one of his vehicles to collect them at Papa's house to take them back to the villa. In a more sombre voice he also informed him that the 'Butcher's Bill' had been heavy. He had lost four men killed and two wounded, one seriously.

A silence settled on the three men as they ran the last few hundred metres each immersed in his own thoughts on the day's action.

CHAPTER 11

.

The following morning Douglas was awakened by a telephone call at 07.50 hrs. It was Francisco Ramirez informing him that they had boarded the beached coaster at first light found McGafferty, the Captain, the Angolan and five crew, dead but that there was no sign of Gallagher or Ponce. There were also two dead UNITA rebels on the quay. Again no sign of the South African bodyguards who were assumed to have survived.

The fire had burnt itself out and arrangements were being made to refloat the ship at high tide, return it to the docks and remove the arms containers.

The Police had picked up two crew members on the shore. The remaining crew, rescued by the minesweeper were simply that - just sailors doing their jobs and following orders.

Apart from the high death toll both Ramirez and Carisco considered it had been a successful operation as the end result had been achieved, with both men being congratulated.

The Captain of the minesweeper was seemingly ecstatic as it was only the second time he had fired his main armament in anger and either by luck or judgement, had scored a direct hit on the Bridge of the 'Maria Luisa' with his first shot.

Douglas expressed his wish that he remain out of the limelight and that his role should be declared as 'advisory' only, he was however concerned over the whereabouts of Gallagher and Ponce.

They would surely work out that the leak of information had come from the conversations held aboard the Hispaniola consequently Sylvette could be in danger. He would contact Alfonso to ask him to station some of his men on board and on the quayside to augment the existing ship's security.

Sean Gallagher, after a night of evasion, little sleep and too much Brandy, spat the dryness from his throat and rubbed his bleary eyes.

He and Ponce had escaped from the ship after she ran aground having miraculously survived the shell exploding on the Bridge with only cuts and bruises. They had managed to dodge the shore patrols.

With Ponce's network and local band of brigands, they had been smuggled out of Luanda in a stinking cattle truck and were now ensconced in a hut in a tiny village some twelve miles North of the City.

Gallagher was furious. Not only had he paid for the weapons in total before the attack but he had now lost the whole shipment and McGafferty was dead. He had to think of something to recover his position.

After a breakfast of maize bread and coffee he discussed the situation in detail with Ponce who was equally bent on revenge and restitution.

They agreed, initially, to send out his spies and milk his sources to find out who had 'squealed' or from where the leak of information had emanated.

Later that day they would move further North to a secluded farm owned by him which at least had running water, a cook and a telephone. It also had a stockpile of weapons hidden in an armoury underground armoury.

CHAPTER 12

Douglas had sent a signal back to General Kendall advising him of last night's operation and had received in return a cursory ' Good, now get back to the job in hand'.

So - to the job in hand. He picked up the telephone and called Edward Anstruther at the Embassy.

"Good morning Ed" he said cheerfully, "I need you to organise something for me".

"Morning, before we discuss anything I want to know if you were involved in that dockyard debacle last night. Everybody is jumping up and down and all I have managed to find out is that it was an Angolan Special Forces Op. HE is hopping mad as there appears to have been 'Brits' involved and it smells fishy enough for you to have been in the thick of it"

"No Edward, you know I am here strictly to review the diamond security. I was tucked up in bed last night and don't really know what you are talking about" (well for a few hours anyway, he thought)

"I have no interest in local operations, so to business. I want you to arrange with your friend Belguerro to get me the necessary permission and documentation to visit the diamond sorting offices in Huambo. I require to review the mining operation, sort rooms, storage and transport prior to the flight down to Luanda so get me on the next flight will you"

"That will be very difficult, only employees of Endiama, CSO De Beers, and Government officials are allowed on these flights. . . . . . ."

"Just get me on the first flight" interrupted Douglas. "I can easily go through official Government channels but it will not look good for you refusing to facilitate matters, understand!"

"All right, I will phone you back".

Douglas replaced the receiver with an amused smile on his face. So Anstruther was not in the loop about last night's operation. Good, he thought, Ramirez' security seemed to be sound but he was surprised that his Police informers had not advised him. Maybe Alfonso had tightened up the sieve that was Police Headquarters.

His next call was to Papa Rock who had now returned home.

"Morning Papa, thanks again for your timely rescue last night".

All part of the service" said Papa, "I'll just add it to my bill. What's up?"

Douglas told him all he had heard from Ramirez earlier and both agreed Sylvette may be in danger. He also told him he was soon to go to Huambo and would be away for a couple of days, in the interim could he go to the Hispaniola, ensure that Alfonso had provided extra Police and check out the security. He would speak to Sylvette directly.

He cut the call then dialled the Hispaniola.

"Sylvette Dubois" he intoned as the phone was answered.

Sylvette came on the phone almost immediately. "Jack" she said, "how nice. Did you see the fireworks on the Lagoon last night or were you perhaps a bit closer, to get a better view of the entertainment?"

Hi Sylvette, yes I heard something about a fire on board a freighter, must have been quite an evening.

I need to speak with you, will you be available for a pre prandial libation around 13.00 hrs.?"

"Always a pleasure Jack. See you at one".

Douglas drove on to the Hispaniola quay at ten minutes to one. As he parked the Range Rover he noticed with satisfaction the blue Police Toyota and three heavily armed Policemen stationed around the car park. A Sergeant, who he recognised as one of Alfonso Carisco's best men, was standing at the bottom of the gang plank talking to the local security guards.

As he went through the normal search and weapon deposit operation he asked the Sergeant if there had been any increase in activity around the ship, the response to which was in the negative but he we informed that there were three Police teams on eight hour shifts so that full protection would be maintained.

Douglas thanked him and strode up the gangway.

Sylvette was already waiting for him in the bar with a bottle cooling in an ice bucket by her side.

"Good morning Sylvette" bending to kiss her on the cheeks "you are looking particularly attractive today"

"Well, thank you kind Sir" she replied, I have a bottle of the 'Widow' here. I felt like a change from Bollinger and I find Veuve Cliquot lighter at this time of day"

"Fine" said Douglas as he opened the bottle and poured two long flutes.

"By the way, thank you for arranging the increased Police presence. Alfonso came down himself this morning and said the teams would be here until I felt there was no more requirement. He also told me in detail, the happenings of last night. I just knew you would have been in the heat of it".

"It was a little warm for a time, but sadly Gallagher and Ponce got away. They must now realise that the information came from this ship and will be Hell bent to even the score. Can you get away for a couple of weeks? Maybe go back to Europe".

"No, nobody drives me off my ship. I will watch out and all my own security people have been made aware of the possible threat".

As they discussed the night before and various security matters Douglas mused that Sylvette really was very beautiful but with a little stab of guilt he thought of his lovely Maggie to whom he had not spoken for four days and made a mental note to phone her from the villa that night.

"Right, must dash. Watch your back. Any problems phone me or Papa. OK?"

Having collected his weapons he drove back to the villa. Sergio was waiting for him with a message that Anstruther had got him on the morning flight to Huambo leaving at 07.20 and returning that evening if that would give him enough time as the next flight, apart from the diamond delivery plane, was in four days.

Douglas asked Sergio to confirm that this was fine and after a light luncheon went in to the drawing room to plan his trip whilst continuing to plan the 'exercise' for an ambush on the convoy after the next delivery.

That evening he spoke to Maggie for half an hour during which he asked her to get in touch with Hamish Duncan's shipping Agent and find out exactly where his ship was currently positioned.

Douglas had known Duncan for years and the pair were great friends. He was ex Black Watch and had had a volatile career since leaving the Army in and out of businesses and trouble. He lost most of his money when a Ferry Company he owned was put to the wall by his Bank.

All he had now was his trawler on which he lived. Douglas knew he was fishing the African shelf and also knew he would be first in on any game which was afoot. A good man to have at your back.

The following morning he arrived at the airport in the darkness around 07.00. There were no formalities and apart from a mining Engineer he was the only other passenger on the eight seat aircraft. The flight was only forty five minutes and the sun was up as they turned finals for the dirt airstrip at Huambo. The aircraft bumped to a halt in a swirl of dust in front of a prefabricated metal hanger. As the door was opened from the outside the heat charged into the coolness of the air conditioned aircraft even although it was barely 08.20 hrs.

As Douglas eased his frame out of the aircraft, he was greeted by two ex pats in Endiama uniforms, one wearing a large revolver on his belt. This was the Head of diamond security at Huambo and the other was one of the Sort House Inspectors. After introductions he was taken to the administration building where he explained his task to the two men and what he wished to accomplish.

"No problem" said John Watson, the Security Chief "we have already been advised by headquarters in Luanda of your survey of our operation and De Beers have also given you clearance to enter all areas including the sort rooms and the strong room.

Let's fix you up with a visitor name tag and I must ask you to empty all articles from your pockets and hand over any weapons you may be carrying"

Jack complied unstrapping his ankle holster and placing it on the table. David, the Inspector, sealed all the articles in a clear plastic bag and locked them in a wall safe in the corner.

"I am afraid you will have to submit to a full search before entering the restricted area. It is a standing order and everyone, without exception, is searched.

"Fine, I want to observe all the security arrangements. Have you a copy of your SOP's (Standing Operational Procedures)?"

There is one in the sorting house which employees must sign once a week as proof they have read the instructions and taken notice of any updates, alterations or additions. You will be given a pad and pencil once inside for your notes" continued Watson.

They walked across to the main area which was located some two hundred metres from the admin. Building surrounded by a formidable, five metres high, steel and chain link fence topped and interwoven with razor wire.

The building itself resembled a single storey, blast proof bunker constructed from reinforced concrete with heavy, one way, armoured glass windows. On the flat roof sat massive air conditioning units, a large freshwater tank and an array of radio aerials and satellite discs.

"The sort office is completely self contained and was rebuilt three years ago with state of the art communication equipment "said Watson with pride. "In the event of an emergency there is sufficient food, water, back up air conditioners and generators for the whole sort team to survive for two weeks with a complete 'lock in' until help arrives".

Having pressed an outside bell by the large steel doors, they were admitted to an anteroom and there all three men were systematically searched. Once clear they wrote their names, badge number and time of entry into a log on the desk which was then countersigned by the attendant who spoke into a microphone requesting the inner stainless steel door, which could only be activated form the inside, to be opened.

Douglas shivered slightly in the cool air as he passed through to the inner sanctum. He noticed that the door was at least six inches thick and had four electronic dead bolts.

Watson continued explaining, "There is only one entrance and exit point. The whole operation is recorded on CCTV cameras and monitored from that booth over there by two men on two hour shifts. They also have keys to the only firearms allowed inside this building. All the security personnel in here are ex pats. The sorters are skilled Angolans who have been vetted by the Company and have been employed for several years. We pride ourselves on our working relationships and we have only arrested one man, some two years ago, for attempting to smuggle diamonds in a place you really do not want to know.

The camera tapes are kept for three months then reused. They are completely renewed each year and the old ones destroyed."

"Impressive" said Douglas, "I would like to check out the security booth first then watch the complete sorting operation".

In the sorting area there were six sorters at the conveyor belt where the diamonds were sized and graded before being packed in small linen bags for storage in the large safe set in to the concrete wall at the other end of the room. The safe was electronic with the door yawning open. It was time locked and set to open five minutes before the start of sorting and automatically locked when the door was closed.

Douglas spent most of the day watching and noting all aspects of the sorting operation. At the end of the afternoon he had made pages of notes but had to admit that he could not fault the existing system and security arrangements. There were some minor weak points which he would highlight in his report but all told, a very secure operation.

At 1640 hrs. John Watson returned to advise him that the plane was leaving in fifteen minutes.

Douglas went through the reverse procedure which he had gone through that morning collected his weapon and personal belongings, thanked Watson and his staff for their assistance, boarded the plane, the only passenger, and was dozing in his seat almost immediately, the bump of the wheels on the Luanda tarmac waking him some fifty minutes later.

As he drove home he went over his day at Huambo in his mind and concluded that any diamond loss could not be from the sorting operation therefore must be in transportation or at the National Bank.

After a shower and supper he filed his report for the General and sent it through.

CHAPTER 13

Some 50 kms. North of Luanda, Gallagher, Ponce and his gang had gone to ground in a deserted village with little food and only two vehicles. Gallagher was furious after the death of McGafferty on the freighter and the loss of his arms shipment most of which had been seized by the Angolan Forces. Fortunately for those concerned the Semtex had not been triggered and the Maria Luisa still lay on the sandbank at a 40 degree list where she would probably be stripped of anything useful by the locals and simply left to rot away as he didn't think there was a tug large enough in Luanda harbour to tow her off or possibly salvage.

"Ponce, I want to know from where the bloody leak came," spat Gallagher. "I know it wasn't McGafferty and he has paid the price so it must have been one of your loose mouthed drunken rats.

I want him found. I want revenge!"

Ponce looked at him under narrowed eyes from where he sat on his haunches under a dried, old tree. His permanent scowl was even more marked today.

Don't worry my friend, I also want him and when I find him I shall skin him alive. Believe me, he will talk and if he is on the Police or Military payroll he will have a long slow death."

"Ok. Get on with it. Take your men and the long wheel base Jeep and find him but keep a low profile. Watch your 6 and don't lead anyone back here. I have to find a phone and contact my people."

Ponce rose, shouted instructions to three of his men who festooned with weapons and bandoliers, fired up the Jeep and roared out of the village in a cloud of dust.

"Thanks", said Gallagher as he spat out the dust, brushed his already soiled clothes and walked over to the other truck to get some water.

Under the truck lolled five more of Ponce's men looking like a bunch of raggedy dolls. Gallagher kicked the boots of one, the souls of which had been re-soled with cut offs from old car tyres. This man had a smattering of English so he told him to get off his arse, take one of his friends and setup an OP 300 yards down the track.

"Don't go to sleep", he said, "or you will feel the toe of my boot and you might find time to clean your weapons", which were filthy and streaked with rust. It is well known that an AK47 is almost soldier proof and will still fire in poor condition but Gallagher saw no excuse for the lack of maintenance.

"No oil", the man said.

"Use bloody engine oil from the truck" Gallagher replied. "You will be relieved in two hours. Stay sharp! "What a joke, he thought.

Alfonso Ponce seethed quietly. He did not like being spoken down to especially in front of his men and he resolved to get his own back on Gallagher with whom he was in bed, only for the money. The truck jarred and jolted down the track not alleviating his bad temper, eventually coming to a potholed blacktop road which led to the North area of Luanda between the airport and "Shanty town" where almost a million people displaced by the war eked out a meagre living and where the 'Market' was held every Thursday and Friday

Here anything could be purchased from weapons, sex, slaves, to lean provisions and broken bicycles. It was also the trading post for all things stolen and the gang ring leaders set up in a large lean to where they drank, smoked the local ganga and waited for their minions to bring them the spoils of the day. Ponce was well respected, and it was within this band of cut-throats he would start his investigation into the betrayal of his plans. His battered Jeep looked slightly out of place alongside the Mercedes ML's, Range Rovers and assorted up market 4 x 4's with their blacked windows.

His armed escort however gave him the presence his vehicle did not, and he despised the others having to show off their misbegotten wealth. He preferred to keep a low profile, show no outward sign of assets and invest his money in buying up property on the hill district which used to be called "millionaires' row" and where most of the Embassies and Missions were once located. Luanda was turning itself around slowly and his properties had already doubled in value.

The stench of the fetid air around the market was palpable – it hung above the stalls and the few thousand people trying to find an affordable 'bargain' or offload some purloined rubbish. Effective Policing was carried out by the gangs – disputes and arguments were settled by the Leaders in the lean to. There was little or no theft as all knew retribution would be swift and terminal.

The smell was even worse in the lean to with no air circulation so much so that even Ponce put his scarf around his mouth and nose.

Once settled with a cold beer he eyed his fellow criminals, spotting a small weasely man who he knew to have his ear to the ground he beckoned him over. The man hesitated as he was one of the acolytes of the 'senior' gang leader who however had seen the sign and languidly waved his hand giving him permission to talk to Ponce.

Without introduction Ponce simply said, "What have you heard?"

Knowing full well Ponce's reputation, the man known as GoMore immediately revealed he knew of the fiasco last night and that it had ended in a disaster. Indeed all the Gang Leaders knew.

"I didn't need you to tell me about last night, I was there! Tell me what you have heard about the betrayal. Who leaked the plan to the Police?" GoMore's eyes rolled white and he started to sweat. "I know nothing about this he said, only a small whisper is going the rounds that it was one of the minor gang leaders who had a score to settle".

"Ah!" said Ponce. "I know which one. Are you sure of your source?"

"Yes", said GoMore visibly frightened – "can I go now. It is not safe for me to be seen with you".

"Get out of my sight you vermin. Be sure your information better be correct or else." as he drew his hand across his throat. GoMore bolted.

The man in question strode in to the Leanto and the air suddenly became colder with the loud conversations on all sides becoming more muted. Ponce knew he could not violate the neutrality of the "Market" but he would make it abundantly clear that he knew the source of his betrayal. This man, Fernando, had a cousin who was one of Ponce's men and the leak had obviously come from there whether by a misguided comment within the family or deliberately, he did not know and did not for the moment care.

He stood up, the conversations around dried up, he walked toward Fernando his hand on the hilt of his knife for all to see. Fernando visibly quailed and turned to leave but two of Ponce's men had quietly positioned themselves behind him at a hand signal from their leader and as they were outside, casually unslung their AK 47s.

Holding his temper in check Ponce strode up and said. "You filthy rat, I know it was you – nothing is worse than a Police stooge. You are protected here. Your family is not. You have three cousins, from now you will have none", and with that he barrelled past shouting for his men who embussed in the Jeep and roared off in a cloud of dust.

At edge of the Market he dropped off two of his men with instructions to seek out Frenando's two cousins and kill them, the third back at camp he would deal with himself.

As for Fernando that would wait for another time – he knew the waiting and lack of action would make him terrified.

Justice had been partly done!

CHAPTER 14

Ten minutes after dawn the Luanda lagoon swirled with a sea har, visibility was down to 20 metres. There was no wind. The stench of the city was not tickling the back of the throat as usual. There was virtually no sound as Papa Rock emerged from his house on the banks of the lagoon, stretched, yawned and rubbed his stomach. He pulled up his canvas trousers, tied them tighter and wandered down to the shore to his small dock where the rigid raider floated without movement.

It was very, very still.

A bit ominous he thought but not unusual to have a har at this time of year. The temperature was already approaching 28 degrees and the humidity pressing down on his head was already about 85%. Going to be a hot one he thought as he somewhat absentmindedly checked the security of the mooring lines.

He had promised Jack he would pull the Raider up the slip today, check over the two massive Black Max outboard engines which could push it along at speeds in excess of 55 knots and check or renew all the onboard equipment.

Papa cosseted his boat and lavished almost all his spare cash on its upkeep. He had owned it now for six years and it had never let him down even on some of the full throttle, more nefarious runs he made. Mind you he thought, there is nothing here to outrun her – the one Customs cutter, an ex Royal Navy fast attack boat of some 120 feet, could only manage around 30 knots from its massive 18 cylinder Paxman diesels and that was if it did not break down through lack of maintenance, and with a clean scrubbed bottom. Papa knew she had not been on the slip for over two years and was festooned with marine growth which slowed her down at least 5 knots.

Gleefully he rubbed his hands together in anticipation of the events to come.

Chapter 15

At his villa on 'Millionaires Row' Jack Douglas had also been up since dawn. He had exercised in the basement gym, showered, shaved and was now sitting down to a sumptuous breakfast prepared by Anna.

Sergio, in immaculate order as usual busied himself in the ante room.

"More coffee Senor "he asked. Douglas shook his head – "Do call me Jack". Only one cup with breakfast had been his routine for as many years as he could remember.

"Sergio, I may have some work for you of a slightly different nature if you are willing to consider it. More suited to your past Military career." he added

Sergio looked at Jack with an implacable countenance but with a slight sparkle in his eyes. "What type of work? Dangerous is ok, illegal is not, although I find the one is usually hand in glove with the other. I have Anna to consider and my future in Luanda when you leave "

"OK. We shall speak about it after dinner this evening".

On that Douglas picked up his satchel checked his weapons and his radio and walked out to the borrowed Embassy Range Rover.

His plan was forming well and today he was going to the main Banco National on the esplanade to check the security operations of the diamond delivery from Huambo and exactly how and where the diamonds were secured in the bank overnight before being transhipped by armed convoy to the airport to catch the outgoing Sabena 747 to Brussels the following morning. Alfonso Carisco was going to meet him there at 09.00 hrs. although he had grumbled a little at the 'early' time. Normally Carisco arrived at his office around 10.15..

Negotiating the potholes on the once beautiful esplanade carriageway, he pulled up in front of the Bank. He was immediately waylaid by a pack of rats – street boys of indiscriminate age, the eldest not more than 15 who wished to 'protect' his car. Jack was well versed in this procedure and knew if he picked correctly the boys would provide more security than an armed Angolan policeman with an AK47. He pointed at a raggedy 12 year old with world weary eyes and a scar on the side of his face and his older and more muscled friend. Normally the fee would be 5 American cigarettes or a couple of cans of beer but Jack knew the coveted currency was the US dollar and always carried a roll of one dollar bills for such eventuality. The local currency, the Kwanza, was still on sky rocketing inflation which rose higher every day, so much so that one never asked how much an item or service cost but simply how many two inch "bricks" of the currency containing tens of thousands of Kwanzas.

As he pulled off two, one dollar bills the boy's eyes lit up. He gave one to the younger, signalling that he would give the other on his return. With great shouts the two selected guards shooed off the other street boys and took station one sitting on the front bumper the other perched on the back.

He knew his car would be safe.

The Bank was not, as yet, open and just as he was about to knock on the massive carved wooden doors, Chief Inspector Alfonso Carisco arrived in a battered, dusty police car driven by one of his force with another riding shotgun in the front passenger seat. The car stopped behind the Range Rover and Carisco alighted in an impressively smart uniform with razor sharp creases on his trousers. His Sam Browne belt gleamed as did the holster of his sidearm on his side.

"Good morning Alfonso, you look well. It is not often I see you carrying a weapon openly" knowing he favoured a shoulder holster with a compact 9mm Makarov, the outline bulge of which could be seen under the left arm of his well tailored tunic jacket.

"Ah well Jack," he said. "after the recent events in the harbour, we are on a heightened state of Alert"

Hiding a smile Jack turned again to the doors, which miraculously opened before he knocked and then they were both ushered in by an old man with grey curly hair rather incongruously dressed in a frock coat complete with wing collar. The doors were slammed behind them and relocked by an armed security guard who looked fit, proficient with pistol on his hip and a well oiled AK47 slung on his back.

The man introduced himself in English as the Manager, whose name was Jose Luis Cantaro de Huelva.

Turning to Jack he said, "We have met before senor, some few years ago when you were a Brigadier attached to the Angolan Defence Force and the Director of DSL."

The grand anteroom of the bank was dim as there had been yet another power cut. He peered at the man who must be nearly 70 and then recognised him as his contact at the Bank, then Assistant manager, who had helped him resolve several tricky fiscal situations many years ago and who had facilitated the transfer of his funds to Switzerland at the end of his last tour..

"Of course I remember. Congratulations on your promotion"

"Ah, simply Dead men's shoes" he replied, "as it will be with my successor"

He then turned to the grand sweeping marble staircase to the second floor with a gesture to follow, the anteroom being through two floors of this once beautiful building built by the Colonial Portuguese, as had most of the fine houses in Luanda – one of the finest being the British Embassy on the hill above the Bank.

Once comfortably seated in front of a stunning rosewood desk and after the obligatory drink or cigar had been offered and refused. Douglas started to explain the reason for his visit. As he was about to speak Alfonso interrupted and advised Jack that he had already briefed the Bank manager in outline. A flash darted through Jack's eyes as he had not wished or not discussed any prior briefing so he could gauge the full strength of the security arrangements. As it was the damage had been done and everybody would be on their toes today.

Saying nothing he turned again to the Manager. "Well, as you now know, I am authorised to carry out a full survey of the Bank's security with reference to the delivery, storage and transfer to the airport of the uncut diamonds from the mines at Huambo. I have already inspected the sorting offices at Huambo and must say I was most impressed."

With a puff of smoke from his cigar Jose Cantaro declared "my staff is at your disposal and they have been instructed to answer all your questions, perhaps you would care to start with the delivery?"

Pressing a bell on his desk which rang somewhere in the great building, an aide appeared to begin the tour.

As Jack rose, he turned to say, "I note you have no log of our visit, nor have you asked for identification. Are all visits so casual?"

Not taking offence, he smiled and said. "No. Casualness is not something we condone, every visitor is checked, searched, signed in and escorted everywhere by an armed guard. You will recall this is not a High Street Bank for the general public but the Headquarters of the Bank of Angola conducting Government, Corporate and Diplomatic business at a high level. The arrangements were waived this morning for you and the Chief Inspector as I was advised that this meeting never took place and is as you say, off the record, Why? I do not know and do not wish to know. Suffice it to say I have known the Chief Inspector since he was a Sergeant and you from our historic association. I trust you are satisfied?"

Umm, mused Douglas thinking there should never be a deviation from SOP's and wondered why his meeting had been deemed off the record.

Cantaro added that he had arranged a light luncheon around 14.00 hrs when he hoped the survey would be finished and he could answer any further concerns or queries.

The tour was quite exhaustive and covered every aspect from the delivery of the diamonds, being secured in the massive steel vault, time locked, and the transfer to the armoured car the following morning. The system was well rehearsed and had Fail safes imposed if one of the two persons required to set and open the vault were absent or incapacitated. The passwords and pass codes were randomly selected by computer every two hours and only the Manager and his two Assistant managers had access.

The massive vault was in the basement and to get to it, firstly you had to negotiate a guard room and four inch steel gates electronically bolted from inside. The guard room had bullet proof glass and steel reinforcement bars through the concrete. This was manned by two armed guards on 4 hour shifts, 24 hours per day. Any person entering the vault room had to completely undress, and don a Bank overall. All personal items including watches were left at the guard room. Such persons were searched again on exit before being allowed to change back to their own clothes. Only the senior personnel plus a bank porter were allowed inside the vault.

The vault was quite old but with a relatively new electronic timelock system which could not be over ridden by anyone once locked. The Bank had its own generators which kicked in automatically when there was one of the many power cuts in Luanda.

Thus the security of the stones once inside the vault was a given. The vulnerability was on delivery to the Bank and on reloading the following morning.

The survey complete and after a pleasant luncheon, Douglas and Carisco took their leave and exited to the bright sunshine. The sea har had long dispersed and Jack's eyes were drawn to the beached Maria Luisa still canted over on her side with black smoke streaks from the fire covering the side of the wheelhouse. Looks as if it has been there for years jack thought and probably will remain there.

"Alfonso, will you join me for a glass at the Barracuda – I have an idea to test the diamond delivery operation."

"With pleasure Jack. I always find the Barracuda such a delightful restaurant although even on my Chief Inspector's salary it is very expensive. Sadly it is the only decent restaurant and what a view from the verandah but prices are geared to European prices for the ex pats. Not Angolan prices."

You old rogue thought Douglas – I often saw you there with business men from all walks of life or oil Company Executives – I am sure you never pay!

"Ok. Dismiss your driver and bodyguard I will drive you then return you to the city or your home if you prefer"

The Range Rover was unmarked, with the two street boys still solemnly on guard. They grinned when Jack approached but visibly quailed when they saw the Chief Inspector and started to retreat. The younger hesitated then held out his hand for the second dollar.

"Well done "said Jack and handed over the cherished note to the grubby paw. The boy rattled away in Portuguese then dashed away

"You spoil these brats" Alfonso said. "Two dollars is far too much "

"Worth it for me to know the car will not be up on blocks with the wheels missing when I return"

He had made a point of introducing himself to the new Maitre on his return with an appropriate amount of dollars enclosed in the first hand shake. He was a great believer in tipping the important functionaries first, not after a meal thus establishing parameters.

They were ushered to the last side table on the Verandah, directly overlooking the beach, which always carried a reserved sign until removed by the Maitre. The beach in front of the Restaurant was patrolled by a couple of well muscled guards carrying night sticks. Their purpose was to ensure the locals would not intrude and start begging below the verandah or impinge on the stunning view. It had always been a contention with Jack as the locals did not intrude, only the prostitutes plying their trade to the ex pats, and if you told them to shove off, they did so with a flashy smile and a saucy wiggle of a rump.

Once settled Jack decided he would treat himself and ordered a bottle of non vintage Krug at an horrendous price. God knows what the price would be if they stocked vintage – he shuddered to think.

He then turned to Alfonso to start revealing his plan, a couple of minutes later the Sommelier arrived with a steward carrying a frosted ice bucket in which sat a bottle of Krug, and a pair of frosted crystal glasses which he sat on the table. This was a Sommelier Jack did not know. He looked at him – The Sommelier then asked Jack if he could pour the wine.

"No, you may not" Jack said in a somewhat steely voice "Summon the Maitre". The Maitre had already sensed something was amiss and was by his side in an instance,

Alfonso could not see any problem and had a bemused look on his face

Turning to him Jack said, "How many times have I been to this restaurant to drink Champagne" The Maitre shrugged. "No matter" he said, "have I ever accepted a bottle of Champagne which has ALREADY BEEN OPENED in the server."

Kindly advise this new Sommelier that I know all the tricks, I am not some oilman with a huge expense account who knows nothing about wine. Take away this OPENED bottle which probably contains some local fizz and bring an unopened bottle of Krug to the table. The Maitre blanched, realised the enormity of the transgression, rattled off a tirade of Portuguese and virtually pushed the cowed Sommelier out of the restaurant. He returned minutes later with profuse apologies, an unopened bottle of Krug and another pair of chilled glasses. Opening the bottle without the undignified pop he poured two inches of the glorious wine in to Jack's flute. His nose wrinkled as his senses recognised the effervescence. Taking a good swallow he turned to the Maitre – Excellent. Thank you. I shall pour"

The Maitre exited in reverse and Douglas could hear him tearing another strip off the two scam merchants in the kitchen.

"You know Jack – it could have been a genuine mistake and it was Krug in the bottle."

"Alfonso, a word to the wise, never accept a bottle of wine, any wine, which has been opened elsewhere, the best is that it can be the dregs from several bottles, the worst is that it could be drugged or poisoned"

Douglas poured two glasses of wine.

Savouring his first mouthful Alfonso said "Ah yes "nodding sagely, "But Jack" he smiled with his palms held out, "It's Africa! "

To the plan. . . . .

CHAPTER 16

Douglas appraised Alfonso Carisco of his plan to stage an assault 'exercise' on the diamond delivery convoy between the Airport and the Bank. For the sake of surprise and reality the only person who would be taken into the Loop would be Captain Ramirez, the troop Commander but he would not be given the details.

Douglas impressed on Alfonso the need for total secrecy in order to test the reaction of the convoy Officers and guards.

"But Jack, you must get permission from Military HQ and CSO (Central Selling Organisation – De Beers) to carry out such an exercise. There will be Hell to pay if you do not and something goes wrong"

"I don't expect anything to go wrong as long as nothing is leaked of our intention, hence no contact with anyone out with our immediate group. This is very much need to know and if there is a glitch we shall simply adhere to the old maxim – adapt, improvise, push on! OK!"

"You are the only one not directly involved in the attack who will know the details as we need you to direct Police resources away from the area at the time as they undoubtedly will think the attack is real, not an "exercise" and start blazing away with live ammunition plus I need you to provide a marked Angolan Police LWB hardtop Land Rover in good nick fully equipped with your police radios. Can you do that?"

Carisco stroked his chin and paused before grudgingly replying "yes I can do that, but if anything should go wrong I shall say the vehicle was stolen – you understand I must have deniability and shall ensure I am away from the area dining with some worthy notables to provide an alibi"

"Have you no Faith" retorted Douglas "I am so pleased you have already mapped out your own 'escape plan' after all this exercise is to assess the vulnerability of the convoy in just such an attack, eventually to your good. I am sure you will not be slow in coming forward when the praise is handed out – might even be another promotion. By the way I need the Land Rover first thing tomorrow 08.00 hrs latest".

The Chief Inspector did not reply but had the grace to look slightly embarrassed.

The sun was just about to dip below the horizon. The day went from dusk to full darkness in five minutes.

Tonight's sunset was spectacular as there were low clouds on the horizon and the flame orange fingers spread out over a roiling dappled sea which was slowly turning to deep cobalt blue. As the sun dropped lower, 'God's fingers' spread upwards to the clouds making the whole horizon look like an enormous Japanese flag although this was not the rising sun but setting. Two minutes later the sun had disappeared completely leaving a brief orange tinge then blackness.

The two rose from the table returning to the Range Rover, Jack having paid the outrageous bill with no discount for the earlier 'inconvenience' but with profuse apologies again from the Maitre. He gave the street boy his dollar and dropped Alfonso at Police HQ en route to the villa.

Showered and dressed in light cotton slacks, a sea island cotton light pink long sleeved shirt with the cuffs turned up just once and loafers without socks. He carried his metal briefcase which contained the secure encrypted computer link to 'the General', sat at a table in the ante room and logged on. Better give the old bugger a Sitrep (situation report) he thought though in fact the old bugger was just two years older than Jack and had been a close friend throughout his military career and thereafter as well as a fellow team member when Jack played polo. Those were the days he thought – young, carefree, having fun interspersed with occasional soldiering – you are looking through rose tinted glasses my lad, he said to himself – there were some pretty hot and hard missions along the way. Ah well!

As he began his report and update on Gallagher and cronies, Sergio appeared quietly beside him.

"Good evening Senor" with a very slight bow "I trust you had an informative day. Anna has prepared a light, white fish supper with lobster to start. Would you care for a drink now or shall I open a bottle of wine"?

Douglas remarked to himself on Sergio's unaccented and correct English terminology, turning he said, "Sergio where did you learn such good English"

"Ah" Sergio replied, "the product of an English public school education – I was six years at Harrow, and had very wealthy parents who insisted I learned English and French, which in those days was still the language of Diplomacy"

"Funny, when I first met you, you didn't seem to have such a colloquial command of the language"

Sergio smiled. "Yes, that was for the benefit of the Chief Inspector, it is better to hide one's true talents from those who need not know"

Douglas laughed, thinking you canny old rogue, but also wondering how such a man from a wealthy Portuguese family had never held a Commission and was now working as a Major domo in this large villa in Luanda. A past indiscretion perhaps. . . . . .

"Something light Sergio, perhaps a glass of Petit Chablis now and then a bottle of Vino Verde from the Algarve with the second course "

"Certainly, I shall bring your Chablis now as you work."

Finishing his brief report he checked his other messages and logged off. Closing the briefcase and rotating the locks as Sergio appeared with his wine. Very interesting man he thought and obviously still fit, we shall see what comes of our discussion after supper.

Having been summoned to the table he attacked his lobster with gusto and quaffed the last glass of Chablis. As he ate, his mind was racing putting in place all the minutiae of the assault exercise. He rarely set anything in writing and fortunately had the ability to retain a vast amount of information in his memory. Almost photographic, but not quite. . .

The second course, also excellently cooked was devoured with the splendid Vino Verde and he rose to relax on one of the comfortable damask covered armchairs in front of the fire which Sergio had just lit. Large marble houses, with no central heating and only inadequate reverse flow air conditioning become surprisingly cold near the Equator and the fire crackled away cheerily giving off a radiating warmth.

It was now 21.30 hrs and as if on cue Sergio returned to ask if Douglas required anything further.

Jack replied in the negative and told him he could now go off duty.

"I would like to have that chat with you now"

Sergio nodded then said. "If I am now off duty, with your permission I would like to be more comfortable "and walked towards his own quarters.

Ten minutes later he returned having lost the double breasted high collar jacket and now wearing a snowy white open necked shirt and an expensively tailored light blue cotton jacket. Douglas noticed he was also carrying a crystal brandy balloon in his left hand.

Without asking, he sat down opposite Jack and said, "this is a fine Armagnac from my own stock, it is not from the house cellar, now what do you wish to discuss"

Straight to the point thought Jack, I like that. "I wouldn't have cared if it was from the house cellar" he said.

"No that would not be appropriate and out of order" he replied.

Strike two, an honest, reliable man with a fine code of ethics – rare indeed to find in such a position where theft of goods and provisions was common place. He was beginning to get the measure of this somewhat inscrutable man, and the more he delved the more he liked what he saw.

"Firstly, if you have no objection, I would like to ask you about your military career and how you ended up here".

Sergio sat in silence for a few moments, he sipped his Armagnac then said.

"Although I have only known you for a few days I think you are an honourable man and anything I may tell you stays with us. I too have been doing some checking of my own for which you must forgive me but it as well to be prepared"

Douglas, slightly surprised at the man's revelation agreed. "As you say, this conversation stays strictly between us and if we do not come to an agreement on what I am about to disclose, will be forgotten"

On this assurance Sergio began to recount his past. When he returned from school in England his Father had remarried only two years after his Mother's death to a much younger woman who he detested as a gold digger, not from the same strata of society and who was only after the family wealth. His family owned vineyards in the Douro region near the great Port houses and produced a renowned typically strong and robust red wine. His Father wanted him to settle back at home and take over the vineyards. On the other hand he wished to take two years off and see the world – sow some wild oats! He was independently wealthy as his Mother's estate had all been left to him, the only child. He was just coming up to his 20th birthday however unusually in Portuguese law his Mother, a perspicacious woman had decreed that he would begin to receive the substantial interest on his 18th birthday instead of his 21st with the Capital on his 25th.

"I tell you these personal details" he said, "as it impacts on the rest of my life and thus necessary"

Douglas just nodded.

He continued: "I had a great argument with my Father, stormed out, packed a haversack with essentials and rode away from home on my motor bike heading for Oporto or Lisbon with no real plan. It was there I literally fell among thieves and started burglarising the grand houses just for the excitement as I didn't need the money although made sure my new friends did not know this fact. Eventually I was caught and sent to prison for one year due to my youth. My Father was outraged and refused even to come and see me saying I had brought great disgrace on an old well respected family which no doubt I had. That one year was probably the hardest of my life. I went in aged 20 and came out one year later aged 45, if you understand.

Again Douglas just nodded not wishing to interrupt the flow.

I drifted from job to job for another year then was contacted by the family Lawyer who had tracked me down working as a stevedore in Oporto to tell me my father had suddenly disappeared, possibly to England and had filed for divorce from my step mother. He also bore the bad news that my Father had, purportedly, written a new will after my incarceration and against his advice, leaving his whole estate to my

Step Mother save one small farmhouse and twenty acres of vines on the banks of the Douro left to me. In light of his pending divorce this was hard to believe. Perhaps a guilty conscience – who knows

I suspected foul play as I think did the family Lawyer but what to do. Finally I decided to return home and confront her, at least I could see the state of my farmhouse which I recalled as being pretty dilapidated.

I left my job and consoled myself in some of the seedy wharfside ale houses for a few days losing myself in the bottle. It was on such a night I was attacked and clubbed senseless. I awoke the following morning chained to seven other unfortunates in a house in Lisbon where we were held for two days not knowing what was going on and being fed one measly meal per day. On the third day a huge barrel chested man with a great beard arrived to tell us that as we had engaged with the French Foreign Legion we were leaving that day by ship to Morocco. We were all shocked by this announcement and I had no memory of any such engagement. Our combined outrage fell on deaf ears until he produced an Official looking scroll headed "Legion Etrangere" on which were all our names alongside our obviously forged signatures. Signed sealed and witnessed three days ago.

It appeared we had signed on for a minimum of 12 years.

At this Sergio excused himself and went to recharge his glass. I sat in some wonderment considering this fairy tale story of high jacking but could see no reason not to believe him, I charged my own glass with last of the Vino Verde from the ice bucket and awaited his return.

He sat down with a larger measure of Armagnac than before breathed out in a soft sigh and continued:

"We were transhipped to a rust bucket freighter on which once in International waters, we were unshackled, given the freedom to roam the ship, showers, decent food and khaki overalls, tunics and boots. The gruff German who we found out was a recruiting Sergeant out of Marseilles and had been in the Legion for 22 years became more amenable and advised us to train hard, fight hard keep our mouth's shut and it wouldn't be too hard.

The initial shock had worn off our group, most of which were resigned to the outcome apart from one lad who I found out was just 17 and had been hit particularly hard over the head so that his left eye seemed to wander all over. It did so till he took a bullet some four years later.

I won't go through the induction, gruelling training and first few years of service. Suffice it to say that once we had become Legionnaires we were actually proud of our status and the fact that we had all survived basic training and had been, as is the Legions practice, posted together to the same Company. We just had to knuckle down and serve our time. One tried to escape in year three across the desert and was never seen again, Some say he made it – I somehow doubt it!

I kept my nose clean, found that I enjoyed soldiering, was good at it and soon promoted from Corporal to Sergeant in my fifth year. In Year nine we were deployed on a disastrous pursuit of nomadic tribesmen who had attacked and looted one of our supply convoys leaving no one alive. Indeed it had been my section that had found the overdue convoy and the manner in which our comrades had been slaughtered had all our blood up for revenge. It was evident it was a sizeable force.

Our full Company was sent in pursuit, under the orders of an old Major who hadn't seen action in many years although the second in command was proficient. He led us in to an ambush, against the advice of the 2ic, both of whom were killed in the ensuing debacle as were 80% of the Company. I was left as ranking NCO and managed to disengage under cover of darkness with 18 surviving men and make it back to the Fort three days later.

I was called in front of the Colonel – praised for my action and given the choice of ending my engagement two years early with an honourable discharge my accrued settlement figure or extending for a further 5 years with immediate promotion to Sergeant Major. The following day I decided to take the former.

At this stage he reached into his inner jacket pocket, pulled out a buff coloured document and three medals and handed them to Douglas. "Just in case you might not believe this wondrous tale" he said.

Douglas opened the document which was a worn and soiled Legion ID card and looked at the medals two of which were Campaign medals the third, the cross of the Legion Medal for Valour

It was now 20 minutes to midnight and although Jack thought, what a story and sensed there was more to come he had not yet started to explain his own plan. Sergio stood up. "Perhaps I am telling you too much" he said "but I think it is necessary you have the full picture if you are going to trust me and anyway it is good and indeed bad to think about the old times"

"Will you join me in a glass of Armagnac"

"Certainly, and thank you" Jack replied. He stood up and placed another log on the fire. This is going to be a long night he thought but realised a barrier had been crossed and respect and blossoming friendship had begun.

Sergio returned carrying two glasses. "Good Health" as he sat down.

The pair sat in companionable silence for a few minutes in their own thoughts then Sergio began again:

"I returned to Portugal with my Legion settlement, knowing that my interest on my Father's Estate which had been untouched for ten years would have accrued to a sizeable amount and with the knowledge that I would now have access to my capital which opened up on my 25th birthday. I was now approaching my thirtieth and was lean, fit and as hard as nails. On leaving the Legion as was their practice I was offered a new identity. This I accepted and I was now travelling on my French passport as Jean Luis Baptiste from Marseilles. Needless to say, my school French had been honed to perfection in the Legion and I could adequately assume 'un accent Marseillaise.'

I had decided to return to my farmhouse on the Douro which now would probably be in a great state of disrepair, renovate to a decent residence of some luxury and consider my next move.

Firstly, I had to meet with my Lawyers and find out my net worth. I had arranged such meeting for the following day having been advised that my Father's old lawyer had passed away some years before but that the Firm would be delighted to carry out any instructions as a retained client. I couldn't remember ever having 'retained' them but what the hell.

On arrival I was immediately shown to the office of the senior partner but had noticed a few downcast looks surreptitiously cast my way as I passed. Perhaps it was just my demeanor and new clothes I thought as my countenance was burnt a deep mahogany from the desert sun and with my permanently slitted eyes I must have looked quite evil.

The senior partner shook my hand and I made my dutiful condolences on the death of my Father's lawyer. Without further ado I asked for a breakdown of my holdings and net worth.

The partner then proceeded to tell me a strange tale of woe. My Estate consisted of the farm on the Douro and the interest on my Father's estate which unbeknown to me had ceased one year after my Father's death thus only a few years interest had been paid. I protested vehemently saying this was impossible as the interest would be paid until the capital was released on my 25th birthday. He then showed me the original deed of settlement of my Mother which had a codicil attached that her capital in trust to me could only be used by my Father for the estate in dire circumstance. Due to the profligacy of my Step Mother and bad management the Estate had fallen in to debt and as his legal wife she had used my Trust funds to maintain her own lavish lifestyle. These had been flittered away by her and there was nothing left.

That is why the interest stopped as there was, no longer, any capital. He showed me a copy of the codicil which was unassuredly in my Mother's fair hand and on which my Stepmother had pounced.

Surely I asked as it was my money which baled out the Estate then I would have a percentage of ownership. I then asked if the Estate had prospered.

Indeed so he said, and yes under Portuguese Law you would have had a claim on the Estate, however your Step Mother sold the Estate as soon as it was back in profit for a sizeable figure, closed all her accounts and now lives near Buenas Aires, married to a cattle rancher.

I was thunderstruck by this run of bad and worse luck. I had thought I was coming home to a life of relative ease and maybe become a gentleman wine grower on my few acres – No such luck he snorted. The Bitch had really shafted me!

What had I left – Liquid funds he said exactly 87, 538 US dollars and 34 cents but there were outstanding taxes due on my house and of course his firms fees which were annotated here and he handed me an invoice for the equivalent of 24, 500 US. I asked how it could be such an amount and he explained there was a standing annual charge for ten years and of course the cost of investigation in to my whereabouts initiated by my Father but never paid by his wife.

You simply disappeared, he said.

As you imagine I was quite upset, cut the meeting short and retreated to the fresh air.

Instead of several 100's of thousands I had approximately 63, 500 US, my Legion settlement which equated to around 15, 000 US and a tumble down farmhouse.

"The mouse had turned again". Sergio said looking in to the dwindling fire.

Jack just sat, saying nothing.

I will summarise the next few years. I spent most of funds rebuilding and modernising the farmhouse which, surprisingly was not in too bad shape . I arranged a lease of my ground to Warre's the neighbouring Port Estate which gave me almost a living income and joined the Portuguese Army using my French identity as for some reason I did not want anyone knowing who I was and it was as if I needed to start a new life.

Due to my Foreign Legion service I was accepted in at Sergeant rank and transferred to the Special Forces Squadron. Yes, he said to Jack, we have special forces in the Portuguese Army, I rose to the rank of Squadron Sergeant Major. Met my wife who was originally from Luanda, married, then returned here after 28 years of military service.

We have been here for eight years and will eventually retire to my farmhouse, once we sell the five properties we have bought which have tripled in value four of which are leased to foreign companies, the fifth in which you are currently resident.

What" said Jack. "you own this magnificent villa?"

He nodded slightly with a grin splitting his face.

"As I said earlier it is better to hide one's light under a bushel" then he laughed out loud and Jack could not fail to join in.

What a story Jack thought.

"Sergio, I must thank you for your honesty and allowing me to know your amazing story. It is straight out of Beau Jeste with strains of the Count of Monte Cristo"

"Agh! I must further enlighten you, I actually am a Count the one thing my Father left me apart from his name is the title which I never use. Maybe when I return to Portugal, I shall use it to reserve a decent restaurant table"

"Sergio, you amaze me! I must now reconsider the subject about which I was going to discuss in light of all your information, tomorrow, actually it is tomorrow" as he looked at his Tag wristwatch which showed five minutes past one, "is a light day and we can resume our talk after breakfast" Standing up with a stretch he extended his right hand, "from now on you call me Jack" as both men clasped hands and then retired their separate ways

CHAPTER 17

Douglas awoke early after a restless night with a slight buzz from the Armagnac consumed during his discussion or rather his listening to Sergio. He was still amazed by the complexity of his life which was undoubtedly true. He had hoped to recruit Sergio as the 'last man' for the team but now knowing his achievements, his apparent wealth and his plans to retire to Portugal he was unsure whether he should involve him although he would dearly love to have such a experienced former soldier by his side.

It was still only 07.00hrs and dawn was lightening the sky over the miasma that was Luanda. The city was unsafe but at this hour no real threat so he decided to go for a run to clear his head but would stick to the high area around Millionaire's Row. Two laps should be around five miles. Nevertheless he would carry his 9mm Makorov and his radio in his waist bag.

Pounding along, there were few persons around in this area although the constant traffic hum from the docks below reached him. It was a pleasant temperature and the air with a slight offshore breeze cooled the sweat glistening on his forehead.

Back at the villa, he showered dressed and went down for breakfast where Sergio greeted him, none the worse for wear from the night before.

He needed another trustworthy experienced man, What to do? mused Douglas. . . . .

CHAPTER 18

Douglas drove down to the Isthmus of Luanda basin, to the home of Papa Rock, to check over the equipment and to finalise the 'double plan' details. The plan was relatively simple although split second timing was of the essence. He was going to use the cover of the exercise to assault the diamond convoy to actually steal the diamonds. He would then after exhaustive search 'find' them and return the stones to CSO (De Beers) from whom he would claim a very fat reward whilst also exonerating his actions and allay any suspicion.

Well, that was the plan – it was a big risk but he viewed it as possibly his last chance to make serious money and to recoup major losses he had sustained four years previously in an operation that had gone badly wrong. He always had Gallagher and his cronies at whom to point the finger.

The 'exercise' would cause sufficient confusion from smoke grenades and noise from the thunderflashes that in the melee Papa and his son would appear from below the old truck which was nose dived in the sewer, blow the rear doors of the armoured wagon, throw in a flash bang to incapacitate the interior guard, bolt crop the single chain holding the strong boxes and disappear again in to the sewer. Thereafter there was only a noxious fifty metres to negotiate before the culvert emerged in to the lagoon.

The rusted steel grille had already been cut the night before by Papa who had silently swum across the lagoon from his home wearing a black wet suit and a rebreather, carrying a portable underwater thermal lance which had cut through the rotten iron in less than six minutes. The overhang above the culvert had shielded him from any casual onlooker who may have chanced to look over the parapet. All the grille would need would be a 'good boot' from the inner side to break the final few strands but just in case he slid the lance through the bottom of the grille to the other side. Nothing to chance he thought. . .

Tonight, under cover of darkness, he would position the semi deflated rigid raider on an underwater ledge near the culvert, weighed down with rocks so that it would sit about five feet below the surface and just in case it decided to rise tethered fore and aft under water which would take a matter of seconds to slice through with his dive knife. The outboards were fully waterproofed as were the battery and electrics although there were emergency pull starts on top of each engine. Once they had lashed the strong boxes to the raider they would offload the rocks until it had negative buoyancy just below the surface, swim it along the bay some sixty metres alongside an old tramp freighter, re-inflate with the new gas bottles and row it deeper in to the docks where a 'tender' would not be suspect, start up and in stealth mode at low revs, motor out to sea before opening up the power of the twin Yamahas.

Arriving at Papa's Douglas saw him down at the slip working on the rigid raider.

"Good morning you old rogue" he said as his hand was engulfed in Papa's huge fist.

"Morning Jack, just fitting the new air bottles to re-inflate and I have one spare in the stern – Belt and braces" he said

"Excellent, she looks in really good nick"

"She is said Rock, she has never let me down," surreptitiously making a sign to ward off evil spirits "Come on get your hands dirty, help me put more grease around the engine seals and the battery box"

As they worked on the boat Jack went over the plan in detail.

"Right, you know the form, the diamond convoy is due to pass by the old truck in the sewer at 18.55 before delivery at the Bank which is scheduled for 19.00 hrs. I will hit it exactly as it is alongside and use my Police Land Rover to push between it and the leading escort vehicle to force it to stop. There will be mass confusion all around as you emerge under cover of smoke and make good the extraction. There will be only two of us above ground making as much noise as we can and firing off our AK's with all the other pyrotechnics. As arranged with Ramirez the convoy guards will have been issued with blank ammo. I just hope to God there is not some cowboy who retains a mag. of live rounds"

"Hold on, two? who is the other person?"

"I have decided to ask Sergio from the villa to help out and he will come in for an equal share – He hasn't agreed yet but I had a long conversation with him last night and he certainly has the experience. If he doesn't wish to be involved then I will go it alone as all I am doing is making a lot of noise and inserting my Land Rover in the convoy. As I am driving a Police Land Rover the convoy guards should not suspect anything until the hit and I am hoping they will be relaxed being less than five minutes from the end of their mission".

Papa Rock pondered this for a moment. "I know Sergio, I also am one of the few in Luanda who knows his background, he is a good man and will watch your six, however, an equal share? do you not think that is too generous?"

"Papa, my old friend all involved will get equal shares although you have agreed that you will pay your son – that's the way I work – all take the same risk of being caught and ending up in a Luanda prison, not a pleasant thought"

"OK, just checking but if I lose my raider you have agreed to replace it?"

"That is our private agreement" said Jack

You had better show me the C4 charge for the back doors'

At that, they walked up the slipway to Papa's boathouse where he unlocked the door and once his eyes had adjusted to the gloom, Douglas saw a rectangular tin on the work bench with about a two inch rubber strip from a tyre inner tube, around the edge. Removing the strip, Papa showed Jack the contents. Inside was a quarter Kilo of C4 with a timer pencil sticking out. The pencil was gradated in seconds not minutes, maximum time being 60 seconds.

'This will go on the main lock. It is not a shaped charge thus most of the blast will be deflected outwards by the armoured doors and the interior guard should not be harmed. I have a follow up flashbang if his ears and senses still appear to be working' and a spare timer pencil just in case. I will set it for ten seconds."

"A bit of overkill, don't you think. Just remember we only want to blow the locks. In the words of Michael Caine in the film the Italian Job 'we only want to blow the bloody doors off '

Both men laughed Jack stretched his hand out again "Ok Let's go over the rendezvous co-ordinates for Hamish's trawler?" Papa nodded. "You have a Navico chart plotter and positioning system on the rib so just punch in the Latitude and Longtitude and follow your nose. Hamish will be there – he has never let me down. Go dual watch on channel 16 and 8 on the VHF radio in case of emergency, He will be monitoring both channels.

Stay with him until dawn then return to harbour after a spot of "overnight fishing" with your son. No further contact unless an emergency"

"Until tomorrow, and may the Gods smile on us" . . . .

CHAPTER 19

Hamish Duncan swept the horizon with his binoculars from the foredeck of his trawler "Highland Mist" – nothing of import, as he turned back to the wheelhouse where his younger cousin, Lachlan Duncan stood with a mug of tea in his hand Lachlan was the only other crew on board and was also the Engineer keeping his beloved Gardner 8 diesel in immaculate condition. They had been steaming from Walves Bay in Namibia for the last four days have given his three local fishing crew their papers after a relatively prosperous season. He had promised Jack Douglas to be at the rendezvous tomorrow evening.

The "Highland Mist" was one of the last of the big wooden Scottish trawlers to come from the famous Jones shipyard in Buckie and was in remarkable condition for her age she was 68 feet LOA and over 6o tons in weight and had been fishing in Namibia for the last two years. Her fishing gear was of the latest technology as was her Navigation and Wireless equipment. She was also equipped with a military quality, 50 mile Furono radar. Driven along by the low revving Gardner she could comfortably cruise at 14 knots all day. Instead of the normal three blade propeller she was fitted with a larger five blade prop protected by a prop shroud which gave her more manoeuvrability.

When Hamish had moved from the cold waters of the North Atlantic to the Med and thereafter the African continental shelf he had slipped his vessel at the commercial shipyard at Algeciras and had them fit copper sheathing to the hull extending two feet above the boot top line, at great expense. This was simply to save his timbers from attack by the boring, gribble worm the curse of all wooden ships in warm waters. This also gave her the added advantage of being more slippery through the water and added a couple of knots to flank speed. He had lain alongside the fish dock at low tide in Walves Bay before departure and pressure washed the hull thus she had a spankingly clean bottom.

"Highland Mist" was painted black on the hull with the upper works and gantries dark grey instead of the usual cream she wore in Highland waters thus with lights off she was virtually invisible at night. Apart from her array of fishing spot lights she also carried two large Francis searchlights on the wheelhouse roof which had a mile's range and which could be operated from inside the wheelhouse as well as remotely from the stemhead.

She made no smoke from her exhaust stack aft of the wheelhouse a testament to Lachlan's engineering prowess.

Hamish Duncan had known Jack Douglas for many years had initially gone to the same school, Inverness Royal Academy and had remained firm friends and kept in touch over the years although their paths had separated when Douglas went to Public school in Edinburgh followed by Edinburgh University, then the Scots Guards.

Hamish had "followed the fish" wherever they took him and wherever he could buy or bribe for a fishing stock licence. His ship was his home and his cousin his family.

He had been involved in a few nefarious enterprises between fishing trips and only just managed to not have his ship seized in the Cape Verde islands four years ago after one such caper.

Another 'Privateer' as Jack Douglas described him.

He had decided that this would be his last "enterprise" as the spoils would be sufficient for him and Lachlan to retire the ship from commercial fishing, run her to Tunisia, remove the fishing gear and have her holds converted to luxurious accommodation thereafter to cruise the Med or perhaps "nip over" to the Caribbean.

Of course all hinged on the success of the mission on which he had been briefed weeks before with the final details received over the ships encrypted satellite system five days ago.

Turning to his cousin who had spelled him on the helm and taken her out of autopilot he said "Well Lachlan and on what are you dreaming spending your ill-gotten gains?"

Normally taciturn, Lachlan beamed at him. "A little white house on an island shore, perhaps the Greek islands where I can just sit and watch the sunset over the sea with a small fishing boat bobbing at anchor – just for pleasure by the way"

Hamish grinned and nodded. "You will have earned it lad, he thought, for your loyalty and skill over all these years He still called him 'lad' although he was only five years his junior.

At that he walked forward once again to take the evening air and watch the magnificent sunset off the port beam.

Chapter 20

Edward Anstruther was irritable and out of sorts. His air conditioner had packed up once again and was circulating lukewarm air. His devious mind considered how to thwart Douglas and regain favour with the Ambassador. He decided to arrange a private meeting with Belguerro, the CEO of Endiama at his office and inform him of the upcoming 'Exercise Ambush' against 'his' and CSO's diamond delivery convoy. Although he did not have any details he knew the next delivery date and timings. By so currying favour he hoped to persuade Belguerro to pass on some praise to HE.and perhaps there may be some financial incentive to keep him appraised of developments and any other information of mutual interest.

With retirement looming, his loyalty and morals had sunk to an all time low.

He picked up the phone and dialled Endiama. Speaking to the Secretary to the CEO, he was advised that he could have 15 minutes with Belguerro at 12.15. Endiama's offices were close to the Banco National, overlooking the Lagoon, and only ten minutes in a vehicle.. He confirmed the appointment then shouted through the open door to his Secretary.

"Judy, get my driver to bring the Land Rover around immediately I am taking an early lunch, and contact the Engineers again to sort this bloody air conditioner"

Anstruther strode or indeed waddled from his office banging the door shut. "Where will you be Colonel in case you are required"

"None of your business" he retorted. I am meeting a 'contact'. "I shall listen out on the radio in case of emergency".

Judy hid her half smile, she was used to his rudeness and self importance 'contact' she thought more likely an early contact with a Gin bottle

Anstruther plodded across the Embassy square to his Land Rover which he noted was covered in dust with its windows open and engine running. He clambered aboard and then harangued the unfortunate driver for the state of the vehicle. "But Sir he said, I washed it inside and out this morning, you know what the dust is like on the roads at this time of year"

"Don't be impertinent. After you drop me off take it back to the Embassy and wash it again"

"Yes Sir," as he rolled his eyes, flicked in to 1st gear and rolled towards the gates. "Where to Sir".

"Drop me outside the Banco National and then collect me one hour later, understand"

Anstruther did not wish anyone to know he was meeting with Belguerro, the Bank being five minutes walk from Endiama Offices.

Having been dropped at the Bank he allowed the Land Rover time to disappear then turned towards Endiama Offices. The Government diamond Company was housed in a magnificent old palatial Villa built by a Portuguese Merchant and which had been restored to its former glory. The bullet proof glass doors hissed aside as he approached and he was transported to another Luanda world. The air conditioning was silent and cold, indeed making him shiver slightly as he approached the reception desk manned by a fully armed security Guard. There were two Angolan Police Officers cradling AK47s on each side of the grand sweeping marble staircase. All right for some he thought as he eased his damp collar from his fleshy throat.

"Colonel Anstruther to see Senor Belguerro" he said.

"Sign in" he said omitting the 'Sir' "Empty your pockets, leave your radio and any weapon"

"I am a Diplomat, I do not have to submit to this sort of behaviour"

"No you don't" said the receptionist, "Not if you do not wish to attend your appointment"

"This is outrageous, I am a personal friend of your Chief Executive" he spluttered but seeing he wasn't getting anywhere with the inscrutable Receptionist he acquiesced in bad grace.

Climbing the stairs to the first floor he was met by Belguerro's Secretary, a stunning woman in her mid thirties with almost translucent "cafe au lait" skin wearing a light blouse and a figure hugging knee length skirt. Her buttocks oscillated jauntily as she walked on six inch high heels which only accentuated the movement. Again – all right for some he mused.

She preceded him to the magnificent Office of the CEO which had probably originally been the saloon or music room of the house with its high vaulted ceiling covered with frescos and inlaid with gold leaf. There were four sets of French doors leading on to a balcony overlooking the Lagoon. The doors were closed and the air was a pleasant temperature.

"Good afternoon Anstruther" said Belguerro without rising from behind his highly polished marble topped desk which only carried a leather bound blotter, two gold pens a keyboard and screen and three different coloured telephones "we shall speak English as your Portuguese is execrable."

Anstruther knew that the blue phone on the desk was a direct line to the office of the President and was always amazed that there were never any files or papers on the desk. He also knew that Belguerro suffered him for the information he could glean from the Embassy but otherwise held him in mild contempt.

"I shall come straight to the point. I am privy to certain information pertaining to the next diamond delivery from Huambo which I believe is going to be larger than the usual delivery, and believe you should be aware, however I must have your assurance that the source is not disclosed"

Belguerro stirred and his brown eyes narrowed slightly "continue, if the information is worth anything you have my assurance"

"There is going to be an ambush exercise on the convoy en route to the Bank which is being orchestrated by a man called Douglas with co-operation from Captain Ramirez, his escort Company and the Police. Douglas is running the show and I believe it has been sanctioned by your Government. Purportedly the reason is to check the reaction and training of the guarding force but I smell a rat and believe there may be a hidden agenda. Douglas is known to sail close to the wind"

"I am aware of Douglas and his remit" said Belguerro "and yes it has Government sanction. I know he has been to Huambo and the Bank to check their procedures, indeed I authorised his flight. I have not however been informed of any 'ambush exercise" although again I know he has spent some time with Captain Ramirez and his men evaluating their performance. I see no reason to suspect anything untoward.

"However I know of Douglas from his time here with IDS – he oversaw all the Endiama security at that time and most of the procedures currently still in existence were by his advice. I was not Chief Executive then, merely a Manager but we had several meetings and I found him to be a forthright but informed man, very proficient in his skills and trusted by many large Corporations and senior persons, CSO to name but one. There has never been an assault on the diamond delivery since then. What makes you think there may be a hidden agenda? "

"The security on his operations is wound down very tightly. Even I as Military Attache am not in the loop, neither is the Ambassador. He seems to have almost unique access to higher authority and can do what he likes. I am sure he is controlled by London"

At that Anstruther stopped talking as he let the last piece of information slip out.

"Interesting, my friend" smiled Belguerro thinking he had better try to give some praise to this rotten little man to keep him on side. "I shall make some enquiries and perhaps we shall meet again in the near future in the interim please keep me fully advised. Now I am very busy. Excuse me"

Anstruther preened himself relishing in being called friend by the great Belguerro who had the President's ear, although it was only a figure of speech. He rose and turning said, "as you know I am winding down my career with the Army and will be looking perhaps for some non executive Board Directorships or form of extra income in my retirement, if there is anything I can do to help . . . .

Belguerro smiled but not with his eyes, "I quite understand" he said "retirement can be hard. I am sure we may be able to consider something for you if you decide to stay in Angola". The fly is cast he thought and the fish has gulped down the bait.

Walking down the stairs he was pleased with the turn of events although he let slip a little too much information. Lost in thought he strode past the reception towards the doors when he was shocked out of his reverie by the receptionist who shouted "Sign out and collect your belongings" Slightly flustered he turned, did so, exited where the humidity hit him like a wet sheet and saw his Land Rover parked 80 yards down the street near the Bank. Climbing in, he was in such a good mood that he praised the driver for having cleaned the vehicle so well and directed him back to the Embassy.

Back at Endiama, Belguerro sat down behind his massive desk. A glimmer of a plan had begun to formalise in his mind as he also was nearing retirement and although he had squirreled away some 2.7 million US dollars in a Swiss account he wanted more. . . . . . .

CHAPTER 21

The lagoon water lapped at the matt rubber sides of the rigid raider lying alongside the dock at Papa's house. He was bent over the bow which was drawn up on the beach when Jack arrived.

"Hi Papa, how goes it?"

"All ready" he said, "but I thought there may be a slight air leak in the stem pontoon however I can't see or hear anything. Anyway we have the extra air cylinders on board to re-inflate. I shall position it by the sewer outfall tonight, submerge it and weight it down with stones".

"Ok. Let's run over the plan once again."

Douglas had already been in contact with the trawler which would be on station tomorrow evening at 22.00 hrs. The position was 14 miles due West of Luanda in International waters and Hamish would have his gear down and his fishing lights on to appear innocent and assist Papa in his navigation. Once he had contact, he would haul his gear, extinguish all his lights and await the rib to come alongside for the box transfer.

The plan was as simple as Douglas could make it. The 'ambush Exercise' would go down as planned with Ramirez and Alfonso and it had been confirmed that the guard detail would have blank ammunition issued. In the confusion and noise of the 'assault' with heavy use of smoke and thunderflashes Douglas and Sergio would be positioned on the right of the route in the borrowed Police Land Rover, would allow the lead vehicle past then, slew their vehicle in front of the armoured wagon with the blue and red strobe lights flashing just as the armoured wagon had to slow down to pass the abandoned truck still nose down in the collapsed sewer. Seeing it was a obviously a Police vehicle the river should not be too suspicious. Once the wagon had stopped Douglas would deploy smoke grenades, scramble on to the roof and drop a CS gas canister through the roof vent which was always open as there was no air conditioning. At the same time Sergio would snap the radio aerials off the front wing then run to the rear to cover. He would be carrying an AK 47 and rapid firing with blank ammo, the banana magazines strapped together in the "69" position, all as per the planned ambush exercise to further increase the noise and distraction however he would also carry twin mags bound with orange tape indicating loaded with 'live' 7.62 ball – just in case

At the same time Papa and his son would emerge from the sewer where they had been hiding in full black lightweight wetsuits and wearing night sight goggles and race the few yards to the rear door of the armoured wagon. There would be only one guard inside, without a gas mask and only blank ammo so hopefully he would be in so much distress he would throw open the doors for fresh air – if not the already prepared C4 charge would be slapped on and the doors blown off. In the darkness, smoke and pandemonium, the internal guard would be subdued with a cosh to the head, Papa would bolt crop the chains securing the strong boxes pass them to Malcolm, his son, who will drop them down the sewer and return with two imitation strong boxes which would be placed on the wagon floor and the broken chain linked through with the cuts simply tied together with black plastic cable ties.

To all on casual inspection the load would seem to be still secure and the "ambush" failed.

Maximum exposure – 80 seconds!

Papa and Malcolm would drag the diamond boxes along the sewer, to the grate outfall where the rib would be quickly re-inflated, the rocks thrown overboard, the boxes secured and the raider swum towards the old dock, towed on both sides by the two swimmers. At 50 metres distance the silenced engines could be started and the Rib pottered forward between the many old, some derelict, vessels and small fishing craft. Stripped off their wetsuits and wearing suitable old fisherman's gear the two would then motor slowly towards the harbour entrance with navigation lights on as if they were simply another small boat joining the nightly exodus of the fishing fleet. Once on the open sea they could open up the Yamahas and rendezvous with the trawler returning in the early morning after a night's fishing, making sure they had actually caught some fish

Douglas would stay within the ambush area, Sergio would disappear into the Luanda night where Anna would pick him up and return to the Villa.

Once the smoke cleared it would take 15/20 minutes for the box switch and theft to be discovered and hopefully not until till the delayed convoy reaches the Bank for offloading.

It was Douglas's plan, once the theft was apparent, to try to switch the blame – i.e. the boxes could have been switched at the airport or indeed at Huambo before take off. He would expect a severe bollocking from all quarters and the blame squarely rest on his shoulders. He would assist in every way to recover the diamonds whilst also laying smokescreens by accusing the Police and the Guard Company of Ramirez for leaking the fact that blank ammo would be loaded that night. Anyway how could he possibly be involved, he was in plain sight at all times running his own "ambush exercise" and was still here!

He finished his 'O' (orders) group with the slightly pessimistic quip that the plan would fail on two factors:

1. A different route from the three variable being selected at the last minute or

2. His failure to stop the convoy immediately after the broken sewer, however he was certain this could be achieved with the unwitting help of Ramirez and Alfonso.

Papa had remained silent throughout the briefing and had no questions.

"All is as already discussed he said, I have no questions and Malcolm is up to speed. You are the one in the most danger so watch your back "

CHAPTER 22

Ponce's 4 x 4 slithered to a halt in the dust outside the safe house where Gallagher and his minders had been hiding out since the debacle at the dock. To say 'house' was risible. It was a two room wooden shack under a rusting tin roof, no running water, a stinking outside loo in a ramshackle shed, and well water which was so brown with dirt that you wondered whether your were washing off are adding to the grime of the last two days.

There was an old stove a couple of worn chairs and two rusting iron frame beds with stained mattresses. The place was quite disgusting but being 12 miles North of Luanda and concealed in the bush down a little used dirt track, was considered relatively safe.

Gallagher was in a more foul mood than usual – he was no longer used to 'roughing it' and still furious over the loss of his containers.

"I have good news" said Ponce as he slumped in one of the broken chairs "almost straight from the horse's mouth, but let us sit outside. I have a cool box with beer in the vehicle"

They both sat on the stoop and Ponce's driver produced two cold beers which were already glistening with sweat due to the humidity.

Gallagher, drafted the bottle and called for another. With his second beer in hand he turned to Ponce, "Go on".

"There is a scheduled exercise to test the diamond convoy guards on the next delivery. I am advised by a Police informer that the guards will have been issued with blank ammunition, although live ammo will be carried in a sealed box in the lead vehicle. It is thought that the leak has come down from Belguerro himself, the Head of Endiama, and that he in turn is getting his information from the Military Attache at the British Embassy who is a devious man. The delivery is tomorrow night."

"I made more discreet enquiries and think that Belguerro is considering pulling out of Angola permanently. If this is true then I think he is approachable He knows of your existence and your reputation, and if we were to consider our own operation to attack the delivery convoy he could assist us for an equal share of the diamonds"

"That's a lot of 'ifs' growled Gallagher, "and a great leap from the initial info to the Head of Endiama helping us. Why in Hell would he do that? He must be on a large salary, lives in comfort and have funds hidden around the world. Why would he wish to get involved with the likes of us? "

Ponce smiled, "That is true but you must understand that Angola is still very corrupt. Belguerro is growing old and even if he has millions hidden away it is never enough. I think he sees a final opportunity to add to his accounts without much personal risk. He can always disavow if things go wrong whereas we will be doing the dirty work. I think he sees it almost as his right to have an end of contract settlement from Endiama. My friend, That's Africa!

The final tasty piece is that the next delivery will be one of the biggest this year as the last two schedules were cancelled due to bad weather. Thus the estimate is 120 million US of uncut diamonds "

Gallagher smiled slightly, the news and the cold beers had temporarily eased his mood and troubled mind and he started to evaluate the info he had just received. He saw the way to recoup his losses and hopefully do for that bastard Douglas at the same time. His mind's eye had already cut Belguerro from the loop. Why couldn't he take the lot he mused.

"Right, I have to meet with this Belguerrro and it has to be tonight, can you arrange that at a mutually secure site"

"Very difficult" Ponce said "he is a very important man and does not usually do his own dirty work. I think it can be arranged for a price through an Endiama contact, but it will cost . . . ."

"If he is a crooked as you say, it will not cost a damn thing, It is in his interest to meet with us asap to get a cohesive plan worked out. Damn it we only have 36 hours. Get it done!"

Belguerro was just a about to leave his Office when his secretary glided through the ornate doors. "you have an unscheduled visitor, one of the Account Managers on the third floor who says he must speak with you on a most important matter"

"What matter" he sighed, thinking his whisky and soda would have to wait.

"He would not divulge the subject but said it was for your ears only"

"OK, ten minutes" as he slumped back in his chair he really had had enough of today and had finally decided to get out but how to gather some more wealth?

He ogled his secretary's rump as she click clacked across the marble floor. He had never dallied with her as he did not believe in such relationships as it was simply too dangerous considering some of his somewhat shady deals in the last five years but he still thought her a very attractive woman. Belguerro was officially married with two children but that marriage had died many years ago and both led their own lives. Indeed he had virtually banished his family to a small estate he owned near Cabinda, which was near her family and he rarely saw them leaving him free to pursue his own discreet pleasures in Luanda.

He had no intention of taking them to Europe when he finally decamped – lucky to get the Estate, he thought.

He looked up to a discreet knock at the open doors. He recognised the man but could not remember his name. He was young, in his late twenties with a lightly pock marked face, wearing a sombre grey suit and was visibly nervous and sweating even in the cold air of the Bank.

"Enter" Belguerro said in an imperious tone, "and close the doors." When he approached the desk he did not invite the man to sit.

"Well, what is so important and secret that you have detained me at this late hour? "

"Sir, began the wretch, I am an account Manager on the third floor and one of my duties is to maintain CSO's (De Beers) delivery records to the Bank. I have been asked to deliver a message to you but it is so outrageous that I don't know where to start. If I don't deliver the message, my uncle who is a bad man will hurt me.

"Go on" said Belguerro his interest piqued, "What is your name" "Ponce" said the accountant.

Ah, he thought, I know that name – one of the serious gang leaders in Luanda an inscrutable rogue who would sell his own Mother for a profit. This could be interesting.

"I am to ask you if you would kindly accept an invitation to an important and immediate meeting with my Uncle and his associate who have a venture they wish to discuss but cannot possibly come to the Bank or be seen in a public place as they were involved in the Maria Luisa incident of which you have no doubt been advised. Any outcome of the meeting would have major financial rewards to all parties concerned"

Instead of being angry the Endiama CEO saw an advantage – he had a structure of Police and Government informers and had been fully briefed on Gallagher's disastrous attempt to export arms and also knew that Douglas was involved in his downfall. Perhaps this is what he had been waiting for.

"And if I were to agree to such a clandestine meeting who is going to guarantee my safety and where will such a meeting take place"

"I am to tell you that it will be at a mutually agreed place, with no weapons and only three people – you, my uncle and one other"

"Give me one reason I should trust these rogues and place myself in danger"

"Sir, all I can say is what I have been told and that if you wish, you may choose the location"

Dangerous thought Belguerro, but intriguing "How is this going to be arranged at such short notice, there can be no telephones used"

"By word of mouth" said the accountant who was now even more nervous and uneasy. "My uncle is close by and if you agree I am to go to him to advise of your decision. He will suggest various locations and timings and you are to pick one or suggest one of your own.. It will take about ten minutes."

It was near to sunset and Belguerro already had an idea about a suitable location where he could be virtually assured of his own safety. The risk he thought is worth it.

"Go" he commanded. "I shall await your prompt return".

CHAPTER 23

The final day, the day of the diamond delivery dawned fine and fresh with an onshore breeze which lifted the slight mist languishing over the lagoon and temporarily relieved the inhabitants of Luanda of its signature smell.

Ponce and Gallagher had met with Belguerro near the darkened "yacht club" on the isthmus at 22. 00 hrs the night before, both parties full of suspicion, however an accord had been reached with Belguerro agreeing to provide all the intelligence on the convoy details and as much information on the ambush exercise as he could glean from his various sources for a third share of the diamonds. They had discussed the plan to steal the diamonds in detail.

They would hit the convoy, after the exercise when the guards would be relaxed, hoping they would not have reloaded with live ammo, and just as it was arriving at the Bank. It had to be fast and heavy with trucks used to ram the armoured wagon and block the route from the other vehicles or reinforcements. Belguerro had disclosed that there was always a secondary unit a QRF (quick reaction force) which was mounted up in full readiness and could be on the scene within ten minutes. Ponce would supply the trucks and the men.

The escape route would be North by road and track to a small dirt airstrip where a light aircraft would be waiting protected by more of Ponce's armed gang. The aircraft would then fly to the Congo where reception for the cargo and onward shipping had been arranged to a warehouse belonging to one of his many 'cousins'. Gallagher would fly out with the cargo and Ponce would join him a couple of days later once the dust, literally, had settled to divvy up the spoils. It was agreed that the strong boxes would not be opened until both were present.

Belguerro had insisted that one of his men accompany the diamonds to 'protect his investment' and that he would make his own arrangements to join them. "No probs" Gallagher had exclaimed thinking, another body en route would be easy to take care of, and really having no intention of honouring his agreement with Belguerro.

Jack Douglas was kicking his heels – in his mind he had gone over the plan time and again and could see no way in which to better it. That morning he and Sergio had rehearsed the 'taking' of the armoured car behind the high walls of the villa. Papa was all prepared.

As long as Lady Luck is on our side he thought.

The waiting before an operation is always the worst time so he decided to contact Ramirez, drive over to the barracks and check on the Guard company personnel.

He drove over to the barracks to find Ramirez and his men again training through an ambush incident with figures streaked in dust and sweat, running everywhere around an old burning car which purported to be the armoured car, shouting and firing off blank rounds. The Company had been split into two forces – Red armbands for the attackers and blue for the defenders and the exercise was just coming to its conclusion with both sides grinning and congratulating them on their own success. Even Ramirez normally impeccably turned out was in faded jungle combats, fully armed and wearing a flak vest – leading his men from the front. He waved at Jack, gave an order to his Company

Sergeant Major and trotted over.

"Hello Jack" he said as he extended a grimy hand, "just keeping the boys on their toes"

"I see that, they seem to be enthusiastic and a bit hyped up. Have you briefed them yet?"

"No, final briefing will be at 16.00 hrs. They will have a couple of hours now to relax and check their equipment until then it is just the routine delivery. They will be told to expect an exercise ambush en route but not where, even I do not have that information. They will also be issued the blank ammunition and searched just in case they have forgotten a magazine of live – it does happen!"

"Fine, "said Douglas with a smile, "No point in telling the CO of the exact plan, that would be too easy, "I am sure they will perform well. See you 'somewhere' tonight "

He turned with a wave of his hand, strode back to the Range Rover and drove back to the Villa.

'H' hour minus two saw Jack and Sergio dressed in dark blue Police overalls checking the LWB Land Rover lent to him by Alfonso. The vehicle was in surprisingly good condition with a powerful 4 litre V8 engine and almost new tyres. There were two hand controlled spotlights bolted to each side of the windscreen with the bar carrying the 'blues and twos' also bolted through the roof. Heavy duty nudge bars were fitted front and back and additional blue lights fitted behind the grille.. two whip antennas were mounted on the front wings with the VHF police radio fixed to the dashboard. A Marine band VHF radio was also fitted. Great, thought Jack, in case I have to contact Papa.

Sergio, on Jacks insistence, was blacking out the passenger front window leaving a small square for clear vision hopefully to avoid recognition. During the raid they would wear lightweight balaclavas and flak vests – just in case.

'H' hour minus one. "Ok let's mount up and cruise down the route, it would be just our luck if the roads department decide today was the day to remove the old truck from the sewer. Unlikely though it was there when I returned from the barracks"

Sergio just grunted. And both climbed in to the Land Rover. Sergio carrying an AK 47 with a folding stock in the forward position already loaded with twin strapped banana magazines and a Jericho 9mm loaded with parabellum in his quick release shoulder holster. His balaclava was rolled to the top of his brow and he had camo cream on his face and hands. He looked particularly competent and fierce.

Douglas was similarly dressed also carrying a Jericho 9mm but he had chosen a belt mounted holster. In his right hand he carried his favourite close quarter weapon – a Mossberg 12 bore, 5 shot automatic riot gun. This he had imported in his gear on arrival and on which Alfonso had warned him that it was an 'illegal' weapon in Angola. 'Illegal' in Angola he thought, awash with weapons of which any and all types could be found, and strewn with uncharted landmines throughout the country still not cleared from the war against UNITA..

The Mossberg was loaded with 'door openers' – these were '00' shells which instead of containing the normal shotgun pellets, had only two large steel pellets which would blow a hole 12 inches wide in any door and cut a human in half – a wicked weapon with a pistol grip and an under barrel pump action, thus it could be used single handed.

Douglas fired up the beefy V8 which settled immediately to a quiet rumble. Both men clipped their weapons to the gun racks and looked at each other.

"Here we go" said Jack as he eased into first gear. . . . . . .

CHAPTER 24

'H' hour! Douglas slowly drove the Police Land Rover along the paseo maritimo towards the nosed down truck which he picked out in his headlights as night fell. He had reconnoitred the route several times to find the best place for him to position just past the truck and he reversed back, in front of an overflowing skip full of foul smelling detritus which would hide his vehicle from the oncoming convoy till they were almost alongside. He cut the engine.

His venerable Tag Heur dive watch read 18.41 hrs - about fifteen minutes to go. The Bank was only another 300 metres down the road where the diamond convoy would 'u' turn to park by the main door.

Sergio reached for his weapon and eased his door to the first stop. The interior light bulb had already been removed. He looked at Jack. "When we first met I could not have realised my being in this position about to commit a massive armed robbery."

"There is still time to pull out if you wish, simply disappear into the night. I can probably manage without you although would far prefer you to be watching my back"

Sergio gave a rueful smile. "I gave you my word – the die is cast – it is time I returned to Portugal"

Douglas leant across and clasped his hand, no further words were necessary.

"Right, lock and load "as he racked the pump action on the Mossberg pushing a cartridge in to the breach. He then loaded another cartridge into the magazine giving him six shots in all and applied the safety catch. He genuinely hoped he would not have to use the shotgun which he would sling over his back to allow his hands free for the smoke grenades and thunderflashes, Sergio cocked his AK and sat nursing it in his lap, butt folded and suspended from his neck by a leather sling. He would be first out, firing in the air as Douglas would pop smoke and throw the thunderflashes. There was little breeze so the smoke should spread thickly.

Douglas fired up the V8. He was watching for the convoy in Sergio's wing mirror and had his hand on the switch for the red and blue strobe lights which was on the dashboard just in front of the gear lever. He caught the lead vehicle headlights some 150 yards back and could make out the larger armoured car tucked in behind. Damn he thought, he is too close it's going to be tight!

The lead escort vehicle had slowed to negotiate the broken sewer and the old truck. Clearing, it fortunately accelerated allowing a wider space between the following vehicle.

"Stand by" Douglas shouted.

The lead escort passed and Douglas flicked on the strobes, pulled out across the front of the diamond wagon and both men debussed. The driver of the armoured vehicle just managed to brake before hitting the Land Rover turning slightly to his left but with nowhere to go as he was soon blocked by the third vehicle which had stopped 20 yards back alongside the wrecked truck.

Douglas threw three smoke grenades then scraped the ignitor over one of the three thunderflashes he had strapped together and threw it to the left of the armoured car. They went off with a tremendous roar. He leapt on to the roof, pulling a CS gas canister from his belt, found the open (thank God) skylight in the swirling smoke, let the pin fly and popped it through the vent.

Meanwhile Sergio was on his second double magazine and had also thrown smoke to add to the confusion.

Douglas leapt off the roof and waited for Sergio to join him at the rear door. He pulled the shaped C4 charge from his pouch ready to slam it on the doors if the CS gas did not have its required effect. A figure loomed through the smoke – Sergio.

"Watch it" the trailing vehicle had debussed its guards and they were being exhorted forward, Sergio threw another triple thunderflash in front of them which dampened their ardour for a few seconds. Douglas checked his watch 28 seconds – where the Hell are Papa and Malcolm they should be here by now. He turned to place the charge on the door which suddenly burst open with the unfortunate interior guard coughing and spluttering and holding his eyes. Jack actually helped him out then stepped back to avoid the loathsome gas. Papa was at his elbow, in his wet suit wearing his mask and rebreather bolt croppers in hand. Malcolm appeared with one of the phony strong boxes. He clambered into the wagon cut the chain close to the floor and threw out both boxes. Malcolm threw one of the phonies in and he and Douglas both carrying a real strong box raced the few metres to the broken sewer. Douglas then returned with the other phony box. Papa still in the wagon placed them as best he could, slipped a black cable tie through the broken links. Exited the vehicle and with a clasp on Jack's shoulder raced for the sewer. The smoke was dissipating so Douglas popped his last grenade. The whole operation had just taken 90 seconds.

Pandemonium and confusion reigned.

Jack grabbed Sergio's AK and told him to leg it. Figures were mulling around in the thinning smoke firing their blank rounds at anything that moved. Jack saw Ramirez on the left flank rallying the guards from the rear vehicle and stepped away from the wagon his hands on his head, AK and Mossberg over each shoulder. He must have looked like 'Pancho Villa' he thought. One of the Guards grabbed his hands and forced him round slamming him into the rear of the wagon, at the same time trying to disarm him.

"Careful" he said my weapons have live ammunition. At that the Guard recognised Douglas and with a rueful shrug unhanded him. Ramirez had trotted forward, obviously not a very 'happy bunny' seeing the rear doors wide open.

"That was fun" said Jack. "The attempt would have failed if your men had live ammo. Well done all round but now get down to the Bank and complete the delivery as you are behind schedule" No damage has been done apart from a few bruises and of course the luckless interior guard but he will make a full recovery in half an hour. We shall have a full debrief later

Ramirez glanced into the rear, saw the strong boxes still intact. Ordered another guard inside, slammed the doors and turned to Jack.

"Underhand using a Police Land Rover to block, my guys would not have been suspicious until the ambush was sprung"

"All's fair in love and war" quipped Douglas." the point of the exercise, deception had to be used as your chaps are pretty good. I shall move my 'Rover and see you at Bank."

Slightly mollified Ramirez shouted at his men to mount, close up and finish the run. By this time a group of locals had appeared as they realised the shooting was over. Looking quizzically at the convoy as the headlights glinted off the massive amount of spent brass spread across the road.

Meanwhile Papa rock and his son had manhandled the diamond boxes down to the mouth of the sewer. Pushing out the cut grille once again, Malcolm entered the water acutely aware that there were now locals lounging against the parapet of the sea wall, although most were still looking inward at the ambush site, talking excitedly and smoking cigarettes the lighting of which would have destroyed their night vision

Swimming the ten metres to the North he reached the rigid raider, lying on the bottom in about fifteen feet, cautiously removing three rocks gave some buoyancy, he cracked open one of the air valves to semi inflate the side pontoons until negative buoyancy was reached keeping the craft just below the surface and making it easier for him to tow back to the sewer outfall. He tied off the painter to the grille and slowly eased himself into the sewer opening.

Only one or two locals now remained on the parapet as the excitement of the evening had died down.

Malcolm removed his mask and rebreather cautioning his Father to remain silent with a finger to his lip and pointing above. Papa gave him the divers 'OK' sign with thumb and finger. As planned they manoeuvred the first strong box to the lip of the sewer and slid it in to the water. Malcolm slipped back in replacing his breathing equipment. Papa slid the second box over the lip which was also dropped to the sea bed.

"Now the tricky bit" thought Papa as he also slid below the surface. One had to lift a box into the rib as the other removed a rock of equivalent weight to keep the rib below the surface. Papa slowly vented a little air with a small stream of bubbles and the rib settled lightly to the sea floor. The first box went in with no problems. Papa bent to lift the second box just as Malcolm removed the last rock, as he turned his feet slipped in the mire the box falling from his hand, Negative buoyancy overcome, the rib started to rise and it broke surface before either could vent an air valve. Malcolm hurriedly cracked a valve but too hard and the air hissed out with a high pitched squeal.

Anyone looking over the parapet would see a large black 'sea monster' hissing and squealing with two disjointed flashing eyes as the weak light reflected from the dive masks before it sank once again to the depths. Indeed that was exactly what was reported by one man a few days later who had been smoking 'ganga' at the time thus his story was laughingly ignored.

As the Rib slowly sank below the surface once again, Papa could feel himself sweating within his wet suit. The second box was successfully loaded. He signalled Malcolm to stay by the rib as he returned to the sewer outfall re-positioned the rusted iron grille and secured it with more black cable ties, cutting off the floating ends and smearing some of the glutinous mud over them.

Good as new, well good as old, he chuckled.

Picking up the thermal lance he had left behind when cutting the grille, he again gave Malcolm the 'OK'. They both positioned at each side of the rib and slowly cracked open the air valves. Once a perceptible buoyancy was achieved they both kicked off holding, the side grab ropes and steered the rib towards the commercial harbour still eight to ten feet below the surface.

Ten minutes of difficult swimming passed and Papa risked surfacing to check his progress. He was bang on track and had surfaced in the shadows of a rusting freighter and an old wooden fishing boat which would never see the open sea again. The fishing boat had a 15 degree list to starboard towards the freighter thus almost forming a canopy above them. Perfect.

Slowly they inflated the rib to full operational pressure and she came out, gushing water through the self drainers in the stern. She was soon empty enough for both men to pull themselves aboard.

After a quick embrace, Malcolm opened the water tight trunk in front of the steering position and stripped out of his wet suit and dive gear. He grabbed old clothes, boots and woolly hat and minutes later was a fisherman. His father did the same. They both lifted the strong boxes into the trunk placing an old net over the top and their dive gear on top of the net. Papa went to the stern wiped the heavy grease from the battery box and eased off the lid.

He swore. "Bloody Hell, the battery box is full of water over the tops of the batteries. I just hope no sea water has got into the electrolyte. There is a manual suction pump in the port fish locker pass it to me."

After five minutes the level in the box was down to a few inches. "Pass me a wrench and some cotton waist, I am going to disconnect the terminals dry them off and regrease them to give them a chance." He didn't think there would be much of a problem as both marine heavy duty batteries were new and had sealed tops, however. . . . . . .

The main problem was time – they were now half an hour behind schedule and would have to motor, once out of the harbour to make the rendezvous with Hamish Duncan's trawler.

Replacing the terminals, he turned on the battery master switch - a flash and crack came from the switch. "Shit" he said as he closed the switch" what now". Malcolm looked at his Father.

"Has this ever happened before" he said. "No" spat Papa "but she has never been underwater for thirty six hours" Get the engine covers off the 'Yammies' and check whether they are still dry.

The engines were fine no moisture had passed the heavily greased seals but Malcolm gave them a squirt of a water displacement spray just in case. He passed the spray to his father.

"Give the batteries and the master a squirt with this."

"In a minute" Papa said in a more conciliatory tone, "sorry I jumped down your throat"

"You always do when things go wrong, I am used to it" he said with a smile

By the light of a small Rolson torch Papa had removed the cover of the blackened master switch which also held sea water. Drying it off he caught a small glint of copper wire at the rear of the switch. One of the connections had worked slightly loose on the switch terminal thus arcing and causing a short. I am sure I checked this last week he thought and with a couple of turns tightened the connection. Replacing the cover he turned to Malcolm.

"Fingers crossed" as he flipped over the master switch. No spark. "Thank God, now let's see if the engines start" he eased the starboard Morse control to Neutral and advanced the throttle about an inch. Turning the key, the engine caught almost immediately and he reduced power. Repeating the process with the Port engine he turned the key, the starter motor churned over but no kick "Please God" he prayed as the noise from the starter seemed to be so loud in the stillness of the evening. He tried again, adjusting the throttle slightly. - Nothing!. In the interim Malcolm had the cover off and said "she smells of gas, I think she is flooded"

"OK" one last time with throttle closed, if that doesn't work we will go on one engine"

He closed the throttle detent. He turned the key again, the starter turned, the engine kicked once, then started, he eased the throttle slightly forward, she picked up and then settled to an even beat.

Switching on the navigation lights and the navigation instruments he said "Let's get out of here" as he slowly ran for the mouth of the Lagoon in full view.

They were now almost an hour behind schedule.

CHAPTER 25

Gallagher sitting in the passenger seat of a stolen 18 ton Mercedes truck, parked at the side of the road 500 yards along from the bank, had a grandstand view of the ambush exercise. The driver was one of Ponce's best men. In the rear were five heavily armed gang members all strapped in to five point harnesses which had been welded to the truck floor. The truck had been fitted with a massive bull bar welded to the front.

Ponce was tucked in behind in a Toyota Landcruiser pick up with a mounted 7.62 General Purpose Machine Gun under a tarpaulin on the flat bed. Their comms. were handheld VHF radios.

The two men had been watching the exercise with interest hoping that the blank ammo mags. were not collected and live ammo issued but through his binoculars from his elevated position in the truck cab he verified that there had been no attempt to re-arm the guards as they were now only 500 metres from the Bank. He watched the regrouped convoy proceeding once again along the Paseo Maritimo where it would pass the bank then 'u' turn at the next gap to retrace its steps and park outside the front door.

Gallagher flicked his radio to transmit.

"Our turn" he said "they won't know what hits them, like taking candy from a baby. Follow the truck when we pull out"

Ponce double clicked his pressor switch to acknowledge.

Gallagher banged on the partition behind the cab to alert his men.

The diamond convoy, now in a semblance of order, passed him by on the other side of the road. His driver blipped the throttle of his seven litre diesel and wiped the steering wheel with a rag to remove any sweat. Gallagher watched in his mirror as the first vehicle turned followed by the armoured wagon and the rear guard.

All three passed him by and slowed ahead to park at the bank for the delivery.

"Hold it", he said to Ponce, whilst tightening the belts on his own harness. "let them park and switch off their engines. Get the tarp off the GPMG now"

Another double click acknowledgement.

There was a flurry of red brake lights from the three convoy vehicles The Guards in the two escort vehicles de-bussed laughing and joking, the adrenalin still high from their successful 'defense' of the diamonds and milled around the armoured vehicle, cigarettes lit and rifles slung on their shoulder. The heavy doors of the Bank swung open to receive the delivery. Gallagher turned to his driver at the same time thumbing his transmit button. "Go, Go, Go" he shouted.

The heavy truck, pulled out diesel roaring and the driver snicked up to 3rd gear, a few Guard heads turned at the noise but took no action, By the time the truck was alongside the convoy vehicles it was doing 40mph. The driver judged it perfectly, pulled out to his left then swung the wheel hard over to the right, striking the armoured wagon with the steel bull bar, forward of the rear wheel with such force that it was slammed across the pavement into the stone wall of the Bank. Gallagher was slammed forward in his harness but quickly hit the fast release grabbed his AK, dropped to the road and opened up.

Ponce in the Toyota had mounted the pavement, as the truck now blocked the road and slewed to a halt behind the rear escort vehicle which was shredded by the GPMG firing over the top of the canopy. The guard detail legged it as it was quite clear that this was not an exercise with the flash of red tracer rounds which were loaded one in five on the machine gun belt, the clap of live rounds passing overhead and the eruption of the rear escort vehicle as a round found the petrol tank. With only blank ammo – 'discretion was the better part of valour'

Douglas, who had transferred to the front seat of the armoured wagon to observe the final delivery was stunned by the force of the collision and trapped, as his door was buckled and would not open against the front of the massive truck whose engine still bellowing, was embedded in the side of his vehicle. His driver had faired worse, having unbuckled his seat belt he had been jerked forward hitting his head on the side of the vehicle and was obviously unconscious or dead as dark red blood was coursing down his face. Even if he could have moved, the driver's door was rammed against the stone wall of the bank. Windscreen only way out he thought.

Armoured glass! He grabbed his Mossberg, shielded his eyes and fired at the glass from point blank range – the glass starred. He racked the slide and fired again. The cracks lengthened. On the fourth shot the window exploded outwards and he kicked out the remaining shards, crawling over the bonnet to take cover. Only two shots left he thought although he still had his side arm.

Crouching in front of the armoured car he tried to evaluate – Who the Hell is this lot he thought, well armed and well drilled. Over his shoulder he saw Ramirez and two of his guards at the forward escort vehicle, dragging a box of live 7.62 from the rear and trying to unload the blanks and quickly reload their magazines. Ramirez was returning fire with his sidearm and yelling in to his radio. The mounted GPMG had now switched targets to the front vehicle and Douglas saw one of guards take at least three hits to the chest collapsing to the ground as the other two took cover behind the vehicle. He moved position slightly and got off his last two shots at the machine gunner now only fifteen metres away. A satisfactory metal clang as one of his lucky shots found the breech of the machine gun which stopped firing immediately.

There was a lull in the firing interspersed with cries for help from the wounded and the crackle of super heated metal from the burning Land Rover.

Douglas took the opportunity to scamper back to Ramirez and his remaining soldier who now had fully loaded AK's. Ramirez was still talking on the radio calling in the QRF and giving them a Sitrep.. Douglas grabbed the dead guards AK, shucked the magazine and was handed a full magazine of live by the remaining guard. Nodding his thanks he turned to Ramirez.

"How many left" he said.

"Four, possibly five but one still has no ammo. The QRF ETA is 4 minutes and I have told them to approach from the North, There must be at least a dozen heavily armed attackers and that machine gun has us pinned down"

"I think I managed to disable that with a lucky shot from the Mossberg, but we must move from here one round in the tank and we are toast"

The roiling smoke from the burning Land Rover gave them some cover as they scuttled back ten yards to a low concrete wall.

Both were surprised at the lack of fire.

"Can't see a damn thing said Douglas as he passed the back of his hand over his right eye, think I have some oil or something in it"

Ramirez looked at him in the red glow. "No it's blood. You have a bad crack above the eye and the skin on your forehead is peeled back.

Douglas pulled a handkerchief from his pocket, spat on it and wiped his eye, His vision cleared slightly and now he could feel the pain as he gingerly explored the loose skin on his forehead pulling it forward as best he could and dabbing the blood with the handkerchief

The QRF Land Rover screamed to a halt and five debussed and leapfrogged forward to their position. Still no fire from the attackers. Suddenly there was a rending and screeching of metal as the Toyota backed out from the pavement, running its wing along the wall. With bodies clinging on everywhere – at least seven – it swung round and raced off into the night.

Ramirez ordered the QRF team to pursue the Toyota. They quickly mounted up and in turn screamed off with sirens blaring and strobes pulsating.

Ponce and Gallagher were in the front of the Toyota, both diamond strong boxes on the floor between Gallagher's feet. There were four of the attackers left bouncing around in the back, there had been five but one was thrown out as Ponce took a wicked corner at speed and he was disinclined to stop to pick him up.

Ponce was laughing.

"I can't believe how lucky we have been" The force of the truck collision had burst open the rear doors of the armoured wagon and under cover of the burning Land Rover it had been a simple job to cut the chains, steal the boxes and get out in the Toyota. The whole attack had taken a few minutes and thanks to Douglas's exercise. No returning fire.

"We only lost two men" he continued "The machine gunner who was decapitated by a heavy round, and one of my foot soldiers who I think was the victim of 'friendly fire' Whatever killed the machine gunner also damaged the gun."

Ponce had now reduced speed as there was no sign of pursuit. He had been weaving in and out of the back streets which he knew so well, doubling back on himself twice, and was now threading through the heavy traffic which never slows even with the sound of heavy firing, almost a nightly occurrence.

"I must pull over to get rid of the gun" he said. Turning in to a dimly lit narrow street. Halting he yelled at his men to unbolt the tripod and ditch the gun. "Throw that piece of meat over as well" indicating the dead gunner lying on the floor. Five minutes later they were on their way at moderate speed with all weapons stowed looking like one of the many pickups taking people to or from work.

Back at the Bank, Douglas and Ramirez discover the cut chains and the theft of the diamonds. His men were slowly returning looking slightly sheep faced at running away. Poor buggers, what could they have done thought Jack.

He immediately realises that this attack would cover up the real theft carried out during the exercise. He would like to be fly on the wall when the attackers open up the phony boxes and find rocks – not the sparkling type!

Ramirez had radioed for ambulances as he had found three more of his men with gunshot wounds. The driver of the rear Land Rover and his front passenger were also dead and burnt out of all recognition. The sweet sickly smell of burning flesh still pervaded the area. The fire service had yet to turn up and some of his men were desultorily throwing buckets of water over the vehicle.

The 'butchers bill' was four dead and three wounded, one seriously.

Alfonso Carisco pulled up in his Land Rover having been radioed by Ramirez.

"What a bloody shambles" he said looking directly at Jack with narrowed eyes. "What the Hell happened? I have despatched all my

Police Force around the city to look for this Toyota – Who were they?

Before Douglas, still holding his blood soaked handkerchief to his forehead, could reply. Ramirez tiredly said. "It is nothing to do with Jack. His exercise went well and he then defended the convoy when the real attack happened, just look at his face. If he had not taken out the machine gun with his Mossberg none of us would be here now. It is just 'unfortunate' that we were loaded with blanks

"Unfortunate, yes," interjected Jack. "Unfortunate that someone in the Guard Company, the Police Force or Endiama leaked the exercise details and specifically that the guard force would be loaded with blanks. Whoever did this has the blood of these brave lads on his hands. The loss of the diamonds is regrettable but secondary and CSO will make up its loss next month.

What is important is that if this was one of the outlawed ex UNITA groups then you have a major problem on hand. These diamonds can purchase some serious weaponry and you could be facing a resurgence of the Civil War"

At that Douglas faltered, stumbled and sat down with a bump. "I think one of your Medics should look at my head if you don't mind"

Ramirez called for a Medic who swabbed away the congealing blood, gave Jack a professional appraisal for concussion and eye damage, cleaned the deep wound, pulling the flap of skin back over and suturing it neatly.

"You will look like a Pirate with that scar" quipped Ramirez with a slight smile, "but seriously you could have lost your eye and my thanks for saving my life! He extended his hand. Jack clasped it "Fortunate I had the correct weapon, Egh, Alfonso"

"I don't know to which weapon you refer" ignoring the Mossberg slung over his shoulder "and with that scar you will look 'more' of a Pirate, Jack."

"Right, I am off to collect my Land Rover and go back home. Enough excitement for today and my head really hurts. I suggest we have a debrief at the Barracks, tomorrow, say around 10.00 hrs. if that's OK with you" looking at Ramirez.

Ramirez said he had to finish up here and then report the situation to his superiors. Alfonso turned to Jack "Come on. I shall give you a lift to your 'rover".

CHAPTER 26

The rolling swell was breaking over the bows of the Rigid Raider in a flurry of spray. It was a factor of the inshore waters of the African shelf. The Atlantic rollers, marching unobstructed for 2000 miles were forced in to shallower waters where the wave height increased, the distance between rollers decreased and consequently the crests became agitated by the onshore wind.

Wind strength had increased and Papa had a 'smell of a pending storm' in his nostrils. They had left the lagoon without challenge and he had ramped the engines up to 80% power on a relatively calm sea. The last hour had seen a marked weather change and he was now running at 30% power – around 14/15 knots. He was not unduly worried as the rib was constructed to take offshore weather but was slightly concerned with the closing weather that visibility would be reduced. He did not have radar, only the RV latitude and longtitude which had been logged in to his GPS which showed 40 minutes 'time to target'. The chart plotter showed 'on track' and a depth below the keel of 16 fathoms – around 95 feet. By his estimation he had made up some of the time lost in the harbour and would arrive approximately fifteen minutes after the scheduled time. He knew he had an hour's window when the trawler would heave to and wait, before continuing its path if there was a 'no show'

The agreed closing signal was to be by light. Papa would flash 'Papa Romeo – (PR) '– in morse. The reply from the trawler would be a simple 'Delta – (D)' if all was well. Emergency contact would be by radio on the open Marine Channel 16 then channel switch to private channel 6 but only in dire emergency. The trawler would be monitoring both channels on dual watch.

Malcolm braced in front of the steering console, scanned the horizon with his Zeiss binoculars for a glimpse of the trawler's running lights

"It will be another ten minutes before we should be in range to see his lights" he said as at the moment there was a blinding flash of lighting followed almost immediately by a clap of thunder indicating the storm was almost on them. The heavens opened and ice cold rain started sheeting down reducing visibility to fifty metres.

At least it has calmed the seas a little Papa thought as he nudged up the throttles on both engines.

The rain stopped as quickly as it started and a wan moon appeared from behind the towering flat topped clouds.

"There she is" shouted Malcolm as the trawlers light came in to a view as they crested a wave about five points off the port bow and three miles distance. Hamish had switched on all his powerful fishing lights and the stern was bathed in harsh blue/white Zeon light.

Malcolm grabbed his signal lamp, directed it towards the bridge of the trawler and tapped out the recognition signal. Almost immediately the fishing lights were extinguished and the 'D' response made.

Papa grunted, notched the throttles up some more and the Rib buried its stern as the powerful props bit..

Hamish Duncan had reduced speed and was idling along at 4 knots. He had rigged a boarding net over the starboard rail just aft of the wheelhouse, the trawler making a 'lee' of calm water for the rib to approach. Lachlan had unshipped one of the gantries which was swung out in case it was needed to transfer the weight of the boxes.

Papa ran the Rib into the 'lee' dexterously closing the throttles to allow it to glide in and bump gently on the trawler hull whilst Malcolm threw the bow line to Lachlan who secured it around a massive trawl cleat. Papa then threw the stern line which was also secured. Only then did he look up at Hamish standing in the sliding wheelhouse door and beamed a big smile. Turning to the console he cut the engines.

"Well Papa, fancy meeting you here. Out for a spot of night fishing are you?"

"Good to see you Hamish. Yes, we have had a great and valuable catch this evening in which I am sure you will have interest"

"That's good news as we have had appalling luck. Perhaps we could share your 'catch' Let's get it aboard. Do you want to use the winch?"

"No, send down a line and we will rope them aboard they are not all that heavy just awkward. I will secure a second line from the rib just in case. . . . . ."

The rib was about ten feet below the trawler gunwhale but the transfer was quickly completed without incident and both boxes carried to the wheelhouse.

Papa and Malcolm then clambered aboard and were roundly greeted by Hamish and Lachlan with claps on the back and many 'well done's.'

"The sooner we open these and hide the contents the better. Don't suppose you have the keys"

"Very funny" snorted Papa just get me a crow bar. Duly equipped Papa used his immense strength to shatter the locks on both boxes and resting in each were found around twenty five bags of diamonds.

"Open one" said Hamish "I want to see exactly what I am smuggling and risking my ship"

Papa untied one of pochettes and emptied the contents on to the chart table. There were a dozen unremarkable matt stones with an almost oily consistency on the table.

"Raw stones" he said "just to be sure" He picked one up went across to the Port aft window and drew the stone down the glass. A deep cut appeared on the window. "Wow! It's all right though, I was going to replace this window glass anyway on the next refit as it is cracked in the corner"

At that they all burst out laughing. The tension of the evening seemingly melted away

In total there were 54 pochettes of uncut diamonds in the two boxes. Hamish said, "right I am now going to conceal the diamonds in various parts of the ship. It is better if only I know where they are just in case of 'awkward questions' if any of us fall into the wrong hands. Lachlan, deep six these strongboxes"

"Agreed" said Papa. You will be able to buy a fine ocean going yacht with your share and still have plenty in reserve"

"Who wants a yacht when I have this lovely old girl" he said as he turned and caressed the mahogany wheel. "She'll do for me although we just might add some creature comforts" He then turned to Lachlan. "stream the Rib astern, we shall stay on low power till 05.00 hrs then if the weather has blown through, Papa and Malcolm can head back to Luanda. In the interim I have rather a special surprise and I think congratulations on a daring and well executed plan are in order"

He stooped to a locker beside the wheel and extricated a dimpled bottle of golden brown liquid. Stooping again he removed a lipped tray upon which were wrapped objects. Lachlan slid the wheelhouse door having secured the rib astern "Agh, " he said "wondered whether this was the special occasion you have been waiting for all these years. It will probably be 'off' by now"

Hamish unwrapped the objects on the tray – four gleaming vintage Stewart crystal brandy balloons winked in the wheelhouse lights as he placed them on the chart table. Holding the bottle, he cracked the wax seal with the handle of his knife.

"This is a 1947 Armagnac" he said, I have had it for 40 years and now seems the time" He slowly twisted the cork which came away with a light pop. The intense aroma immediately escaped from the bottle. "Wow "said Lachlan "I can smell it from here" licking his lips in anticipation.

Hamish poured two inches of the liquid into each glass and handed them around.

"To us" he said "and that rogue Douglas. Take 'the nose' Gentlemen. . .
. . . .

CHAPTER 27

Luanda is a maze of small unlit streets and it was almost hopeless to attempt pursuit. The Toyota and the diamonds were long gone and Alfonso Carisco was not a happy man when his various forlorn patrols returned having scoured the area with no success. He was still unsure what exactly had happened and how. The only fact was that strong boxes had been stolen by, at the moment, persons unknown and although he had requested information from his usual troop of snitches, no one had come forward.

Either, too scared he thought, which pointed to one of the main gangs being the culprit, or they really did not know.

Looking at his watch he saw that it was now approaching 04.30 hrs. Home for a couple of hours sleep, then, hopefully refreshed, matters might be clearer when all parties met at the Barracks for the 10.00 hrs debrief. He called for his driver and wearily made his way to his Land Rover.

In the interim Douglas had returned to his villa where Sergio, already showered and changed in to his white jacket awaited.

"Hi Sergio, any problems"

"No, none whatsoever" Sergio replied. "Anna picked me up as arranged and we slipped back around 20.00 hrs. Nobody saw us, my weapons are cleaned and locked away and the vehicle used has reverted to the proper registration numbers. But what have you done to your head, When did that happen?"

"Agh, of course you will not yet know. There was a second attack on the diamond convoy just as the delivery was being made to the Bank. Several of Ramirez's men are dead or wounded and it was only by the grace of God I had the Mossberg and managed to extricate myself. The good news is that the attackers got away with the phony strong boxes so our deception and the actual theft will be covered"

"Good God" said Sergio, "I did hear some more rifle fire after I had left you to find Anna but thought it may have just been the exuberance of the Guards firing off the remaining blank ammo. Have you any idea who were the perpetrators?

You had better let me attend to your wound which looks as if it has seeping again"

"Thanks Sergio, but have you something cold and wet, I have a drouth"

"Ah, a thirst?" he said, "I have a bottle on ice in the drawing room on the table by the fireplace. Are you sure you are OK? "

Douglas flopped down in one of the armchairs as Sergio opened the bottle and pored two glasses. "Probably a bit soon and maybe tempting the fates" he said, "but I think we owe ourselves a toast, not forgetting Papa and Malcolm who will now be hopefully well out to sea."

Douglas accepted the frosted glass with relish, "to us" he said "here's to us, wha's like us, damn few an they're aw deid" Sergio crinkled his brow with obvious lack of understanding. "In English, here's to us, who is like us, very few, and they are all dead".

"A good toast" he said.

Douglas, emptied his glass in two long swallows, stood up and headed upstairs for a shower, he handed Sergio his sidearm and Mossberg – "grateful if you could give these a quick clean and return them upstairs if you don't mind. I will be down in half an hour. Perhaps Anna could prepare a light supper – an omelette and salad would be just fine"

Stripping off his soiled clothing, he ran the shower for a few minutes, stepped inside and let the hot water rinse off the dried blood around his head and face. He removed the dressing and saw the vivid weal with the tramline sutures above his eye. God he thought, that feels good as he put his head up to the flow. Ten minutes later he soaped up then reduced the temperature for a further couple of minutes to cool his body down. His forehead was still weeping blood. Stepping out of the shower, he grabbed a tissue and stuck it to his forehead, towelled off and dressed informally in a pair of jeans and a cotton Safari shirt. He slipped on his Gucci loafers without socks then grabbed the case with his secure satellite comms.

He fed in General's Bruce's private email and typed out a short report on the nights activities. He was not in the mood to be quizzed on the phone line and would speak to him after the de-brief tomorrow. The message was encrypted automatically, the green light came on and he pressed send, thereafter closing down and locking the case

Going back down stairs he helped himself to another glass of Bollinger and went in to the dining room having forgotten to take the tissue from his forehead he caught sight of himself in the ornate gilt framed mirror and could not halt a chuckle. Bloody fool he thought, what do you think you look like as he peeled the tissue off his face, little bits still sticking to the cicatrise like little pink flies. He dipped his finger into his wineglass and gingerly dabbed the area, screwing up his eyes at the sting. Bloody waste of champagne, he thought, but at least it should sanitise the wound until tomorrow. Dipping his finger once again, he noticed he was now drinking 'pink' champagne!

Sergio came through from the kitchen carrying his supper.

"Grab another glass Sergio and sit down, have you eaten yet? "

"No, I shall dine with Anna later. We have much to discuss"

Jack nodded. "excuse me as I eat," surprising himself that he was quite hungry.

They sat in companionable silence as Jack quickly finished his meal. "excellent, my thanks to Anna, just right. Now let me fill you in"

Jack then recounted the attack on the convoy as it arrived at the Bank. When he had finished without interruption, Sergio said, "You are right, it will certainly disguise our own deception and throw suspicion on others. It saddens me however that there were so many deaths in the Convoy guards especially as it is likely that the attackers were fully aware they had only blank ammunition. Cowards" he spat. "the person who leaked the information has their blood on his hands, may he rot in Hell. Did you recognise anyone?"

"Wondered when you were coming to that" Jack said "Yes, our chum Gallagher was riding shotgun in the big truck and the driver I am sure was one of Ponce's Lieutenants although I didn't see Ponce himself thus it is safe to assume that it was his gang. It was an efficient and quick operation. Gallagher had acquired the information, probably from Endiama, either here in Luanda or maybe at Huambo, or indeed Ponce probably has sources inside the Police or Ramirez's guard Company. Gallagher obviously saw a way to recoup his losses from the 'Maria Luisa' "

Sergio nodded. "It looks as if we are in the clear, what will you do about Gallagher and have you heard from Papa or the trawler?"

"No, strict radio silence, I shall meet with him on the isthmus after the de-brief tomorrow, Gallagher can wait, and now my friend let us finish this bottle and early nights for both of us. . . . .

CHAPTER 28

Douglas awoke early and went for his run in the breaking dawn. He considered how best to approach the upcoming debrief with Alfonso and Captain Ramirez. Attack is the best form of defense he thought and lay more smoke screens. On his return he had a light breakfast, asked Sergio to stay around the villa and drove to the barracks.

He decided to drive past the Bank, the burnt out 'rover was still there with a police vehicle and two Officers lounging against it looking bored, There was a black scorch mark on the Bank stone wall and fresh chips on the stone facade from the attackers' rounds.

Arriving at the barracks, the barrier was down and instead of the normal two on Guard duty, five of Ramirez's men under a grizzled Sergeant Douglas had not seen before, were deployed, looking alert and well armed, security was obviously at a heightened state.. He flicked down the electric window, showed his ID and asked how the injured soldiers were fairing. "Injured" said the Sergeant curtly, signalling to open the barrier and waving him through.

As he pulled up to the Orderly Room Alfonso's vehicle was already parked outside. It was still just 09.45 hrs. Looks like the boys are getting their stories correct before my arrival, he thought, this could be a 'tad' uncomfortable.

"Good morning, Gentlemen" as Ramirez rose from behind his desk. It looked as if he had been there all night, was unshaven and still had not changed his soiled uniform. Alfonso on the other hand appeared fresh and immaculately turned out as usual. He did not rise, simply nodding a greeting.

"Any news before we begin?"

"Another of my men died during the night "said Ramirez, "he was a good man with a wife and four children. I really want the bastards who did this." He continued, "The Toyota remains unfound after an exhaustive search overnight and a ring thrown around the city to ten kms. out. Vanished into the night – they could have gone in any direction"

"From Intel. received it appears that Ponce and his gang were heavily involved as they have all gone to ground and only the lower minions are in evidence. We have one in the cells but don't expect him to know much, if anything. What he does know he 'will' tell us "he said with a grim face.

"What about you Alfonso" said Douglas "Anything from Police sources?"

"Nothing he replied. The QRF vehicle soon lost touch with the fleeing Toyota in the North East of the city and other patrols report a 'No show'. I still have eight patrols out quartering the City and as Francisco said we have road blocks on all the main roads but there are hundreds of dirt tracks we simply cannot cover. We did find the discarded GPMG in an alley. I am afraid they are clean away"

Douglas sat down on the vacant seat in front of the desk. "OK let's begin, see if we can make sense of the information already on hand and plan damage limitation.. Firstly the 'ambush exercise' went well and" turning to Ramirez, I thought your boys handled themselves well. Any comments.

"Only your insistence that we have blank ammunition" said Ramirez, barely hidden anger and suspicion on his face. "That was the direct result of the deaths of my men"

"Back it down" said Douglas shortly "I am sorry about the casualties inflicted on the Bank ambush, but that was nothing whatsoever to do with the 'ambush exercise'. If anything the failure and responsibility is yours being too complacent to call in the blank ammo and re-issue live for the last 500 metres of the convoy run. If you had done that your men would have stood some chance of surviving"

Ramirez jumped to his feet his face contorted with anger. "My fault, My fault? "he shouted with a fleck of spittle at the corner of his mouth. "Where the hell were you the first couple of minutes?"

"You may recall" Douglas said, "I was semi knocked out in the diamond wagon, and then too busy saving your ass. If that GPMG had continued firing you would have been spread over the road and would certainly not be mouthing off now, so sit down and calm down. This does nothing!"

Alfonso then spoke. "Jack is quite right" he said "We are not here to apportion blame, no doubt our Superiors will do that. We must work together to try to recover the diamonds and establish the identities of the thieves. More importantly for me and the Government is whether this operation was for personal gain or was it Political and the funds going to someone's war chest. The Exercise and the Attack are two completely separate entities and have no bearing on each other"

Douglas eyed them both. "Firstly, I am of the opinion that it was Ponce who attacked the convoy at the Bank but am pretty certain the mastermind was our old 'friend' Gallagher as I am certain he was in the front passenger seat of the Mercedes truck. I lost him in the smoke and confusion of the firefight, but it seems realistic for him to take the chance to recoup his losses inflicted upon him by us and rub our noses in the mire. He has outmanoeuvred all of us.

However, he could not have done this without secure classified information being leaked from a high placed source either in the Army, the police Force or Endiama. He knew the route, he knew the timings, he knew that the Guards had loaded with blank for the exercise and hopefully would not have reloaded although he had the firepower and the numbers if they had. So look to your own commands first – it must be a senior position as you were all sworn to secrecy, so look up the chain of command not down. I am not saying it was deliberate – perhaps a document left on a desk, perhaps a slipped word but whoever it is, he is the one directly responsible for the loss of your men and the 'stramash' in which we now find ourselves.

All were quiet for a moment then Ramirez said "We only switched the ammo ten minutes before leaving the airport. Only me and my Company Sergeant Major knew this. None of the convoy detail knew when or indeed if there would be an ambush as you Jack had given no details. All my men knew was that they may be tested on the run. I command a secure independent unit with only upward reporting to the Brigade Commander. He was aware of the training and the Exercise but none of the details so I am pretty certain we can rule out the Army"

"Likewise," Alfonso said. I was the only one who knew of the Exercise ambush, not even my second in command was informed and I saw no reason to inform the top brass. I can assure you," he said with a half smile, "It was not me! . . . and remember Jack you chose the route but that really is irrelevant as all the routes obviously end at the Bank. That only leaves Endiama or perhaps a source we as yet, do not see.". I have a photo of Gallagher from his visa application and will circulate it to all my stations."

"Yes, Endiama" said Jack, "But how did they get the information? Even CSO were not informed and they were their diamonds. Alfonso can you contact Belguerro and ask for his assistance, i.e 'grill him'.

"Already in hand", he said "but being Saturday he is not in his Office and there is no response to his phone. I have sent an 'immediate' email to the head office requesting his whereabouts. Now if there is nothing else, I am beginning to perspire in this office. I don't know how you can bear that clattering old aircon. unit Francisco. It just circulates warm air"

Douglas smiled, held out his hand to Ramirez and then Alfonso. "No hard feelings" he said "We had to say what we were all thinking and I am truly sorry for your lost men. Ramirez gripped his hand. "I too must apologise for my loss of temper, it has been a long night." As he turned to leave Alfonso caught his elbow. "Walk with me" he said.

The two walked out into the stifling air it was past midday and heat and humidity had soared. No breeze disturbed the dust on the hard baked parade ground where two soldiers were languidly sweeping. As they reached the Range Rover Alfonso said. "Jack something is not right with Belguerro. I did not wish to speak in front of Ramirez as he has the President's ear but Belguerro has disappeared . No one has seen him since yesterday afternoon. His servants at home have been given the weekend off, his car is in his driveway yet there is no answer to the house phone or his mobile. I am now going directly there and if necessary will break in with my men. We can always apologise later. Do you wish to come"?

"No, That's Police business. I have a lot to do today but keep me posted". With that he flicked the key fob opening the locks, fired up the V8, put the aircon on full and opened all the windows to dissipate the interior heat, closing them a minute later before he set off for the Isthmus with his shirt sticking to the leather seat back.

He pulled into the track down to Papa Rock's house and quay and was relieved to see the Rigid Raider lying quite still alongside the dock with both engines tilted up There was hardly a ripple on the lagoon surface and the air was even heavier here. The minute he stepped out of the vehicle it was like walking into a warm shower and his shirt was soaked after a few steps. Papa had heard the vehicle and banged out of the cabin with Malcolm behind him clutching four ice cold beers. "Here" he said, "One for the throat and one for the forehead" Inside, and cool down. There is going to be a thunderstorm later"

Douglas followed him in to the dark cool of the shuttered cabin where the air con units were running full chat. In fact it was actually cold and Jack shivered in his sweat soaked shirt. Papa threw him a clean white T shirt and a towel. "Put that on"

Somewhat refreshed and holding his cold beer can to his damaged forehead, which was throbbing badly, he took a long pull from the other can in his right hand.

"Where did you get that" Papa said indicating his wound – some husband return too early?"

"No. Collateral damage" and proceeded to tell him of the attack on the convoy and Gallaghers involvement. When he had finished his tale. Papa got up from the sofa and withdrew another couple of cans of beer from the cooler. Throwing one to Jack he said. "That explains all the chatter on the Marine net as we were returning to harbour. Seemingly several vessels had seen and reported the firefight and the attack outside the Bank. At first I thought they were referring to us until I heard reports of tracer rounds and a vehicle on fire. We motored in just before dawn, unchallenged and yes before you ask we had some fish on board" Looking at Jack he smiled his wide smile showing off pearly white teeth. "Oh, that's not what you were going to ask? Yes, of course all went well, do you not trust my seamanship after all these years? We met Hamish and the cargo is now steaming North at 14 knots. I must say neither you nor Hamish have told me the port of destination. He said ask you. I am a bit miffed"

"Need to know" said jack, "for yours and Malcolm's safety. I know you are a tough old bird but if you had been stopped and interrogated in the usual Angolan manner, how long do you think it would take Malcolm to break. Even the threat of his beating would have been enough for you to give up the information, and rightly so" he added

"Anyway, all looks good on our side and Gallagher's attack has covered our theft of the diamonds. I think it unlikely he is going to 'report' the phony boxes to the Authorities when he eventually opens them and finds he has the wrong type of rocks

Papa guffaws and wiping his eyes he said "By God, he is going to be one angry man"

CHAPTER 29

Sunday saw Douglas with nothing to do. He had spoken to General Bruce when he returned from the isthmus and briefed him fully on the Gallagher situation together with his suspicion of Belguerro. He had been told to keep digging and establish the source of the leaked information and if possible assist in the recovery of the diamonds.

Alfonso Carisco had telephoned him first thing to advise that there was still no sighting of the escaped Toyota and that his search of Belguerro's house had not yielded any clue as to his whereabouts. His clothes were still in the wardrobes, shaving kit in his bathroom and a well stocked fridge in the kitchen. There had been no contact on his Mobile which was switched off.

Douglas mused over this and then was disturbed by the shrill ring of the landline. "Douglas" he said. "Good morning Jack" as Sylvette Dubios's silky voice flowed into his ear, "How are you after Friday's excitement?"

"Fine, with a souvenir of yet another scar, this time on my forehead, but otherwise fine. What are you up to?"

"Would you swing by the Hispaniola this morning, perhaps stay for luncheon on the stern as I have been contacted by one of that gangster Ponce's Lieutenants saying some very unpleasant things and I am concerned for the ship and a little bit for my own security. Alfonso has kindly agreed to maintain the police presence at the gangplank but I have this uneasy feeling "

"Of course, Sylvette, I can be right over if you wish"

"No I have few matters to attend to and wish to update my own onboard security staff, Say around 12.00 hrs?"

"Ok, see you then"

Replacing the receiver he wondered what Ponce and therefore Gallagher were up to and what nastiness they were cooking up. He phoned Papa and asked him to meet him at the Ship, then went upstairs to dress in a pair of light blue slacks, blue suede loafers and pale yellow lightweight sea island cotton shirt. He slipped on his ankle gun, grabbed his satchel with his phone, VHF radio, wallet and glasses. He went through to the kitchen to find Sergio asking him to put the Mossberg shotgun and a box of double 'O' cartridges on the front seat of the Range Rover.

"Sergio, it appears that the rats are stirring, Sylvette has had a nasty call from one of Ponce's minions which has upset her. I am going over to the Hispaniola now and have asked Papa to meet me there. Tell your boys on the gate to sharpen up, close the gates after me and allow no one to enter till I return. I shall give you two short blasts and one long blast on the horn"

"OK Jack, I shall also retrieve a couple of AK's from the gun box, leave one in the hall and one on the first floor landing with half a dozen extra magazines just in case. . ."

"Good thinking" as he strode to the Range Rover signalling the gate guards to open up.

The temperature was more pleasant today, Papa's forecast thunderstorm had only lasted for fifteen minutes but had certainly cleared the air and the humidity was down to around 80% still 'sticky' but manageable. Firing up the V8 he drove down towards the Paseo Maritimo, then around the 180 degree curve on to the finger of land at the end of which on the seaward side, was the Barracuda with the Hispanioala almost opposite on the Lagoon side some 100 metres South of the rather grandly named 'Luanda Yacht Club' There were still around twenty assorted pleasure craft moored on the pontoons, mostly motor boats or high powered speed boats. In pride of place was a 52 foot, Taiwan built, sailing ketch belonging to the British Ambassador which Douglas knew was not somewhere just to sit on deck for cocktails. The Ambassador was an experienced sailor with one circumnavigation and two 'crossing the ditch' to the Caribbean under his belt.

The remaining craft either belonged to the oil Companies or very affluent Government Officials. Indeed, the President owned a sleek and powerful 36 foot Sunseeker which gleamed at the end of the dock sporting the Presidential Angolan flag on its stern which hung limply in the still air. The two permanent crew were on deck swabbing and polishing the bright work.

Douglas had stopped at the Club just to check on the number of fast vessels lying there. Apart from Dos Santos's yacht he could only see three others which would have a decent turn of speed and logged the information away to discuss with Papa later if a need arose.

Driving down to the "Hispaniola" he was pleased to note that Alfono's Police presence were alert, rifles at the high port not slung over their shoulders and immediately started towards the Range Rover with one talking on a hand held radio as he parked. As he alighted one of the Officers recognised him and with a cheery wave retreated to the shade of the two trees under which the Police Land Rover was positioned.

Douglas made for the security room at the foot of the gangplank, went through the normal procedure of depositing his 9mm Makarov but this time going through a full frisk search even although, again, he was recognised. Signing the ledger, he nodded to the guards and climbed the gangway to the lovely stern deck of the ship with its taut white canopy giving welcome shade. As he walked towards the curved highly polished rail he reflected that Luanda must have been a lovely city under Portuguese colonial rule, as it was, situated around the lagoon with the many fine 19th century houses and palaces along the paseo maritimo. The sun glinted off the pink stone of the British Embassy, on the hill and to the right of the national Bank, one of the finest buildings left and resolute behind its 15 foot walls topped with twinkling razor wire, steel bomb proof gates and own armed guard force ably assisted by the resident SAS team, rarely seen. The city was slowly recovering from the decades of civil war and lack of maintenance but sadly many of the fine old buildings were either too damaged or in such a state of disrepair that they were being bulldozed and new, office or apartments blocks of glass, steel and concrete erected on the sites. Burying the soul of the City he thought – ah well, it's Africa.

A waiter appeared silently at his side. "Good morning Sir, May I get you a drink?"

"Morning, a bottle of Bollinger non vintage and three glasses please and could you advise Miss Dubois that I am here at her disposal"

"She already knows you are on board and will join you directly"

Eyes everywhere thought Jack but good security systems, he knew he would have been monitored and recorded from the car park.

The waiter returned bearing the glistening silver ice bucket in a two legged ring which he clipped over the rail Opening the bottle he proffered the glass to taste. Douglas took the nose and handed the flute back. "To the brim" he said "I am thirsty." He half emptied the glass in one large swallow.

A light hand fluttered over his left forearm, he had not heard her approach even though her four inch heels should have tapped on the immaculate deck.

"Morning, didn't hear you"

"That's because I keep to the central carpet. Do you think I am going to damage my lovely teak decks with these heels" She is a vision he thought as he took in her light silk shirt open to her cleavage and the shimmering light cotton skirt in pale yellow. She had piled her hair up to combat the mid day heat which accentuated her graceful neck. Her skin glowed with a light suntan.

"I must say you look quite beautiful" he said.

"Why thank you kind Sir" she said laughingly.

He filled a glass to the shoulders and handed it to her, "your health" as both sipped the delicious ice cold wine. It was his foible that he never clinked glasses, simply raised his glass to the other whilst looking directly in to the toast recipient's eyes. The old superstition was 'clink a glass and another sailor dies' He never said 'cheers'

"I have asked Papa to join us, hope you don't mind but think he could prove useful"

"Of course I don't mind, Papa and I go back almost as long as you and I, we normally see each other once a week or so. He is a dear friend. Come and sit in the shade "

They had just eased onto two immaculate blue and white striped canvas chairs when Papa loomed soundlessly behind Jack. For a big man he moved very quietly. Papa was elegantly dressed in a dark blue silk shirt, black cotton trousers, bright red socks and gleamingly polished black slip on shoes.

"You clean up quite nicely when you are not up to your elbows in engine oil" Jack said with a twinkle in his eye, Have a glass "

"I always dress appropriately when I am meeting a Lady, you, you are not important" as he held up his glass in silent toast. What's the problem"

Sylvette recounted the telephone conversation she had had earlier from someone purporting to speak for Ponce. "They know Jack and I are friends and that we may have eavesdropped on Gallagher and McGafferty whilst they were staying on board. They have put two and two together and made five in the hope of exacting some financial compensation from the 'Hispaniola' to soften their loss of the cargo on the 'Maria Luisa' whether we passed on relevant information or not. If no satisfactory payment is received within 72 hours then me, my crew and the ship will suffer. It is just bully boy gangster tactics. I will certainly not pay one sou."

Papa said. "I think you are pretty safe here, shore side your security is excellent, seaward side not quite so good and it would be a simple exercise for 'professionals' to come aboard from another craft in the hours of darkness but they are not professionals just thugs. You keep a lot of cash on board?"

"Yes, because of the Casino and of course crew wages which are all paid in cash. There is normally two hundred to two hundred and fifty thousand, mostly US dollars in the strong room overnight with around 50, 000 Euros. But you have both seen the strong room and the systems it is virtually unbreakable when locked down and requires my eye and thumb print to over-ride the time clock"

"Capture you, force you to co-operate – that is the weakness "Jack said "Your men would stand down if you were in harm's way. Gallagher is an evil man and has had no compunction in mistreating or indeed killing women in the past. I believe he has left Luanda for the moment but will probably return shortly."

Sylvette shivered slightly "I will not be forced from my own ship" she said, signalling the waiter to pour another glass from the almost empty bottle. "another bottle please"

"No you are a brave woman but it may be prudent if you were to come and stay with me and Sergio at the villa for a few days. Call it a holiday

– you can still control your Empire from there" He smiled

"I suppose it would be quite nice to see Sergio and Anna again and take a break from the ship routine and having to talk to all these guests and clients "

Whilst they had been talking the Sunday lunch crowd had arrived and almost half the tables were now occupied by diners.

"You must excuse me I have to go meet and greet, I shall join you for luncheon later. We are on table number one, your old table Jack on the starboard quarter" she said with a small sad smile.

Jack and Papa moved to the lunch table, the waiter brought the second bottle. "Watch yourself Jack, just remember you are spoken for" said Papa.

"I am very well aware of that but thank you for reminding me in your usual fashion, but seriously I think she is in danger and more so when Gallagher realises he has been duped when he opens the diamond boxes, if he hasn't done so already. He will hot foot it back to Luanda to seek vengeance and I shall be his prime target. Any friends of mine will also be in his sights. Could you also move in to the villa for a few days to back up Sergio. Malcolm will be ok but he can move in too if you wish"

"I shall move up, Malcolm will stay put to protect my home and interests, he can look after himself"

They ordered luncheon as Sylvette returned to the table, told her of the plan and that Papa would collect her in the Range Rover when she was ready to leave later today. She acquiesced quietly then brightened as a cold fish salad appeared on the table.

Chapter 30

Sylvette quietly moved in to the Villa taking pleasure in renewing her friendship with Anna and Sergio who she had known for several years but had not seen for some time.

Sergio insisted she should have the main guest suite which was only slightly smaller than Jack's however more feminine being decorated in light shades of lemon yellow, one of her favourite colours. With a white and yellow marble bathroom.

Indeed she had been instrumental in planning the interior decoration of the Villa at Sergio's request.

The balcony had a spectacular view across the lagoon to the 'Hispaniola' moored on the far side.

Surprisingly she felt at home and secure.

She and Jack had taken a light supper and although early, retired.

The following morning a leisurely breakfast was interrupted by the arrival of Alfonso.

"Morning all, Agh, Breakfast, do you mind if I join you, been up since 05.00 hrs and have had nothing to eat".

Douglas waved him to a seat with the inscrutable Sergio arriving from the kitchen to take his order, appearing again within ten minutes with a light savoury omelette, grilled tomatoes and mushrooms.

"What news?"

Alfonso paused to wipe his mouth with his linen napkin, "It appears that Belguerro has taken a permanent leave of absence - done a bunk! His bank accounts have been closed with all funds transferred offshore and it looks as if he left in a hurry.

As you know the house was comparatively undisturbed with the Mercedes in the drive but we have interviewed his Houseman who told us all the staff were given two week's holiday on full pay - unusual, also that Belguerro told him he was going up country to check on mining operations.

One of Endiama's long wheel base Land Rovers is missing".

"Thought so" said Douglas, "I already smelt a rat. I think it highly likely that Belguerro is in league with Sean Gallagher to steal or re-route his own country's diamonds and leave Angola"

"Highly likely" Alfonso agreed, "after all he is the Head of Endiama with unlimited access and control over collection, stockpiling and movements. I think he was aware of your 'Exercise'. If this is so he has been planning his flight for some time that is why the last delivery was much larger than usual.

He has recently come under suspicion but I have no proof as carat weight appears to be accurate unless the ledger security has been breached.

I know he has several Bank accounts abroad and a large house in Lisbon but that is not illegal in Angola.

I have put out a priority trace to find him but I am not holding my breath. He has a good head start and indeed I doubt he is still in Angola".

Breakfast over, Alfonso and Douglas decide to go to Belguerro's office to scan his computer and files whilst the protesting Sylvette is persuaded to stay secure at the villa under the watchful eyes of Sergio and Papa Rock who has arrived as back up.

At Endiama, Belguerro's Deputy initially refused to give them access to the office but after a few quiet words from Alfonso along the lines of 'art and part' conspiracy to commit theft and fraud, to which he vehemently protested his innocence, he moved, with some alacrity, to unlock the office and filing cabinets then scurried away to find the password to Belguerro's computer.

The two worked through all the files which seemed to be in order and contain normal corporate business. Douglas attacked the desktop computer whilst Alfonso made telephone calls to his HQ.

Douglas brought up the last two years diamond deliveries and compared them to the Huambo mine's ledgers. The carat weight and quantity appeared to check out but there was a 'nag' in his mind. Every 3rd or 4th delivery, there was an annotation, 'HUhel' in brackets, in the ledger. There was no explanation, key or other reference.

Alfonso had no idea and he told Jack that his outposts had reported no sight of Belguerro and no lead.

Douglas printed out the manifests and other data to study later. Alfonso would order a full audit of Endiama and the Bank accounts the following day. He had been given full authority by the President to invoke his name in any part of the investigation where bureaucracy or high handed Officialdom impeded.

The afternoon had flown by, the sudden African sunset was upon them and it was now dark as both men left Endiama's Offices making arrangements to meet at the Villa the following morning.

CHAPTER 31

Gallagher was in a foul mood, even more so than usual as he crouched over an open fire outside a ramshackle farmhouse five miles North of the border between Angola and the Democratic Republic of the Congo. He was waiting for the big pot of water to heat so that he could have his first decent wash and shave for the last three days. The wind changed blowing acrid smoke in his face and he cursed.

Ponce was huddled down on the other side of the fire, saying nothing, gripping a mug of coffee in his left hand.

The remainder of their motley crew were scattered around or on sentry duty further up the track.

"That fire is a dead give away" he mumbled, "we are supposed to be hiding out"

Gallagher looked at him grim faced. "Most of the cock ups so far have been down to you, just shut up and keep your ears open for Belguerro's chopper. The minute it arrives our cover is blown anyway.

Go and kick some life in to your so called mechanic and get him to check over the vehicle"

Ponce rose grumbling just as the recognisable beat of a helicopter some distance away, intruded on the domestic scene.

"That sounds Military to me, the rotor beat is too heavy for a commercial machine. Put out that damned fire and take cover till we are sure"

Gallagher kicked over the water pot which immediately doused the flames and engulfed them in steam. He cursed again, kicking himself that he had agreed not to open the diamond boxes until Belguerro had arrived. He thought that it would have been so easy just to leg it with the diamonds and cut Belguerro out of the deal but had decided, he may have use of him, so reluctantly had stood by his 'honour amongst thieves'.

The rotor noise became louder. It was obvious it was coming in from the South, from Angola, and soon he spotted an old Huey H1D military helo, low level about a mile away.

"Down to the LZ," he shouted. "that's him" as he ran the 100 yards down the track to the open area they had prepared yesterday. "Fire the green flare"

The flare arced up to the sky and burst. The helicopter slightly altered its flight path and overflew the LZ in a crescendo of noise with the distinctive, whump, whump, whump of the old two bladed Huey. The pilot did a severe 'wing over' and pulled up to eyeball the area, circled, then flared into wind to reduce speed before settling in a cloud of dust. He did not reduce power and kept about half pitch on the blades ready for immediate lift off if anything was suspicious

Gallagher approached at 12 o' clock, saw Belguerro in the front seat and gave the instruction to cut his engine by drawing his hand across his throat. The half pitched rotor was still kicking up a recycled dust storm. He saw the Pilot drop the collective and immediately the dust began to clear as he reduced power to flight idle. Belguerro threw off his harness, handed his headset to the pilot and opened the door to get out, whilst the pilot went through his shut down procedures. The whine of the turbine suddenly ceased and the rotor blades decayed their rotation till the pilot could apply the rotor brake.

Apart from the ticking heat from the turbine it was now very quiet.

The two men approached each other.

"Well we did it" said Belguerro proffering his hand. Gallagher ignored the outstretched hand "No, we did it" he said indicating Ponce and his men, "all you did was to provide some information, sit back and let us take all the risk and then fly in in a bloody chopper like Lord Muck. We have been in this stinking shithole for nearly two days. Where did you find this old relic anyway" as he looked at the Huey which he could now see had no markings or registration whatsoever over its patchwork camouflage paintwork.

"My friend" said Belguerro. "This chopper was the workhorse of the American Army and was retired from the Angolan army some four years ago along with its pilot who bought it for commercial work. I assure you although old, it is very well maintained and ideal for our needs"

"Belguerro, I am not your friend only an associate in this endeavour, after this I have no wish to see your black arse again"

Hearing a sound behind him he turned again to look at the helicopter, where the side door had been slid open revealing a harnessed machine gun manned by a second crewman, the pilot standing beside him.

"What the hell" he said as the barrel traversed towards him.

"Just a little bit of insurance so that we may conduct our business in an amicable fashion, as you say we are not friends" Belguerro turned to the pilot telling him to stay with the aircraft and the gunner jumped down with an automatic carbine slung over his shoulder to give him protection.

"Fair enough" growled Gallagher "I would have probably done the same, ".

The three men, joined by Ponce started to walk back to the farmhouse Belguerro confirmed that the man behind the failure of the arms shipment was Jack Douglas, ably assisted by Chief Alfonso Carisco as told to him by Anstruther the idiotic British Military Attache. He further informed him that Douglas was a former Officer in the Scots Guards and that his and Gallagher's paths had crossed before in Belfast

"I thought I knew the bastard. Now I can place him, the event and circumstances. Well, well, the wheel turns. . . But he has egg all over his face now. He was supposed to be enhancing the security to increase protection for the diamonds. Serves him bloody right. Let's open these damned boxes.

The diamond containers were dragged across the rotting stoop on to the beaten ground where Ponce's men set to work with crowbars and hammers but the locks would not break.

"Enough of this, any of your boys got AP rounds?" he said to Ponce who replied in the affirmative. "Get me an AK with some armour piercing rounds"

The weapon having being handed to him he stepped back a few paces then proceeded to blow the locks off the containers causing a whirlwind of dust and flying metal chips one of which cut Belguerro's right cheek. "There" he said with a smile, "now your blooded!"as he turned back to the strong boxes, the lids of which had been twisted off he let out a shriek.

"Bloody rocks, a switch, a bloody switch - nothing but fucking rocks" as he dropped to his knees. "I'll get that bastard Douglas and it will be messy". then as an after thought "Are you double crossing us Belguerro?"

Belguerro looked at him in contempt as he dabbed his cheek with a snow white linen handkerchief.

"How could you be so inept, your pitiful revenge is no consolation to me. I have burned my boats and am now on the run without the several millions I expected from this operation. Why would I be here if I knew of the switch? I personally saw the diamonds through the airport they must have been switched during the exercise."

Gallagher tried to rationalise. "That crafty bugger Douglas pulled the stunt himself during his exercise then we hit the convoy ten minutes later taking all the blame and giving him a clean slate. The diamonds will be long gone by now but nobody plays me for a sucker"

"I think they just have" said Belguerro. "You owe me Gallagher" and with that he signalled to his crewman who had unslung his weapon to guard the rear as he stalked back to the helicopter.

Minutes later the whine of the turbine started up and the Huey lifted off in a roar heading North and leaving the others with their 'rocks'.

Chapter 32

At the villa, Jack Douglas was on the sat phone to Maggie Grosvenor. He gave her a brief summary of the events of the last few days and apologised for being out of touch. Maggie well knew that when he was on an 'Op' she was lucky to hear from him at all and was just relieved to know that he was OK, so far. . . She knew she was safe in their home at 16 Kensington Court in London and also knew that she could never persuade Jack to slow down and stop taking unnecessary risks on his 'adventures'.

He told her that he hoped to be clear within a week and asked if she could book a suite in the Krasnapolsky, in Amsterdam, one of their favourite hotels, and await his arrival.

"Hamish Duncan should be there before me," he said, "so he can take care of you. Don't worry if I am a day late"

In his mind he could envisage her, sitting by the French doors of the drawing room leading out to the terrace with its old trailing grapevines, leading to the double garage and the steps to his private entrance in De Vere Gardens. Her head would be forward, a slight frown of concentration on her face and a wisp of her ash blonde hair over her right eye as she cradled the phone. No doubt she would be in her normal pose with her right leg tucked underneath her. An uncomfortable position he had always thought however she was very supple.

He considered himself to be very lucky to have such a beautiful and at times very feisty partner - he hated the word partner and had asked Maggie to marry him some years back but she had declined the offer being the fiercely independent person she was and of course having her three children from a previous failed marriage.

This was a time when Douglas was still in the Scots Guards and they had drifted apart - a period he deeply regretted, when she had married a charlatan on the rebound.

Enough of this he thought as Maggie having consulted her diary said, "Cowboys and Indians again Jack. I shall see what I can do but I have family commitments"

"Maggie, for once in your life just do as I ask. You are in for a surprise and if all goes well this may be the last time I have to play Cowboys"

It had been a day of relative inactivity and all were rested and in good spirits as Douglas descended to the drawing room for dinner. Anna had attacked his unruly long hair which was now brushed back in a classic 'Cavalry cut' - not as short as the Brigade haircut being longer at the back although Douglas had always favoured this style in the Regiment, receiving many reprimands from the Adjutant when he was a junior Officer and suffering extra Piquet Officer duty as a result.

He was casually dressed in open neck shirt and slacks.

Sergio, unprompted had opened a bottle of Krug and proffered a glass to Jack "So far so good" he said with a half smile lightening his face.

At that moment Sylvette appeared at the head of the stairs, paused for dramatic effect and glided down towards them. She was wearing what could only be described as a figure hugging 'sheath' which accentuated the lovely curves of her body. The dress was calf length, split to the thigh on one side, cut to outline her perfect bosom, and swept over one shoulder with an elegant swoop down to the base of her spine leaving her back bare. The material was a shimmering deep blue silk with gold embroidery and she wore gold and blue heeled shoes.

"Gentlemen" she said, "do close your mouth Jack, we are not a goldfish. You would think you had never seen me in evening dress before"

She was quite beautiful.

Feeling somewhat silly and underdressed, Jack took her hand, kissed her on both cheeks and turned to Sergio who was poring a glass of wine his half smile now increased to a wondrous full smile which shone from his eyes and crinkled his face. Jack had never seen the normally taciturn Sergio in this mood.

Sergio handed the glass to Sylvette. "A fine wine for a fine Lady," raising his glass in a toast, "you look quite lovely".

"Why thank you kind Sir "she said with a coquettish smile "I . . . . . .

She was interrupted by the sudden knocking on the front door then opened by the gate security guard mumbling an apology. "There is a Lady to see you Sir"

Papa Rock appeared out of the courtyard gloom with a somewhat dishevelled Judy Wiltshire in tow in an agitated state, and who had obviously been crying.

"You should hear this" said Papa.

Sylvette came forward, "Firstly let's make Judy comfortable and Sergio, a stiff brandy" the two ladies then withdrew to the downstairs cloakroom to repair Judy's somewhat ravaged face and give her time to compose herself.

They emerged some five minutes later, outwardly Judy appeared much calmer.

In the interval Jack asked Papa what was going on and why had she come here. "Best to hear it from the horse's mouth" he said "it is not pleasant"

Judy and Sylvette sat on one of the sofas by the fireplace Jack sat on the other sofa opposite, Sergio and Papa remained standing and Anna had come in from the kitchen to enquire about the commotion.

Taking a large gulp of Brandy, Judy began her tale.

"I didn't know where to turn Jack, I have just had the most frightful argument with James who became furious and in his apoplectic state revealed some vile and frightful facts. At one stage he raised his hand to strike me but fortunately did not.

I knew there was something amiss but did not suspect the depth of his depravity and betrayal of me and the Service." At this she half sobbed and lent back on the sofa.

"Easy Judy" Jack said, "take your time, you will stay here tonight and if it is too much for you, you can tell us tomorrow"

Judy took another large swig from the Brandy balloon "No, I must tell you now"

"James has confessed to being homosexual and has been having an affair with a black Portuguese who works in Endiama and is in fact Belguero's nephew. He is leaving the Civil Service to stay in Angola and wants a divorce. He wants a divorce. . . I never wish to see him again and told him to leave which thankfully he did"

"God, that's frightful. Don't worry, you will stay here as long as you like" glancing at Sergio who nodded discreetly, "I shall speak to the Ambassador tomorrow and take things from there"

"No, no, you don't understand" she groaned, "there is much more. He told me that Colonel Anstruther knew of his proclivity and had blackmailed him into criminal acts otherwise he would expose him. He has been including illegal packages for Anstruther in the Diplomatic pouch which he knew contained 'blood diamonds' and has also been instrumental in arranging meetings with Belguerro and him. Belguerro bribed him for information about you, your team and your operations in Angola." Both James and Anstruther have been working behind your back"

"The little weasels" said Jack angrily. "I'll settle their hash"

Turning back and moderating his tone of voice he said softly, "Now Judy, off to bed with you, perhaps another Brandy to help you sleep? You have had a really rough day and thank you for telling such a difficult and personal story"

Sylvette, helped her up from the sofa and propelled her upstairs. Jack asked Sergio to telephone Joe Walsh, the chief Security Officer at UNAVEM (The United Nations Mission in Angola) asking if he could join him for a late breakfast tomorrow. Papa was despatched to find Judy's car and bring it in to the villa compound.

It was now 22.00 hrs and the thought of a pleasant sumptuous dinner now long gone. Jack went in to the kitchen and asked Anna if she could just rustle up omelettes and salad for those who wished and serve on the big scrubbed pine kitchen table. Sylvette re-appeared having changed in to a black trouser suit.

"God, I need another glass "she said, "Judy, quite naturally is wrecked. I have given her a sleeping pill and she has gone to oblivion. Hopefully she will not have too many bad dreams. What an appalling tale, I can not imagine how she must feel. Her husband is a weak minded little shit"

Jack raised an eyebrow. It was not often he heard Sylvette swear and glancing at her, suddenly she looked tired. He realised that the years of living in Luanda had taken their toll on her and behind the always bright 'party face' was a lonely, whilst still beautiful, tired middle aged Lady. Poor kid, he thought, time for her to leave this country.

After a quiet supper with all five not saying much around the kitchen table and the girls toying with their food, Sergio and Papa did last rounds of the villa compound agreeing to spilt the night shift between them and all retired.

Douglas undressed, decided he was too tired to have another shower and rolled in to bed naked and was asleep in in an instant.

His trained sixth sense alerted him to his bedroom door being opened softly and a figure appeared stealthily crossing the room towards him, He reached for his Makorov 9mm on the bedside table at the same time switching on the bedside light.

Sylvette was caught in the glare and seeing the gun, froze like a deer in a car's headlights. She was virtually naked apart from a wispy, ethereal night dress.

"What the Hell, Sylvette" said Jack.

"Thought you may like some company, this evening has un nerved me and I don't want to be alone"

Jack replaced the Makorov on the table and watched her carefully. She was breathing heavily and the cool air had made her nipples stand out hard and firm under the silk material. He felt himself becoming aroused as she sat down on the bed beside him, leaning over to gently brush his lips Her delicate scent was half her in her nakedness and half a very expensive subtle perfume. Jack reached for her and kissed her tenderly, then with more passion. He cupped his left hand around her breast teasing the swollen nipple with his fingertips. A soft moan escaped from Sylvette. She reached under the sheet for him with a small cry finding him hard and ready.

Jack Douglas' mind was in turmoil - his brain saying no way but his body betraying his every thought.

He looked over her shoulder to catch the moonlight glancing off Maggie's photo on the dresser. The photograph he always takes on every operation.

"Damn it Sylvette, I can't do this" as he gently pushes her away. "I am sorry, you are such a beautiful woman, but betrayal is betrayal and it is not a path I walk"

Sylvette's shoulders slumped as she gathered her night dress around her.

"I am sorry too Jack, you know I have loved you for a very long time. I just hope Maggie knows how lucky she is" and with a sniff and a brush away of a threatening tear, she got up and silently left the room.

CHAPTER 33

Douglas was up early, already thinking on the day ahead and planning his stratagem. He thought of Hamish Duncan ploughing North on the trawler. He would now be closing on the South West coast of Portugal if all had gone well. He would maintain radio silence until he reached his final berth in Holland.

Firstly was the breakfast meeting with Joe Walsh and Papa.

At that moment, he heard the noise of a vehicle entering the compound. Opening the front door he saw a white Toyota land cruiser with large blue 'UN POLICE' signs on the doors and bonnet, festooned with radio aerials and flying the UN flag from two small staffs on the front wings and on the longest whip aerial. This was Joe Walsh. Chief Security Officer and an ex New York cop - a hard man but scrupulously honest. Douglas had known him for many years and the two were firm friends.

"Hello Joe," he said extending his hand to take Walsh's huge leathery paw. Jack thought he was nearing 60 the mandatory age for retirement from the UN force but he knew he had had a "stay of execution" for a couple of years as he was so efficient in his role and had a wealth of contacts throughout Angola.

"Morning Jack, How are ya"

"Fair to muddling" Jack said with a smile "you can shuck your combat belt and sidearm on the hall table, presume you wish to keep your radio live?

"Yeh, operational necessity, I carry two of the damn things switched on 24/7"

He unbuckled his heavy belt, dropping it on the table and eased his spine, stretching to his 6ft. He was a well built man with massive shoulders and chest from years of gym and weight work and his head seemed just to sit on top of his shoulders with a short bull neck. He still had steel grey hair cut in the Marine style Number 1 which looked like a fuzz on top of his pate. Combined with flint blue eyes, an aquiline nose and pointed jaw he looked a bit like an eagle about to pounce. This look was enhanced by his habit of 'stooping' his head slightly forward and his eyes never resting in one place but constantly and sometimes unnervingly, scanning.

A hard man and definitely a force to be reckoned with. No wonder the UN wish to keep him on, Douglas thought.

Going through to breakfast he shook hands with Papa and Sergio and was introduced to Anna.

Sweeping off his blue 'powder puff' UN beret he took her hand and with a slight bow said "Ma'am, a pleasure"

With niceties over they ordered breakfast - eggs over easy on waffles and grits, black coffee and orange juice

"I haven't much time Jack" muttered Walsh through his first sip, no gulp of coffee, "been up since 04.00, bit of a flap at the base but under control so get to it "

Douglas then summarised the events of the last few days, the fact that Sylvette had moved from the ship to the villa for safety from Gallagher and Ponce and that they expected reprisals.

He also told him, although he hated doing so, a little white lie that Gallagher had attacked the convoy and stolen the diamond strong boxes. Not really a 'lie' he thought as they did actually steal the strong boxes but not the diamonds he thought with an inward smile.

"Yeh, I know about the attack, seems like there was an insider. Was that shady bastard Belguerro involved as I hear he has done a moonlight"

"As ever you are well informed" said Jack. Yes Belguerro was involved and also some Members of the British Embassy. James Wiltshire and Anstruther to be exact. I have an appointment with the Ambassador today to present our evidence.

"Jesus" said Walsh. "no wonder you are 'forted up' here. Wondered why there were quite a few weapons lying around"

"What I need from you Joe is some extra security if you can swing it. We are short handed here, just us our gate guards and the Angolan Police patrol courtesy of Alfonso. Any chance of a squad of your UN cops for internal security - ideally six would help tremendously whilst also being a visible deterrent of blue uniforms, white UN vehicles and a UN flag above the gates "

Walsh thought for a minute. "I'll have to run this through HQ at the camp, Pity there are no UN personnel living here and in danger"

"Ah, but there are" as Jack flicked his old UNAVEM identification, still current, across the table. "and Sylvette has UN accreditation as well"

"That 'll make things easier", getting up from the table. "I must get back. Call you in a couple of hours and if it is a go I'll give you an UN Police radio. Thank Anna for a great breakfast.

At that he threw his belt over his shoulder, marched out to his Landcruiser and disappeared in a cloud of dust.

Good to his word he telephoned two hours later with the news that six UN police and two vehicles would deployed within a couple of hours. They would be armed but with precise 'terms of engagement' only to open fire if fired upon and in defence of the villa residents. They would initially be deployed for five days and would require food and accommodation.

Conferring with Papa he told him the good news, to brief the gate guards and Sergio, make sure that he or Anna would keep Sylvette and Judy Wiltshire in sight and that under no circumstance would they be allowed to leave the security of the villa compound.

He retired to the study to continue going through Belguerro's files and await the arrival of the Chief Inspector. After an hour he leant back in his chair, squinting at the mass of paperwork on the light teak desk some of which had overflowed to the floor and peering at Belguerro's laptop. He was again scrolling through the schedule of shipments and being niggled by the highlighted delivery, once every three or four weeks, seemingly on random dates, highlighted by the the word 'HelHU'

Alfonso arrived and he appraised him of his findings, indeed lack of.

Alfonso gave a short chuckle. "Jack you have been looking too hard, it is right in front of you, 'HelHU' means Helicopter from Huambo. Obvious really!

He went on to describe the 'short loads' from the outlying mines which were insufficient in quantity to require the fixed wing aircraft thus every now and then, an unscheduled 'short load' would be transported directly to the bank by helicopter, landing at Ramirez's barracks and being delivered by an unmarked vehicle which would not attract attention.

"Of course" exclaimed Jack, "why had I missed that"

He checked the files again comparing weight and number of pouches transported and delivered to the Bank - identical.

Alfonso pulled out his pipe and tobacco pouch. "Don't mind do you?" Jack waved his agreement still staring at the screen.

He again leant back and ran his fingers through his hair. "This must be where the diamonds are being stolen" as he watched Alfonso mechanically fill the bowl of his pipe from a heavy looking leather pouch. Alfonso lit his pipe and disappeared in cloud of smoke which the air conditioner swiftly dispersed. Satisfied it was drawing well he casually threw the pouch on to the desk which slithered towards Jack.

His eyes were drawn to the pouch as emblazoned on the front was 'Endiama'

"Alfonso, is that a diamond pouch?" Alfonso confirms.

Suddenly a light is switched on in Jack's head. "I think I have it" he said "When I was reviewing procedures at the sorting office in Huambo the diamonds coming in are in lightweight textile pouches. Go and get me a scale will you?

On his return with the scale, Jack had emptied his tobacco out of the pouch on to the desk top and weighed the leather pouch - just under five ounces. The textile pouches could only weigh one or one and a half ounces

"Eureka, there's the answer and so easy we overlooked it. There is no discrepancy in weight or number of textile pouches. The weight and the number of 'leather' pouches match the delivery account. Nobody has realised that the pouch weight is so different allowing 3 to 4 ounces in diamond weight to be removed on the direct flight from Huambo by helicopter. Thus the onward shipment exactly matches the schedule of delivery.

So simple but so effective - it must have been going on for years with Belguerro squirreling away millions in uncut stones and that bastard Anstruther helping him to export them via the diplomatic bag.

There are roughly twenty pouches per shipment thus around 60 ounces of diamonds are stolen on every Helicopter delivery in the textile pouches.

"That's a Hell of a lot of diamonds!"

Thinking quickly Jack added, "Belguerro must be in league with the terrorists some of whom we are certain work the mines, their share gives them the funds to buy them more modern weapons and explosives. There also must be some of the Helicopter team involved, if nothing else to turn a blind eye. Of course security at Huambo is not violated as it is simply an "accounting matter", the diamonds never leave the helicopter.

The Courier changes the diamonds from textile pouches to leather pouches under supervision in the helicopter at Huambo where the full 'textile bags' have been weighed and recorded on arrival. The leather pouches are NOT re-weighed. The courier then simply removes some diamonds from each leather pouch en route to the bank - he probably carries a small scale measure - Landing at the barracks he hands over his burden, gets a signature and walks out of the gates his pockets full of diamonds. He might even have his own car on the base. As part of the normal security detail it would be most unlikely he would be stopped or searched. On arrival at the Bank the stones and pouches would again be weighed and match exactly the weight and number as in the schedule.

"Over to you," he said to Alfonso who was already on the telephone ordering his helicopter and a small assault team for immediate departure to Huambo

Now to beard Anstruther in his den as he made ready for his appointment with the Ambassador . . . .

Douglas decided to brief the General on the sat. phone prior to going to the Embassy. Activating the machine he typed in the secure number which was answered on the third ring. A monosyllabic "Yes". He summarised the last few days expressing his concern over Belguerro's disappearance and that Gallagher had not re-surfaced. He was told not to worry, that Gallagher had probably scurried back to Belfast to face the music for his double failure and that extra eyes were on the street. The minute his location is confirmed he will be advised. Anstruther will be re-called immediately and dismissed the Service if not Court Martialed. The Civil Service would discipline Wiltshire but as it would appear he also has done a bunk it may be difficult.

The General finished with the advice that he would call HE at the Embassy to discuss the matter before he arrived and further advised not to 'stir the pot' too much as there is significant embarrassment already. Always the under statement Jack thought, 'embarrassment?'

Jack signed off, stowed and locked the phone, slipped on a buff coloured linen jacket for the Ambassador's meeting and with a nod to Papa and Sergio who were both in the drawing room walked out to his vehicle. No further words were needed!

As he emerged into the glaring sun and high humidity, he reached for his Ray Ban Pilot's glasses at the same moment the compound gates were swung open and two dusty UN jeeps drove through. A Police Sergeant debussed form the front vehicle approached Jack and asked him if he was Colonel Douglas.

"Plain Mister now Sergeant" he said as he introduced himself to the other five, heavily armed officers. All wore the light blue UN Police shirts, dark trousers, armoured gilets with their combat belts sporting 9mm Colt automatics in tied down holsters, wicked looking combat knives, water bottle, VHF radio and first aid pack. In place of the blue UN beret they all wore blue Kevlar military helmets. They all carried M16 carbines.

"Looks like you have been briefed on the situation" he said with a slight smile. Go in and find Sergio, he will show you the accommodation for your guys and will walk you through a 'famil' of the property. I shall be back in a couple of hours when we will have a combined briefing.

The Sergeant snapped up a parade ground salute, told his guys to back up the Jeeps to the rear wall, three to stand down, two to start a roving patrol inside the walls and to fly the metre by metre and a half sized UN Flag from the post above the gate. With a last command to rig up a spotlight for dark hours he clumped towards the villa door.

Douglas exited the villa compound and swung left along the top of the ridge heading South East towards the British Embassy. He had half a mind to make for the 'paseo' where traffic would be lighter then turn up from the lagoon but rejected that as he wanted to drive by Ramirez's barracks to check on the activity.

The air hung languidly between the buildings, the humidity was almost visible as a fine mist interspersed with dust kicked up by the vehicles. There was not a breath of wind A 'five shirt day' as we used to call them, he thought. God it will be nice to leave this country behind for the last time. Fortunately his aircon was working well but he knew that when he arrived at the Embassy and walked the 30 metres to the front door it would again be like walking through a tepid shower with his clothes on. Ah well - not a courtesy call!

The time was approaching 13.40 hrs. The traffic was appalling as everyone sped home or to a restaurant /bar for the siesta. There was no order. Vehicles sped past in both directions on either side. If the oncoming lane was clear you drove in it. Rarely did you see a vehicle indicating - most of them didn't work or were smashed anyway and all vehicles seemed to have dents or scuff marks on most of their panels. All were a uniform dust colour, only his had a gleam of polish underneath. Regretting his decision to take this route he emerged in the square opposite the barracks where two Military UMM's were parked either side of the gates with five watchful guards controlling egress and ingress. The UMM was a dreadful vehicle - Jeep like, soft skinned 4 x 4 with an underpowered Peugeot 1.9 litre diesel engine. No air con and constantly breaking down mostly from the bad electronics. Douglas remembered them well as he had three of them when he was stationed with IDS and had covered many uncomfortable miles although he had an Isuzu trooper for his own use. Although they were not fit for purpose he had a fondness for the ugly things a bit like some people having a fondness for the 'corrugated iron' 2CV Citroen with the sardine can roof the 'Deux Chevaux'.

Flinging the remembrances aside he decided that Ramirez had upped the Security alert level as passing the gates he saw a long wheel base Land Rover just inside the barrier with the canvas top off and a mounted GPMG with two further guards in the rear.

Interesting he thought, maybe Ramirez has more current Intel. I shall have to give him a call or get Alfonso to pay a visit.

Barrelling out of the square he narrowly missed a heavily laden donkey cart, rejoined the cacophony of horn and engine sounds and turned up the hill. At one time in the Colonial past it would have been a lovely approach road to the imposing residence which was the British Embassy, beautifully cobbled avenue with tall palm trees down either side. Now it was rough and broken with areas of missing cobbles just filled in with rubble, most of the trees had gone and rubbish and broken cars lay in abandon. The last 50 metres to the gates had been cleared to give uninterrupted field of fire from the Embassy walls and redoubt. A further two metres in height had been added to the original walls and you could only see the roof and third flower of the gracious Palladian mansion inside. The large double gates were five inches of hardened steel.

The whole vision was like a bad 'Beau Geste' film with a hastily constructed Foreign Legion Fort on a Hollywood film set, However this illusion was simply that. The Embassy was indeed a small Fort and its walls and defenders had saved many lives during the civil war as Jack well knew, especially when Savimbi's forces had assaulted the North of the Luanda, meeting little resistance they had swept aside the Government troops reaching Millionaire row and the smaller Embassies and almost breaching the Presidential Palace defences before grinding to a halt as their only three T52 Russian tanks had been incapacitated, one throwing a track on the slopes just outside Jack's villa. The following days had seen hard hand to hand fighting and looting throughout the city with considerable loss of life before Savimbi withdrew. Of Course the President had been secretly helicoptered out to Namibia until thought safe to return

That would be Savimbi's last attempt to take the Capital.

Today the gates stood open with one ex Gurkha and two Angolan guards on duty, although the red and white barrier pole was down. Recognising the Range Rover the Guard glanced at Jack, who had rolled down the window to be assaulted by the heat, saluted and ordered the barrier to be raised.

Parking in front of the main portico which was held up by four beautiful marble columns, he kept the engine running to cool down once again. Marshalling his thoughts, he switched off and strode towards the double bullet proof glass doors in to the security area, before secondary doors allowed him access to the main Hall or ante room of the Embassy. Having verified his identity with the door guard he signed in, checked his weapons, radio and satchel, adjusted his shirt collar under his jacket and headed for the Ambassador's Office.

A side door swung open with a crash and a somewhat dishevelled and sweating Anstruther appeared.

"Douglas" he half croaked "Could I have a word before you see HE" pointing to his office.

"But of course, Edward" said Jack with an imperturbable smile on his face following him and silently closing the door behind.

"Before you start", Jack said in a cold, clipped, steel tinged voice. "I know!" Not only do I know but I also have a deposition from a person of good character, unlike you, confirming your duplicity, theft, abuse of position and acceptance of bribes"

You are a disgrace to your uniform. "

"No, No, you are wrong, I have only done what I considered to be for the good of the Embassy and the Ambassador. You don't understand. Sometimes we have to find devious ways to get along with these people.

"Shut up you snivelling little man. No you are not a man but some loathsome creature, I am done with you. I have my report to make to the Ambassador. Keep on eye on today's signals, I am sure you will find something pertinent to your sudden recall to the UK"

Turning towards the door, Anstruther grabbed his elbow to plead with him and seeing no mercy in his eyes pulled himself together with a great effort and shouted "Get out of my Office"

"My pleasure" said jack "I can't abide the smell, but there is just one other thing." at that he pivoted through 180 degrees with the force of his turn adding power to the long Jab from his right arm which connected with Anstruther's jaw, hammering his fist in to his chin.

Anstruther's head snapped back and he careened off his chair before dissolving in a heap on the floor - Out cold!

I have been wanting to do that for a long time thought Jack as he dropped the Range Rover keys on the desk.

"Oh, by the way, it will need a wash and an interior clean - smells as if somebody died in it, smells a bit like you . . . . ."

Nursing his knuckles Jack approached the Ambassador's office, knocked and entered without waiting for a reply. HE was behind his desk. He did not stand up.

"Well Douglas this is a fine mess with allegations flying everywhere, I have had a telephone call from General Bruce advising me of the facts as YOU see them -preposterous! What have you got to say for your self"

Jack sat down without waiting to be asked. "Good afternoon Sir, could I trouble you to ask your Secretary for a glass of your excellent lemonade with ice. Devilishly hot outside"

"You've a nerve Douglas, well all right" as he lent to the intercom to place the request.

"As we wait I suggest you have personnel start the works for a replacement military Attache from the MOD and of course a replacement Commercial Attache"

"Now look here, Douglas," started the Ambassador as there was a discreet knock at the door and two glasses of lemonade were delivered.

Taking a sip. Douglas shot HE a withering look. "No you look here and don't interrupt. I am not impressed or concerned by your position nor am I impressed by you. Your lackadaisical attitude to your responsibilities has jeopardised my operation, put lives in danger and besmirched the name of Her Majesty's Government To say it is a political hiatus is an under statement. Indeed as I sit here I wonder just how much you are personally involved. . ."

The Ambassador's face had been steadily becoming more infused with blood and was now a livid purple red in colour. "How dare you besmirch my name and this office, he exploded. "Get out!"

"Gladly" said Jack when I have finished what I came here to say and of course my lemonade.

"Out, out now. I will have you disciplined for this crass insubordination and disrespect"

"You forget, Sir, I am a civilian not subject to censure by you and quite outwith your control so don't make silly idle threats. If you insist on me leaving I shall simply advise General Bruce that I now consider you may have been involved in one way or another. True or not, mud sticks and I think you will receive advice to seek early retirement"

The Ambassador had gained some composure and his facial hue was returning to his more normal light pink.

"Very well Douglas - I am aware you have the lead in this matter and almost plenipotentiary power, which by the way I abhor, Continue "

Douglas then outlined the collusion and betrayal of his Military Attache and his Commercial Attache together with the theft of blood diamonds and the abuse of the Diplomatic bag. He also advised him of the security risk involved, that Judy Wiltshire was being protected in a safe house and would not be in for work until the situation was rationalised and that he should take no action until he heard directly from the Foreign Office or General Bruce.

The Ambassador slumped back in his chair. "God what a mess, I simply had no idea. What do I do?"

"Clean house Sir," said Jack. "Take more interest in your staff and their comings and goings" Your new M.A. should instigate completely new security procedures and standing orders including being approached by outside sources all of which contacts must be reported. However it is not my job. I have informed you. I have returned your Range Rover with thanks. Anstruther has the keys and is aware he has shot his bolt. Perhaps these keys should be retrieved immediately in case he considers doing a runner."

"He will have done so by now" said the Ambassador.

"No. I believe he is, ah, resting" said Jack with a smile, "but I would secure the keys sooner rather than later"

Douglas stood, as did the Ambassador. "You are a hard man Douglas, you don't pull punches and are certainly not Diplomatic, but I have to say, thank you as he extended his hand. Jack shook the proffered hand and said

"No. Your Excellency, you are right no time for Diplomacy. Not my job, but I do actually still retain respect for your position and the of course, the Crown.

Douglas gathered his equipment and walked out to one of Alfonso's hard top Police Land Rovers which had been earmarked for his use. Apart from the driver who greeted him with a wide grin, there were two other Policemen in the rear armed with the ubiquitous AK 47 assault rifle. All looked alert and the weapons clean and oiled. Alfonso had insisted on a three man team as the threat level had risen and they were at his disposal until Jack left Angola. A fresh team would switch every 24 hours.

Jack was impressed that the Land Rover provided appeared quite new and was again, the powerful V8 rather than the somewhat sluggish 110 diesel.

Another thank you to Alfonso, he thought.

"Back to the villa boys" he said

On arrival he told the team to remain on stand by but go to the kitchen for some food and water. "Get some rest but be ready to reinforce your compadres" he added.

Getting a bit paranoid he thought.

He met Sylvette as she was coming down the stairs accompanied by Judy looking rested and much calmer. The former was as bubbly as ever, dressed in peach coloured slacks and a white silk blouse. Judy also looked well and had borrowed a filmy summer frock from Sylvette as they were both similar size, and actually smiled a welcome.

"Bollinger I think girls, and a late luncheon or have you already eaten"

"No we were waiting for you" as she took the proffered glass with a her head cocked over and a slightly bemused smile on her face"

Douglas was relieved that the indiscretion of the night before had seemingly been forgotten, or at least filed away, He wished to remain firm friends with this lovely Lady but God, she is pretty he thought as she flashed him another smile over the top of her crystal glass.

After luncheon an Embassy car arrived to convey Judy Wiltshire back to her home. Jack had pressed on her his invitation to stay longer but she had gracefully declined and seemed now to have a firm resolve to sort out her life. He promised her that she would be reassigned within the Embassy and would not be returning to her position with the Military Attache.

Thereafter Jack contacted Captain Ramirez and asked him to join him and Alfonso for supper at the Barracuda that evening.. He really just wished to check on any new Intel Ramirez had received and commend him for the way he had acted during the exercise and after the theft of the diamonds. His troops had acquitted themselves well but he still felt guilt that if the exercise had not been on and the squad not loaded with blank ammunition, then several more of his men would still be alive.

He liked Ramirez and his professionalism and wanted all ends to be 'squared away'.

Papa was also going home to check with his son that all was secure, to which Douglas had agreed knowing he now had the further support of the UN Police contingent but told him to be back by 21.00 hrs.

CHAPTER 34

Douglas had decided to leave the next day on the TAP flight to Lisbon then on to London and had booked his usual seat. He would report to General Bruce on arrival for a full debrief and then fly to Amsterdam for his rendezvous with Hamish Duncan and Maggie at the Hotel Grand Krasnapolsky.

He had almost finished packing for the flight, Anna had laundered all his clothes and he had arranged with the Embassy that he would drop off his weapons to be sent back to London in the 'diplomatic bag'. Alfonso had insisted in personally driving him to the airport. He felt content and also realised that nothing more could have been achieved on either operation, official or clandestine without the great assistance of his friends and Lady Luck who, for once had been on his side.

He was looking forward to his last meal at the Barracuda.

He dressed, had a glass of wine with Sylvette who made a 'moue' about being excluded from dinner which nearly changed his mind, kissed her lightly on both cheeks and holding her hands said, see you later for a nightcap.

His police Land Rover and guards were ready, he spoke quietly to

Sergio about the guard disposition at the Villa reminded him that Papa would be back by 21.00 and glancing at the large, spotlit UN banner drooping on the flagstaff above the gate, set off for the Barracuda.

. . . .

Gallagher and Ponce watched from the shadowy cover of the trees below 'Millionaires Row' as the Land Rover pulled out from the compound and the gates swung closed. They could not see who was inside but counted two bodies in the front.

"That reduces the defence a bit" Gallagher spat "the bitch is in there and Douglas should be there too. We'll wait another ten then go".

He looked over at the two and a half ton truck which had been fitted with three huge steel upright bars welded on to the front bumper and at the .50 calibre machine gun mounted on the cab roof already loaded with a belt of ball and tracer. The brass links gleaming in the early moonlight.

The back cover was off and he had seven of Ponce' s men excluding the machine gunner, heavily armed awaiting the assault. Ponce would drive with him riding shotgun.

Ten men he thought and with the .50 Cal. should be more than enough.

The time was 19.59 hrs

With the powerful engine roaring the truck charged from the trees, bucked up the slope towards the gates and as soon as it was on level ground the base baritone of the .50 Cal opened up hosing down the Angolan Police sentries on the outside who were tossed aside as if they were dirty unwanted cloths and then concentrated fire on the gates.

The truck rammed through the gates which splintered and yawed open, skidding to a halt in the compound. Another Police guard had been unlucky to be running across to aid his companions and was crushed under the wheels.

The attackers debussed and the machine gun chewed away the centre and locks of the front doors then switched to the UN Truck backed up to the wall whose tank ignited in a whoosh lighting up the scene. Two UN Police appeared from the side carbines blazing but fell to murderous concentrated fire a third UN officer opened fire from the balcony above the door and dropped two of Alfonso's men but the .50 Cal found him and with rounds chewing up the stone balustrade with little puffs of white dust, found their mark.

A Lull! An all enveloping, sudden and piercing silence, the smell of cordite, blood and death heavily in the air. The fire from the burning truck outlined the harsh ruthless features of the attackers.

"Come on" yelled Gallagher. "Attack" as he paused to allow three of his troops to crash forward in to the villa as 'cannon fodder'

Inside, Sergio had been in the act of loading one of the AK47's when the attack started. He urgently signalled to Sylvette and Anna to keep down behind the marble centre console and Anna grabbed the other AK slammed in a 30 round banana magazine and cycled the action eyes blazing. Sergio switched off the main lights in the fuse box and hit the outside floodlights and the alarm which immediately started to wail. Phone for help he said to Sylvette who grabbed the kitchen phone off the wall - if you can't get through use the radio as he slithered his VHF set across the floor. We are heavily outnumbered.

Get through to the Police, Military, Embassy - any one - we need immediate assistance.

He belly rolled through the batwing kitchen doors coming up behind the heavy drinks cabinet which was part of a low stone wall. He triple tapped short bursts from his rifle at the now back lit attackers dropping two but was immediately targeted by four or five other rifles. He was caught by a ricocheting round in his left thigh which he knew had cut the artery as blood fountained from the wound. He changed magazines, switched to full automatic and fired at two more figures one letting out a cry and somersaulting backwards over a sofa. He was then punched several times in the chest by the sheer weight of incoming fire and died with his finger still curled on the trigger emptying the magazine.

"Find them" Bellowed Gallagher. "I want Douglas and the bitch" Opening the kitchen door he was met with withering fire from Anna, a round nicking his cheek and opening up a 4 inch long crease.

"Wait till she changes mags" he said "then you three go".

They heard the distinctive click of the firing pin falling on an empty magazine. The designated three charged through rifles blazing but Anna had re-loaded and killed two before Ponce took off the back of her head with a long burst.

Gallagher found the fuse box switched on the house light to see Sylvette crouched on the floor, telephone in hand mouth open in a silent scream.

Ponce reached her and ripped the phone from the wall.

"Miss Dubois" he said in a cold voice from the pits of Hell, How nice to renew our acquaintance" How many more in the house and where's Douglas? "

Sylvette. Stood, looked at the bloody mess on the floor which had been Anna and screamed" you murdering pig you bloody bastard. . . ." Gallagher backhanded her across the mouth and then hard again from the other side.

"Search the house" he said to his last remaining gunmen, quickly. Sylvette raised her arm to strike him which he deflected easily then she spat straight in his face.

"Well, you got spirit girl. Pity "

Ponce returned with his men, "the house is empty, let's get out of here before all hell breaks loose"

Gallagher lowered his pistol slightly and shot Sylvette through the right knee who collapsed to the kitchen floor. He stepped behind her and double tapped her in the back of the head, blood and tissue splattering over the tiled wall.

"God" said Ponce "did you have to do that? It was Douglas we were after"

"A lesson, this will hurt him more" as he picked up a chef's pastry brush, dipped in her blood and scrawled 'a diamond for a diamond' across the kitchen wall.

"Vehicle coming" said one of Ponce's men.

"Take cover" as the incoming headlights hit the yard and lit up the truck and bodies. The vehicle lurched to a stop.

"Hit it" yelled Gallagher recognising the Range Rover Douglas had been using as all four opened up. Bits flew from the Rover the side windows and windscreen shattered, the engine wheezed to a deathly rattle, shot to pieces and the figure behind the wheel was thrown back by multiple hits.

"Cover me" he shouted as he crouched in a half run to ensure the occupant was dead. He immediately saw that it was not Douglas but some British Officer, a Colonel with several holes across his chest and neck.

"Hard luck laddie, wrong place, wrong time and wrong car" but at least that's another British Officer dead - call that a bonus.

"Lets go" His truck had been turned to face the gates by the machine gunner who now scrambled to re take his place loading another belt into the gun. The engine was still running.

Ponce dived behind the wheel his men scrambling for the rear and Gallagher just managing to get in the passenger door as the truck picked up speed.

The second UN Police truck slewed across the exit half blocking the road and rapid fire stitched across the truck windscreen which starred and shattered covering the occupants with flying glass shards. Almost blind Ponce floored the accelerator and with bellowing engine the heavy truck shouldered the jeep aside flipping it over, skidded around it and disappeared in to the night.

One of the UN Policemen was mangled under the jeep the other two had superficial wounds only.

The time was 20.12!

The whole assault had taken less than thirteen minutes.

Papa Rock was returning to the villa when he saw three police vehicles with sirens and lights blazing, speeding up the road.

An icy hand clutched at his heart as he knew something was very wrong. He accelerated up behind them reaching for his sidearm.

One Police unit had stopped outside and debussed four armed Officers the other two were in the compound as was a fourth Police Rover and an ambulance. The vehicle doors were ajar, the blue and red lights and the headlights throwing macabre shapes of colour on the utter devastation which met his eyes. Having skidded to a halt in front of the gates he produced his ID recognised one of the Sergeants to whom he explained he worked for Douglas and was living here and was urgently waved through.

He took in at a glance the burnt out UN vehicle the smashed gates and doors, the many pockmarked building the ripped up bodies on the ground and that all pervasive smell of death.

Two Angolan Policemen came out the front door, the younger of whom was violently ill

Papa and the Sergeant were pointed towards the kitchen. More bodies sprawled on the marble floor in the twisted throes of death. The grisly scene was even more stark as all the dimmers had been turned up. To the right he saw Sergio, obviously dead, but with one hand still clutching his rifle pointing over the bar as if to say 'I am still trying to protect you'

He steeled himself for what lay behind the kitchen doors. The house was silent as if holding its breath disbelieving the terror of the last hour.

He eased open the bullet splattered doors which shrieked in protest. Stepping over two of Ponce's men he went to Anna crumpled in the corner with her rifle still in her hands, the tears came to his eyes, then he quailed as he saw Sylvette's body on the floor behind the island and the writing daubed in vicious red on the wall.

He fell to his knees and gently lifted her in his bear like arms cradling her damaged head and a harsh keening sound came from his mouth. His eyes were now flooded by tears and his chest was heaving up and down. Ever so gently he picked up a fallen linen napkin from the floor and tried to bandage her devastated face. She was already cold!

"You shouldn't touch her" said the Sergeant.

"Get out, get out, leave me" he said and the Sergeant quietly left the kitchen.

Ten minutes later he heaved a great sigh and gently let Sylvette slip back to the floor. He emerged from the kitchen tears still shining on his face as one of the surviving UN Police approached "Jeez fella, where are you hit" seeing the mass of Sylvette's blood all over the front of his shirt.

"Not mine" as he pushed aside whipped a white table cloth from the dining room table and returned to cover Sylvette.

His brain clicked up a gear. Ok first tell Jack and Alfonso at the Barracuda. Second try to get some idea of how this had happened and third "revenge", grieving will come later.

The UN Sergeant was still by his side. "Do you know what happened? The chain of events., and where were you."

Looking slightly uneasy he explained that his patrol only arrived at the end of the action but we took out at least three. Our radios had been playing up so I had taken one of the Jeeps further up the hill for better reception and was speaking to HQ when the shit hit the fan. We could see and hear the attack clearly and my driver in his haste to turn our jeep dropped the rear wheels in to a culvert in the dark. It took three to four minutes for us to rock it out but I was on the radio at all times giving a contact report and a QRF was despatched although it would take 30 minutes from camp.

We arrived back here just as the enemy truck came barrelling out with a bloody great machine gun blazing away. It bulldozed past my vehicle flipping it on its side killing one of my men.

We two, pointing at his companion receiving attention for a flesh wound in his arm were already out and firing.

The Angolan Police arrived a few minutes after.

"I have lost four men KIA." he continued.

Papa turned from him brusquely thinking I have lost much more then turned back grasping him by the shoulder.

"You did the best you could - just circumstance. Wait here for your own QRF then throw out a perimeter. Nothing moves from this house, nothing and nobody. I don't care if the Angolan police disagree. You have command "as he pointed up to the UN flag now stirring in the light breeze.

CHAPTER 35

Papa stumbled to his truck and drove to the Barracuda. Mounting the kerb and scattering the street urchins who screamed at the sight of him covered in blood he left the engine running, the headlights on and the door swinging in the breeze. One of the taller boys, recognising him shouted "I look after car Papa, no worry"

He pushed past the doorman and two waiters who, seeing his state, tried to stop him entering. He saw Jack, Alfonso and Ramirez and made straight for the table. A hush descended on the restaurant with all eyes staring at him, aghast.

Jack saw him, saw the blood got half way to his feet then slumped back down with an anguished look on his face.

"The Villa's been hit". Papa just nodded.

Ramirez and Alfonso grabbed the big man to steady him and shouted for a Doctor and a Brandy not realising that the blood was not his and that he had not been wounded.

Papa sat.

"Sylvette?" Jack asked with a pleading look in his eyes. The big man just held up his hands covered in her blood, still taking great sobs and gulps of air to try to assuage the pain.

Jack's face was ashen.

Alfonso strode to a phone shouting for his driver to get on his radio for a SITREP.

Ramirez was out on the verandah speaking on his radio, returning with a grim, set face. "I can do more from my headquarters, anything you need right now?" looking at Jack who returned his look with a blank stare and a shake of the head.

A waiter arrived at the table with a large Brandy balloon half filled with Cognac which Papa swallowed in two gulps, and a bowl of warm water to wash his hands.

He immersed his hands immediately turning the water pink.

"The executed her Jack, they bloody executed her!" he finally said, "and killed Sergio and little Anna".

Douglas stirred and snapped himself out of his stupor. His eyes turned to flint.

He suddenly understood that Papa in his way had been in love with Sylvette from afar, all those many years.

Plan, think, regroup, he thought, revenge is a dish best served "HOT".

He stood up, took the big man by the hand and quietly led him from the Barracuda.

"Ready Jack? I will drive you up".

"No, I will take Papa's truck, could you take him home to his son?" Alfonso nodded stating that he would come to the Villa later.

Douglas walked towards the truck his mind in turmoil. The street urchin was sitting on the bonnet, unbeknown to Jack he had turned off the engine and lights and had the keys in his hand.

"You friend of Mr Papa" he said. Jack nodded "OK here keys. You tell Mr Papa we all sorrow for troubles. No charge tonight"

Jack nodded. Bush telegraph he thought, but that's the only way these youngsters can show sympathy. I shall certainly tell Papa when he is more composed.

At the Villa the two surviving UN policemen approached him. "We're truly sorry Mr Douglas, we did what we could. It's carnage in there".

Again Jack simply nodded and walked past grim faced hardly noticing Anstruther's body behind the wheel of the riddled Range Rover.

Inside the house he followed the battle line towards the kitchen where Orderlies were carrying out the bodies of Ponce's men to the waiting ambulances. Sergio, Anna and Sylvette had not been moved.

He caught his breath as he saw Sylvette's crumpled bloody body on the kitchen floor.

Gently, he eased the blood soaked sheet from her body. Looking at her cruelly smashed head and knee. He knew without a doubt that it was Gallagher's handiwork, confirmed by the blood smeared message on the wall

"You bastard, I'll get you, vengeance is mine"

Alfonso appeared, standing a little way behind to allow some privacy. He had also been a long term friend of Sylvette and was grief stricken at the waste of this vibrant young life.

"Help me Alfonso" Jack said as he bent to take the lifeless form under her shoulders.

"My honour" Both men carried her upstairs to her bedroom with as much quiet dignity as possible.

They laid her shattered body on the bed.

Straightening, Jack asked Alfonso to instruct his men to do the same for Sergio and Anna after all this was their home now dreadfully violated.

"Certainly, I shall await your further contact later". quietly leaving and softly closing the bedroom door.

Jack looked down at the ravaged, once beautiful face and wept. He took up a towel, wetting it from a glass of Bollinger by her bedside, and cleaned her face as best he could.

She would like that, he almost smiled, not water, her last 'nightcap'.

Taking another towel he bandaged her shattered head as if she were wearing a turban having just washed her hair, took one long last look at her once sparkling eyes now devoid of light, closed them gently, softly kissed her lids and her cold lips and vowed his silent oath.

He sat beside her for half an hour holding her hand till her body became ice cold. His thoughts and emotions were tumbling in his head but mostly, My Fault, my fault - I should have been here!

There was a soft knock on the door. Alfonso and Ramirez both came in to pay their respects and say a personal Goodbye, then silently left.

Jack arose, and with one last squeeze of her lifeless fingers, softly closed the door.

Chapter 36

The following day dawned with haze over Luanda and a sea har over the Lagoon softening the outlines of buildings and ships in the harbour. The Hispaniola appeared to be floating on a cloud as only her upper works and funnel were visible. There was not a breath of wind.

It was as if the City, appalled by the happenings of the night before was trying to cloak them in this soft ethereal light to soften the anguish and sadness.

Douglas had been woken from a restless sleep by Judy Wiltshire expressing her shock and insisting she come over to help with the arrangements. He asked her if she could cancel his flights for him, re book for tomorrow and go to the Embassy to send a brief signal to the General. He was not in the mood to talk to anyone.

Papa arrived dressed as was his mood, in a sombre fashion. It was obvious he too had, had a hard night with little sleep. His face was lined with grief.

Jack shook him by the hand. "I didn't know" he said "I had no idea you loved her, why didn't you tell her?"

Papa looked at him with big sad eyes "Better to love from a distance rather than be spurned. She was out of my class"

They settled down in what remained of the drawing room which was being cleared up and returned to some semblance of order by two of Alfonso's men. Carpenters were working on the house doors and the gates effecting temporary repairs. Cleaners were tackling the hideous state of the kitchen and washing down the walls.

Jack had been in contact with the American Mission who had taken over the funeral arrangements, Sylvette was Catholic and they had a Priest on their staff. She was to be flown to Switzerland after the funeral and interred in her family crypt in the little village of St Cerque perched on the mountain overlooking Lake Geneva and Mont Blanc

The Service was to be held on board the 'Hispaniola' at 15.00 hrs after which she would be transferred to the ship's launch which would take her across the lagoon to a waiting hearse and escorted to the airport. Papa Rock was going to travel with her on this last journey.

Sergio and Anna were to return to Portugal to be buried on the family Estate.

He had had a long telephone call with Maggie which had picked him up a little. The two girls had never met but she knew that he had been, and was very fond of Sylvette. Her support, concern and love which flowed down the line strengthened his resolve for the day ahead.

With this strength he faced the day.

Douglas had forgotten Anstruther's death until a Recovery truck arrived to take the shredded Range Rover back to the Embassy. He felt no sympathy for the 'mistaken identity' He had disliked him intensely but even he should not have suffered such a death. He thought his whole involvement would be hushed up. There could be no Courts Martial, post mortem. He would no doubt be buried with Military Honours and the files on his wrong doings buried with him.

Judy Wiltshire arrived with a nurse from the Hospital to attend to Sylvette's wounds and clean her up the best they could. An unpleasant and difficult task.

They had all concurred in the decision for a closed casket.

The undertakers arrived with a beautiful sand coloured hardwood coffin with brass and black roped handles. At Jack's instructions and after conferring with Papa, there was a simple brass plate on the lid which bore the words:

'Sylvette'

A flame extinguished, now

Another bright star in the night sky.

Judy appeared behind him deeply upset by the task she and the Nurse had just completed.

"She is ready Jack" she said softly. "would you like to say a final Goodbye"

"Yes" he said hoarsely, "and thank you both "

He turned for the stairs mounting them with bowed shoulders. He entered her room where the drapes had been half closed and saw her lying on the bed dressed in a simple white shift. Her head had been expertly bandaged and was dressed in a silk veil. Her neck was bound in another soft yellow silk scarf, her favourite colour, covering the hideous exit wounds.

Her pale face wore no make up and Judy had cleverly arranged her hair which had lost its deep sheen, to frame her face and lie across her breasts. Her hands were crossed on her chest and she wore one sapphire ring on her right hand and a gold and platinum chain bracelet on her left wrist

Jack stood beside her for some time. God even in death you are still beautiful he thought.

He stooped down and lightly brushed her cold lips with his.

"Goodbye, dear Girl" he said "Fly with the Angels"

He softly closed the door and nodded to the undertakers. "You can go in now. Be gentle with her and take her downstairs. The lid shall be put on there"

Ten minutes later they re-appeared with the casket and placed it on two trestles they had provided.

Judy took Jack's hand and went forward. She had picked some yellow and white flowers in the gardens and made a small bouquet which she placed in Sylvette's hands. Her face seemed to have softened, seemingly at peace.

Neither spoke and stepped back to allow the Undertakers to secure the lid and take her in the hearse with the waiting Police motorcycle escort to her 'last party' on the Hispaniola.

Papa had declined to see Sylvette again. "She will always be in my mind's eye "he said "I shall remember her loveliness in life not in death"

Judy left, returning home to get dressed for the Service. She would be travelling with the Ambassador and his wife.

Douglas had arranged to meet Papa, Alfonso and Captain Ramirez at the Barracuda for a private toast before the funeral. His Police driver dropped him off just as Alfonso arrived with Ramirez, both in dress uniforms sporting black armbands. Papa arrived a few seconds later immaculately dressed in a black suit and tie and a pale yellow shirt and handkerchief in his top pocket. He noticed Jack's slightly raised eyebrow.

"For Sylvette" he said with a soft smile "her favourite colour".

The four friends entered the restaurant and were immediately shown to their usual table overlooking the Ocean. A respectful quiet pervaded the room and there were few other clients that day.

Sylvette often frequented The Barracuda when she needed to escape her guests on board - it was only 800 metres away - all knew of her shocking death.

The Maitre, shook hands with all four, saying what a tragedy, then ushered the Sommelier forward with a bottle of Vintage Krug in the ice bucket. "The best in the house for Miss Dubois"

The mist and sea har had suddenly cleared with a soft onshore breeze. rippling the waves and sparkling the Ocean. It was a beautiful day.

The four charged their glasses and stood, all looking out over the sea. Jack looked at Papa who shook his head imperceptibly,

"To Sylvette" he said "Brutally taken from us. The world is a far darker place without you. May you have fair winds at your back, the sun shine on your face and soft rain on your hair. Sorely missed!"

 "Sorely missed" echoed the other three.

They emptied their glasses stepped to the railing and with Papa first, shattered them on the rocks below. Returning to the table in sombre mood fresh glasses were recharged and they sat in heavy silence all lost in their own thoughts.

The funeral on the Hispaniola was elegant yet informal. The huge new Ensign at the stern fluttered at half mast, and the guard rails were draped in black. The burnished coffin sitting on trestles before a temporary altar gleamed like gold in the afternoon sun. The Company flag draped the coffin and also flew at half mast from the main cross trees.

The Catholic priest led the Service with Papa giving a soft spoken, emotional Eulogy.

There were probably two hundred people on the aft deck that day, where Jack had sipped champagne with her those few short days ago, from Ambassadors, Government Ministers, Members of the police force, Military and Navy, friends, to staff and crew members in their whites. Even the President had sent a message of sympathy.

She had touched so many lives.

The Service over, the coffin was moved to the ship's side where a section of guard rail had been removed, attached to two davits and slowly lowered by two immaculately dressed ships' Officers to the waiting launch below. Barber's 'Adaggio for Strings' had been softly playing on the ship's music system.

A Police Piper on the top deck, courtesy of Alfonso, played the haunting lament 'Flowers of the Forest' as the coffin reached the ship's launch where it was carefully placed on the fore deck by four more of the ship's crew who the stood at each corner with heads bowed. The Launch's ensigns were also at half mast.

Jack and Papa stood at the rail looking down both choked with emotion. The launch cast off and slowly bore away across the smooth surface of the lagoon towards the waiting hearse.

One long blast from the ship's horn shattered the silence, answered by a similar blast from the launch and the Angolan gun boat who dipped her Ensign.

"Gone away" thought Jack as he gripped the rail Other vessels around the Port also sounded their own salute. He was actually unnerved by just how many people wished to pay their respects. It was as if the whole of Luanda wished to bear the grief.

Papa, Alfonso and Ramirez left to join the cortège to the Airport at the other side of the Lagoon to accompany Sylvette on her last journey on Angolan soil.

As they rounded the causeway, the coffin was being placed in the hearse behind which stood three gleaming black Mercedes on Government plates. The Company flag had been removed and the three flags of Angola, France and Switzerland now draped over. There was one simple bouquet of white and yellow flowers on top.

Somewhat perplexed at the Government vehicles Papa turned to Alfonso with an unspoken query.

"The Commissioner himself, authorised the use of the cars. Sylvette did a lot of good work for our Government and was a close friend of many in high places. A few of those you saw on the ship"

"I know" said Papa "Sylvette worked for the Angolan Government?"

"Let's just say she was a good friend to Angola!"

Douglas, having changed his mind, arrived as the three were talking. Papa took his hand "Good, you made it Jack" he said "Sylvette will be pleased."

They approached the second car. "who's in the first car he said, it looks armoured, not Dos Santos?"

"Yes" said Ramirez with a deadpan face "it is the President and the First Lady. The people know his car this way he shows his support and personal grief for the death of Sylvette who I believe dined with him on several occasions but he will not be alighting at the Airport.

That is why all cars are flying the Angolan flag as does the hearse, and the strength of the military and Police escort as he indicated the armoured cars and motorcycles around.

"Well I never Sylvette" he said through his sadness "a spy for the

Angolan Government"

"She didn't want you to know Jack. We were even working together when you were last here. Who do you think helped in your extraction"

The cortège wound sedately away from the water's edge. Police outriders in front and Officers on every junction holding traffic, who saluted as the hearse went by. At the airport they swept through the open gates at General aviation straight on to the apron where the cavernous rear door of an Illuyshin transport in Angolan colours yawned open, awaiting their arrival.

Eight of Ramirez's men were there to receive the coffin and with military precision and with bare heads raised it to their shoulders and slow marched towards the ramp.

Douglas again heard the mournful drone of bagpipes and saw two ex Ghurkha pipers, now working for IDS at the Embassy, stood, in full dress, on either side of the ramp.

The lament sounding eerily in the evening darkness.

It was almost too much for him and certainly too much for Papa as the tears rolled down his huge face.

Alfonso and Ramirez came to attention and snapped up a salute as the coffin disappeared in to the cavernous hold.

The lead Mercedes turned away with its outriders as Alfonso and Ramirez again saluted, their President.

Douglas had no idea that she had been so important to the Angolan Government and so well liked.

As the tail gate began to close the great engines started up ready for immediate take off.

His eyes turned to steel

"No more tears, Sylvette" he said aloud "just a promise, I'll get him no matter how long it takes"

At that the two old friends turned disconsolately to their car for the ride back to the City.

CHAPTER 37

Douglas had managed to get a seat on the TAP flight to Lisbon, courtesy of Judy who had cajoled the local Line Station Manager. His connecting flight to Heathrow landed at 19.45 hrs. He admitted to himself that he was tired and somewhat drained and thus decided not to go home but stay in his Club, the Cavalry and Guards Club on Piccadilly. Maggie would already be in Amsterdam and his flight the following day was at 10.40 hrs.

He only had cabin baggage as his other case and 'specialist' baggage was being delivered courtesy of the Foreign Office.

He had been unable to reserve one of the larger 'single Officers rooms' on the third floor overlooking Green Park but had managed to get one of the lovely 'married Officer's rooms' on the fourth floor.

He was looking forward to a long bath and a relaxed dinner in the Ladies dining room. The 'Coffee room' which was the Member's dining room was only open for breakfast and luncheon and single Officers staying in the club dined at a large rectangular table set for fourteen at one end of the Ladies dining room overlooking the park. This was commonly referred to as 'the Cad's Table'. One could either engage in conversation with fellow Members or dine silently without the necessity of small talk. The latter option was what he hoped to achieve.

Striding towards the airport exit and then to the taxi rank he found a Government Daimler waiting for him with the driver outside holding a white card with Col. Douglas written in large red letters.

"I'm Douglas" he said.

"Fine sir" said the driver who from the bulge under his loosely tailored uniform jacket, was wearing a shoulder holster. "May I see some ID"

Douglas handed over his passport and after a careful check he was ushered towards the black windowed rear door which was held open to find General Kendall in the rear wearing dinner jacket and white silk scarf.

"Thought I would meet you myself" he said extending his hand. "I'm on my way to a dinner in the City. Sorry it was so rough and so sorry about Sylvette Dubois. I know you go way back and were good friends"

"Yes Bruce, we were." as he settled into the sumptuous cream leather. He always dropped the General's rank in private.

"Thank you for meeting me on such a foul evening but it matches my mood" The heavy rain drummed on the roof and the wipers were on fast action to clear the windscreen but the big car was still doing over 80mph on the M4 into London, effortlessly controlled by an obviously very experienced driver.

"Debrief tomorrow early then David, nodding at the driver, will take you back to Heathrow for your Amsterdam flight. Checked with the Club no rooms on the third floor but you have a double on the fourth.

How the Hell did he know I was going to Amsterdam he thought. I didn't tell him and made the booking myself. Oh well I suppose it is his job to know.

"By the way. Told Maggie you were arriving this evening. Get in touch" he said with a twinkle in his eye, she is worried about you."

"Yes I also told her I was back today but she is not here - some family stuff, hence me not going home. I just hope the valet has my trunk out of the locker and has sponged and pressed my suits and ironed the folds out of some shirts. I do look a bit disreputable" looking down at his wrinkled cotton trousers and creased linen jacket.

Arriving at the Club he retrieved his key from the Porter and walked down the corridor to the lift. On the fourth floor he was just putting his key in the lock when the door was flung open by Maggie who launched herself at him, grabbed him round the neck and gave him a long kiss. His momentary surprise gone he held her tightly and bent down to kiss her again - she was a good 12 inches shorter in stature.

"God" he said "it's good to see you. I thought you left for Amsterdam yesterday. Maggie pulled him inside the door where he dropped his bag and kissed her again. "a sight for sore eyes"

She looked ravishing, ash blonde hair glistening, blue eyes sparkling with just a faint heightened redness on her cheeks She was already dressed for dinner in a simple dark blue cashmere dress, wearing his Father's locket around her neck which he had given to her many years ago.

He couldn't take his eyes off her and still clutched her hand.

"Go and have a bath" she smiled at him in a coquettish way, I'll open the Bolli. Jeffrey kindly let me have the silver ice bucket from his bar, the one he thinks is his own property"

Jack laughed. "have you another dress with you" he said.

"Why, do you not like this one?"

"Yes I do but it's going to get a bit wrinkled" as he lunged towards her and as she let out a shriek they both collapsed on the bed.

Half an hour later, lying entwined, passion spent, he eased himself from under her arm and walked naked to the bottle of Grand Annee.

"It looks as if you are ready for the second round" she said with an impish grin.

"Uh, Uh, wine, bath, supper and then to bed we have a lot to discuss." Pouring the wine he said "just the one Mrs Wembley?" using an old joke between them.

"Just the one Sam" as she raised her glass in silent toast. God I'm glad you are back safe . . .

CHAPTER 38

The morning dawned bright and still. Douglas had arranged to meet with the General at his Mews house just off Gloucester Road in Petersham Mews and as it was only a mile from the Club decided to walk through the Park past Knightsbridge barracks.

He told Maggie to have a leisurely breakfast and be ready to leave for the Airport at 11.30 hrs.

Walking briskly through the park he marshalled his thoughts and the details of the past frenetic days in Angola isolating what not to include in his report to Bruce Kendall.

Knocking on the Mews door at two minutes to nine o'clock it was opened directly by the General. A smell of fresh roasted coffee assailed his nostrils.

"Morning Jack" said the General, "coffee?"

"Morning, yes thanks, black with a spoonful of honey if you have any"

"Yes, I recall your preference"

They both moved through the exquisitely furnished drawing room to the surprisingly large kitchen at the rear which was as expensively spartan as the drawing room was elegant. It was obvious to the eye that the General lived alone with his Valet/bodyguard who had been with him in the Regiment. There was no sign of female influence his wife having sadly died some six years previously

They sat down at the centre island which was strewn with classified files.

"I made an early start" said Kendall. I am fully up to speed just need to hear about a couple of aspects of the operation from the horse's mouth" He then began dissecting the various reports and intel. with exacting precision and clarity. It was 10.30 hrs when they finished.

Rising from his chair he said. "Last two things. I now appreciate I should have told you that Sylvette Dubois was in fact a double Agent working both for the Angolan Government and me. Her tragic death is most regrettable. She was a lovely person and very skilled. There will be posthumous decorations in line"

You hard old bastard, Douglas thought, you don't really care about her death just that you have lost a valuable asset, or, looking him directly in his eyes he thought he glimpsed a flash of sorrow, quickly shielded - or maybe you do. . .!

"I knew you two had history and didn't want to cloud matters.

The second thing is that Gallagher is still at large and we believe he is now in central Europe so watch your back. I'll have my driver take you back to the Club then Heathrow for some well earned leave.

Thank you Jack. I don't suppose I can entice you back to the fold after you are rested"

"Not a chance," said Douglas, "hopefully this will be the last time I am involved in your Machiavellian intrigues."

"Well, I wish you good luck. Give my regards to Maggie. You know where I am if you ever change your mind"

There was a tap at the door, both men shook hands. The same driver from last night was waiting with the General's gleaming black Daimler.

From the silent luxury of the big car Jack reflected on the last hour and a half. The General was a good man doing a hard job and someone who could not afford sentimentality however the two of them were firm friends and he was sure that he would be kept an eye on for the next few months in case trouble surfaced. It was a good feeling of extra security.

The Daimler swished to a halt in front of the Club on the double yellow lines.

"I'll be about half an hour, if you are moved on and have to go around the block"

"Don't worry about that Sir, No one moves this car. I shall be right here"

No, they probably don't he thought, exited and strode across the Club hall towards the lift, asking for his account to be prepared.

He knocked on the room door as he had left the key, swiftly opened by Maggie all set to travel and almost all packed. She was used to his exactness as far as timings were concerned and unlike most women was normally ready.

He gave her a light kiss and said. "Right, let's get out of here, the car's at the door"

"How was your meeting with Bruce"

"Fine, just fine. Business over, pleasure awaits" as he picked up his carry on bag and her suitcase. His own clothes still lay around but the Club Valet would ensure all were laundered, pressed and consigned once again to the trunk in his locker ready for his next visit.

Maggie, knew not to press him for detail as he simply would not disclose same. His was a mind of one door closed, next one open, Sometimes it vexed her but today, forward to the Krasnapolsky.

CHAPTER 39

Hamish Duncan had been staying at the Krasnapolsky for two days before Jack and Maggie arrived. He was waiting for them in the elegant Foyer.

"Good to see you both" he said in his soft Highland twang. Looking searchingly at Jack and kissing Maggie on both cheeks. If you hadn't arrived today I would have had to check out. Have you any idea how much this place costs?"

"We were a bit delayed - family business" he said with a grin "and I had to see the General. I believe we have adjoining suites"

"Suites is it" said Hamish. "my room is bigger than my flat at home"

"Good to see you dressed in something better than jeans and that old oily Fairisle sweater. I'll just check in, see Maggie settled then come through to your suite.

"Aye, OK."

Approaching the Reception desk the Head Porter appeared at his side with a hand delivered letter addressed to him c/o the Hotel. "Welcome back Sir, this letter was delivered this morning with specific instructions to place it immediately in your hands on your arrival"

Jack was impressed he remembered who he was as he hadn't stayed here for over three years, or maybe he had been discreetly pointed out as his passport lay open on the reception desk.

"Thank you" placing the envelope in his inside jacket pocket.

The formalities over they proceeded to their respective rooms.

Maggie and Jack decided to shower and change. It was always amazing how dirty one felt after air travel even although one had only showered 4/5 hours before. The suite had two bathrooms but that didn't stop them sharing the one shower and soaping each other's backs. Refreshed, Jack told Maggie he had to have a word with Hamish then they would all go for a late luncheon at The White Room on Dam Square, a short walk from the Hotel.

"More secrets and 'derring do' Jack" she said. "Fine with me I shall have my hair done. See you later."

Douglas went next door to Hamish's suite taking the unopened letter with him. Hamish pulled a couple of beers from the fridge and they both sat down on the soft cream leather sofas. Jack then gave Hamish details of the last few days in Luanda after Papa had made his delivery to the trawler including the facts on Gallagher, Anstruther and Belguerro's involvement in the second convoy attack and the subsequent attack on the villa resulting in the execution of Sylvette, and the deaths of Sergio and Anna.

"God the Bastards" said Hamish. I only met Sylvette that one time with you many years ago when you were in Angola with DSL. - a nice Lady!

Does Maggie know the full score?"

"No, and I don't want her to so use 'veiled speech' OK? Suffice it to say this was my last contract and it should prove very lucrative indeed for all concerned. I presume no trouble with Customs when you docked?"

"No none, the pouches were well hidden in the fish hold underneath our last catch which was frozen and was unloaded to the fish factory on arrival. They are still covered by a few fish and a layer of ice but accessible within half an hour. Might smell a bit though when we retrieve them"

"They will smell like bloody roses" said Jack when you know the estimate - "120 million dollars".

Hamish nearly dropped his beer. "God, you said I could re-engine the old girl with funds to spare but not that I could buy two new boats!". Both men stood up, grins splitting their faces, shook hands again grasping each other's shoulders then Hamish decided to attempt a jig, failing dismally.

"Enough" said Jack "a lot still to organise" removing the letter from his pocket. "This should be from our buyer with instructions where and when to meet. I will need a couple of pouches of diamonds for tomorrow morning as samples. Can Malcolm bring them in to the City or do you wish to do it yourself"

"Malcolm's a canny lad, he can handle it"

Jack slit open the envelope, read the instructions and returned it to his pocket.

"Well" said Hamish.

"Best if only I know for everyone's safety. Remember that bastard Gallagher is still around and somewhere in Europe he will be trying to follow the trail.

"OK" said Hamish a bit miffed, "need to know, it is"

We will only achieve at best 50% of the real value because of the size of the delivery and of course the fact that they are stolen. These people will only trickle feed the stones on to the market over the next couple of years. Our payment will be in unaccountable cash in a mixture of Sterling, US dollars and Euros. The split will be four ways which will be around 12.5 million each. You, me and Papa Rock."

That's three" said Hamish.

"The fourth share is for operational costs - I am going to war against Gallagher and I will track him down no matter how long it takes - I promised Sylvette so call that her share. Any left over balance will again be split three ways."

Papa also does not want all that money He wishes half of his share for himself and his extended family the other half to go in to the 'War chest' - he was very, very fond of Sylvette.

Understood, and no argument from me" said Hamish, I'm starving. Let's get Maggie and you can take us to that great restaurant you've been going on about" and until I see the colour of money, you're paying."

Chapter 40

The initial meeting for the contact to the diamond dealer was to be made in the foyer of the Diamond Museum on Paulus Pottersrat. This was a man known by Douglas and who had dealt Blood Diamonds out of Angola many years ago. He was well connected to the massive under level of illicit diamond dealing in Amsterdam and Rotterdam and could 'almost' be trusted

His introduction fee was 10, 000 Euros which Douglas had asked Hamish Duncan to withdraw from the trawler account in bills no bigger than 100 Euros and which was now burning a hole in his pocket. He did not wish a paper trail to directly lead back to him.

The meet was at 12.00 noon, thereafter they would be taken to the Diamond merchant at as yet an unknown address but as he had been informed, within walking distance of the Museum, where the transaction would be finalised

Malcolm was to meet them at 11.50 hrs to hand over the two specimen pouches and then to drop back and shadow them from a discreet distance, watching their backs and watching out for any possible surveillance from third parties. They both carried hand held VHF

Marine radios taken from the Trawler which were fitted with two encrypted personal channels.

Douglas expected the whole operation to be complete by 14.00 hrs.

They arrived at the Museum at 11.45 hrs, spotted Malcolm lingering at one of the exhibits, looking slightly nervous but dressed as any other tourist with a camera around his neck and an Amsterdam guide in his hand. Jack sidled up to him and with a simple 'good morning' the two pouches were switched from jacket pocket to jacket pocket outwith the view of the many security cameras. Malcolm then made an irritating look at his watch and made for the entrance, engulfed by a visiting coach party of Japanese tourists.

Exactly at noon Jack saw his contact walk leisurely through the front door he was also casually dressed and mingled with the crowd. The two made eye contact and with a sideways nod of the head the contact indicated a side door to which all three made their way and exited into the sunshine. No words were spoken, no handshakes offered. To a casual observer there was no connection between the contact and the two men following.

Turning left he quickened his pace and in fifty yards entered a small roadside café which was very busy. Jack and Malcolm followed and found him sitting at a corner table towards the rear with his back to the wall.

Good trade craft, Jack thought. Still hasn't lost his touch.

As they approached the contact stood up and greeted them like old friends, they ordered coffee.

"Jans" good to see you after all these years "your looking fit. This is Hamish." There was no need for surnames. Jans was South African and had been a member of the security team of the South African Mission in Luanda in the early 90's

"And you Jack" he said in his slightly guttural Boer accent. "No time for pleasantries, we drink our coffee and go.

The less we are seen together the better. We are not far away. I shall leave first then you two follow some twenty paces behind on the other side of the road - just amble along like the 'tourists' you are. When I reach the house I will knock and be admitted you will follow and enter, the door will be unlocked just push it open."

"Fine" said Douglas" at the moment we are in your hands but don't you think our meet at the Diamond Museum with all that security was well advised."

"Hiding in plain sight, Jack. Who would expect Diamond smugglers and contacts to meet there"?

Douglas smiled.

"Once I have made the introduction and all is secure I shall leave you to your negotiations" Jans continued

"OK, let's move" said Douglas.

"Ah yes, but you forget you have something for me?

"Of course" said Douglas.

"Just take it out and hand it over quite openly smiling as if it were a present - well I suppose it is" Jans said with a lopsided grin.

With a nod from Jack, Hamish passed the bulky envelope across the table confirming the denominations were as requested which swiftly disappeared into a brown leather lap bag around Jans' waist which he saw also sported a small automatic pistol.

"Can't be too careful. A lot of rogues in this city"

"A canny man" said Hamish. Jack simply nodded his agreement finished his coffee left a ten Euro note on the table and walked back outside.

Jans had turned right and he was easily spotted walking slowly along the road. Jack looked left and saw Malcolm on the other side looking in to a shop window but watching the road in the reflection, He gave a slight nod. Jack reached in to his pocket and pressed the pressor switch on his radio twice. He immediately received one click back from Malcolm. All's well. The only other signals they had arranged were three clicks to be careful, something is not right and five clicks if there was inherent danger.

As instructed the two friends crossed the road keeping Jans in sight until he stopped at a single black door in an old and relatively small three storey building. There was no outward sign as to what lay behind and there were heavy steel bars over all the windows. He knocked and disappeared inside. Jack and Hamish re-crossed the road and with a final glance at Malcolm, swiftly entered the building being surprised by the weight of the door which looked like old wood but was in fact three inches of solid steel. The door softly closed behind them and dead bolts automatically activated.

They were in an ante room beautifully furnished with old highly polished pieces, Persian carpets on an old oak floor and comfortable leather club chairs in front of a elaborate fire place bearing a coat of arms on the mantel. There was a claret coloured thickly carpeted stairway to the right but before gaining access to this staircase a young man, obviously fit and more obviously ex military, arose from behind a desk, immaculately dressed in a charcoal suit white shirt and claret tie matching the carpet.

"Gentlemen" he said. Please empty your pockets in this tray and remove your wristwatches you will receive everything back before you leave.

Jack and Malcolm did as requested. The two diamond pouches he left on the desk. "these will be scanned separately" said the gatekeeper, "and returned to you once you have passed security"

"Now" he said "please face the bottom of the stairs one at a time" As Jack turned he realised that there was an ingenuous scanner set in to the wall and stairway banister which lit up as he approached. At the same time steel plates had silently descended from the ceiling across the stairway and on the stair side of the banister making it impossible for anyone to gain access to the upper floors

Impressive, Jack thought.

Having passed through he was met by Jans on the half landing. The security plates had once again slid in to place waiting for Malcolm to take his turn. The plates rose, Malcolm appeared holding the two diamond pouches.

With a nod from Jans they followed him up to the first floor where they saw a pair of finely carved doors one of which was half open. Jans did not knock but pushed the door open ushering them through. The sun was gleaming through floor to ceiling windows and even although also heavily steel barred did not obstruct its brilliance.

The room was a library with all walls covered in old leather bound books and one magnificent Gold Ormulu Louis Quinze desk facing the door behind which was a small man dressed in Hasidic black.

It was difficult to see him with the sun at his back. He made no attempt to rise.

"Good afternoon" he said in heavily accented English. "Please sit. There will be no introductions I only know your first names and you may refer to me simply as 'the Merchant'. From your presence here you have obviously had a successful trip. What have you to show me"

Malcolm slid the two pouches over the fine desk on top of which he now saw was a black velvet cloth in front of the merchant with one large and one small loupe at the side.

The merchant carefully poured out the uncut stones on to the velvet which sullenly appeared more like soapstones, not reflecting the brilliance yet to be released. There was one particularly large stone which Jack leant forward and set aside.

The Merchant looked at him quizzically and continued his examination without a word.

Eventually he straightened up "Of fine quality he said and untraceable - no laser imprints. The amount and carat weight is as already advised?"

"Yes" said Jack "and in Amsterdam"

"Good, let us begin" and lapsed in to silence waiting for Jack to open

"We have 120 million dollars worth of diamonds" said Douglas. "we expect a large slice to be deducted due to their source and for cutting and polishing. A realistic figure we could accept would be 70 million"

The merchant wheezed and without looking up said "Twenty"

Jack stood up slowly. "gather the stones Malcolm we will not be doing business here"

As Malcolm stretched to recover the diamonds an arthritic hand came out covered in dark liver spots and clawed them towards the Merchant.

"Sit, Sit" he said, "one has to try, that is the game, no offence was intended. Call it my opening Gambit.

Damn near your closing gambit thought Jack but both retook their seats

After an hour of tooing and froing an accord was finally reached at 62 million about 10 million more than Douglas had expected so he was well pleased but kept his features stern and cold. Hamish just sat dumbly.

Arrangements were made for the transfer of the stones and the cash, 12 million, for tomorrow, 16.00 hrs at the Fishing dock where the Trawler was moored.

The cash would be accompanied by the Gatekeeper and in the required currency and denominations who would also verify the diamonds. The balance would be in irreversible Bank Bearer bonds drawn 50% on The Dutch Bank 'ING' and 50% on Deutsche bank, redeemable anywhere in the world.

Douglas had considered an encrypted CHAPS bank transfer but again this would leave a 'paper trail'

Hamish had arranged for some cordage and ships supplies to be delivered by a local Chandler known to the Merchant thus there would be no problem in adding two trunks of 'ships stores' to the delivery nor in transporting the diamonds back to the City

"There is one more matter with which I require your assistance" Douglas said picking up the large raw diamond. "I would like this cut, polished and mounted on a platinum chain"

"That is easily done, all our cutting and skilled technicians are on site and the workshop is on the top floor. I can have this for you within a week"

"Thank you, but I require it by 19.00 hrs this evening. It is important to me"

The Merchant, looked at Jack somewhat askance. "These things should not be rushed, one slip and the diamond will be ruined, however if you insist. . . ." He removed a small phone from his jacket pocket which seemed to be answered immediately, spoke for three minutes in his own language, then nodded to Jack.

"As you wish, but at your risk. If the diamond is damaged through undue haste it is your loss. However as I will have to stop my team on their scheduled work it will cost you 20, 000 Euros. If you wait one week there is no charge. Call it professional courtesy".

"Fine, take 20, 000 from the cash delivery"

The pair got up to leave, silently the Gatekeeper had entered behind them. The Merchant did not rise and said a simple Goodbye.

On the ground floor they retrieved their belongings and radio which Douglas switched on again and transmitted two clicks expecting to receive one click back - all's clear. Instead he received a definite three clicks - be careful. Looking at Hamish he turned to the Gatekeeper.

"Do you have street surveillance?"

With an affirmative nod he pointed at the screen on his desk, he rolled his mouse to bring up the street scene immediately outside the front door and expanded the picture. Malcolm was sitting on a bench on the opposite side of the road apparently consulting his Tourist map. Rolling to the right all seemed normal until he spotted two men of indeterminate origin simply standing outside a shop window but looking at the front door of the Merchant's house. They stood out from the tourist crowd as both were wearing ill cut suits, somewhat crumpled as if they had just stepped off an aeroplane. Both were swarthy with dark hair. One was smoking.

"Trouble?" asked the Gatekeeper.

"Possibly, can you help?"

"There is a secure delivery entrance from the basement which comes out from the house next door and leads to a lane at the rear. Wait whilst I scan the Lane. All clear" he said.

Jack and Hamish followed him down to the basement and up steps to another solid steel door. The Gatekeeper pressed in a code on the security pad and the door swung silently inwards giving access directly on to the lane. He looked both ways, told them to turn right then next left which would take them back towards the Diamond Museum, signifying all clear he ushered them out with a quiet Good Luck.

In the lane Douglas quickly called Malcolm on the radio. Which was answered by one click. Malcolm had an earpiece so all he had to do was listen and respond by clicking the pressor switch in his pocket. He asked if the watchers were still in place, confirmed. He then told him to amble back down to the square, check he was not followed and take two taxis back to the trawler, getting out and walking about a bit before flagging another. They would join him later. Malcolm confirmed with a double click.

Hamish had heard the one sided conversation and was relieved that Malcolm was returning to the dock he asked Jack who he thought the watchers were.

"No idea" could be local 'mafia' who have somehow got a whiff of a possible nefarious deal. Could be Gallagher's foot soldiers. Could even be under cover Dutch police.

We shall just have to be more vigilante"

The two returned to the Hotel agreeing to meet later to go to the Dock for the arranged delivery at 16.00 hrs.

There was a cryptic note from Maggie saying she had gone out to buy him some 'decent' clothes as he had only carried the bare essentials from London, she would be back around 17.00 hrs.

Chapter 41

After a quick freshening up, Jack met Hamish in the Foyer and exited to find a taxi. There was nobody around resembling the earlier watchers lurking at the Hotel entrance but just in case, they would switch cabs half way to the Port.

The Trawler was berthed near the North Sea marina at lJmuiden on the North Sea Canal some 20 miles away. The journey would take around 50 minutes.

Hamish had radioed Malcolm with an ETA and instructed him to prepare for departure around 17.00 hrs. On arrival they found the vessel prepared for sea, the diesel fired, the ship's lines singled up and the aft deck derrick swung out with a cargo net to the dock awaiting the 'ship's stores'. Malcolm confirmed he had been in contact with the Port Authorities who had given permission to depart subject to a cursory last Customs check and verification of the ship's papers. This had been arranged for 16.40 hrs. Ample time!

As they were talking a panel van bearing the insignia of the Chandlers pulled up, the driver verifying the ship's name reversed up to the cargo net. In the front passenger seat was the Gatekeeper now appropriately dressed in seaman's clothing.

The 'real' stores were offloaded and swung on board the driver getting a signature from Hamish, ripped off the top copy and ambled to the front of the van to light a cigarette studiously avoiding the next phase.

Malcolm had deftly swung the cargo net back on the quay and it was now spread immediately behind the van. The Gatekeeper manhandled two heavy black aluminium cases into the net, which was immediately swung inboard. All three went back on board the trawler where the cases now sat on the aft deck.

Douglas had already positioned the fish box containing the diamonds on the deck temporarily hidden by an old heaped net

Being given the keys, he opened both cases and saw packed bundles of currency in cellophane bundles and all bearing authentic bank seals. He couldn't possibly check them all so randomly selecting three from each case, slit them open with a wicked switch blade handed to him by Malcolm. The currency was authentic and he was then handed a single plain unheaded sheet of paper in clear plastic which detailed, amounts, in which currency, and denominations. He noticed with amusement that the Gatekeeper now wore black linen gloves - no fingerprints.

He had to take on trust that the rest of the currency was genuine and noted with amusement the last item on the page was a deduction 'for services rendered' of 20, 000 Euros.

Signalling to Malcolm on the winch the relocked cases were swung through the saloon hatch. Both he and Hamish had agreed that no attempt should be made to hide the cases, they would be scratched and dented and then stowed beneath the sleeping berths as if they contained personal clothing.

Douglas pulled aside the net and dragged the fish box across to the Gatekeeper, indicating with a wave of his hand he said

"Your turn"

Swiftly he opened the box removing a cleverly constructed top tray of frozen fish, firstly counting the number of pouches and opening again a random selection to check the contents. He removed a small weight measure from his pocket and weighed several of the pouches adding their weight on a small calculator. The whole operation had only taken some fifteen minutes.

He grunted his satisfaction and then handed Jack a steel briefcase.

Opening it Douglas saw the most important part of the deal - the Bank bearer bonds all signed and sealed. He rifled through them and quickly did the mental arithmetic.

"Fine" he said. "looks as if we are both satisfied.

They loaded the fish box into the cargo net, Jack throwing in the old fishing net as cover which were then hastily slid in to the back of the van.

"Turning to Hamish he said "you know what to do. I shall meet up with you in a few days" and shaking hands with both he picked up the briefcase and walked back to the van.

"Could you give me a lift back towards town" he said. My taxi wouldn't stay. I can pick up a cab en route."

"Sure" said the driver and they all slid into the front with Jack in the middle, briefcase on the floor behind his legs. Good move he thought quietly, the driver has already bribed the gate guards thus they won't stop us going out. At that moment a blue and white Renault of the Port Authorities arrived carrying two men in Customs uniform who would carry out Hamish's departure check.

They passed through the Port gates, the driver giving a cheery wave, and set off back to the centre of Amsterdam.

Douglas eased his position, let out a breath he did not believe he had been holding and began to relax.

CHAPTER 42

Douglas entered the hotel carrying his metal briefcase. He walked across to Reception and asked the pretty girl on duty to lock the case in the strong room. Accepting his receipt he then crossed to the Porter's desk,

"Could you book me a table at L'invite Restaurant on Bloemgracht for 20.00hrs this evening. I would like one of the corner tables outside overlooking the Canal and a taxi for 19.45"

"Certainly Mr Douglas, I shall confirm to you by telephone to your suite".

Douglas nodded his thanks. He was looking forward to his meal as he had not been there before and it was highly recommended as one of the best French cuisine restaurants in Amsterdam.

Entering his suite Maggie was just coming out of the bathroom a towel round her hair and wearing one of the fluffy white Hotel dressing gowns.

"Hi, she said, a successful day?"

"Hmm" he replied "yes, all went well" Maggie stuck her tongue out at him knowing he would not tell her anything else. "I thought you were having your hair done?"

"Cut" she said "and now washed by my own fair hands"

The telephone rang. It was the Head porter confirming his reservation and choice of table.

"Come and see what I have bought you"

Hanging in the bedroom was a beautifully cut dark blue, double breasted, lightweight suit by Armani a cream silk shirt and a blue silk tie with red spots. She had also bought him a pair of black loafers from Bally, black silk socks and even new underwear.

"The full outfit" she said "and much more modern than your Saville Row suits from Meyer and Mortimer"

Douglas slipped on the jacket which fitted well and tried one of the shoes - a perfect fit.

"Fantastic, I thought you were only going to buy me a casual jacket. This must have a cost a small fortune. Did you get anything for yourself?"

"Wait and see. And don't worry about the cost, I used your Debit Card from your Coutts account"

Douglas swept her into his arms and gave her a long kiss. "Thank you" he said simply.

We have approximately an hour to get ready and much as I would like to tarry, with you almost naked, I need a shower and a shave"

Reluctantly he disengaged his embrace and Maggie scooted back to the bathroom. leaving his new clothes in the sitting room with the words you shall dress here, I do not want you in the bedroom whilst I am dressing.

After his ablutions, and being banished to the sitting room to dress he was now resplendent in his new suit in which he specifically sat down to add a few wrinkles before going to the fridge to open a bottle of vintage Krug he had instructed room service to place inside. The crystal flutes were also in the fridge, which misted over immediately he removed them.

"How are you getting on" he said through the closed bedroom door.

"Two minutes" was the reply.

He poured two glasses of the smoked amber liquid.

Maggie opened the door and appeared in all her finery. She was dressed in a stunning, calf length, blue and cream silk dress with a plunging decollete, no stockings on her tanned legs and dark blue leather mid heeled shoes. The dress was slit to her mid thigh on one side. Her hair was up, with two curled drops on either side of her head framing her face which had the lightest of make up, blue highlighted eyes and cerise lip gloss. She wore no jewellery other than single diamond studs in her ears and her signet ring on her left hand. Around her neck was her favourite pendant given to her by Jack's late father, of a miniature classical painting mounted on white gold, suspended on a thin chain of link and rectangle alternating in yellow and white gold.

She did a half curtsy, twirled around and waited with her lips slightly parted.

"You look stunning" he said "quite beautiful! "

"Thank you Sir, you don't look too bad yourself"

"Would you mind taking off your pendant I don't want you to wear it at the moment"

"Why ever not, I like it, you like it"

"Could you just for once do something without asking why. Indulge me" Maggie unclipped the chain and carefully laid the pendant on the side table.

Without further explanation he handed her a frosted glass. "To us" he said and kissed her lightly on the lips.

Sampling the delicious wine and looking at Maggie Douglas thought, what a perfect ending to this operation..

There was a discreet knock at the door and on opening Jack saw a younger version of the Merchant dressed in Hasidic black who it transpired was one of his sons. He withdrew a finely tooled blue and gold leather box from his pocket and handed it over.

"I am afraid we lost over 30% in the cutting but the diamond is still over 7.5 carats in weight. It is a 'clear blue' of the finest clarity. You chose well. My Father also asked me to say that he is very pleased with the quality of the other stones and if you ever require 'assistance' in Amsterdam in the future, we are at your service.

He wishes you Good fortune and a long life"

"Thank you, and give my best wishes to your Father"

They shook hands and the Merchant's son walked back down the corridor towards the lift where Jack saw the Gatekeeper was waiting, ever watchful.

"Who was that?" said Maggie.

"Just Room Service, I have something for you - a small gift to thank you for your love and support over all those years and for putting up with me and my bad moods. "as he stretched out the blue leather box.

"Oh you haven't bought me another watch, you silly man the last one you gave me is just fine "as she opened the box and gasped. Her eyes sparkled with moisture or the reflection from the most beautiful diamond Jack had ever seen. It danced with flashes of ice blue as

Maggie lifted it from the box. It was quite flawless and beautifully mounted.

For once Maggie was speechless as she looked from the diamond to Jack's smiling face.

"Allow me" said Jack as he took the pendant from her hand and fastened it around her neck. By the way, don't think there is an endless supply.

He kissed her gently recharged their glasses and lifted his in silent toast as the diamond sparkled on Maggie's chest. "I love you very much"

She brought up her hand to touch it and fire flashed from the stone. "It looks so hot and is yet so cold"

"Hot Ice" Jack said laughingly, but don't ever ask.

He turned catching his reflection in the ornate mirror - a spectre seemed to appear in his mind. Sylvette's face flashed into focus head wrapped in a towel. No, I won't forget you Sylvette he thought. I'll get him, the image faded, and he turned back, but not tonight.

Tonight, is for you, my beautiful Maggie.

Printed in Poland
by Amazon Fulfillment
Poland Sp. z o.o., Wrocław